The Great Hippopotamus Hotel

ALEXANDER McCALL SMITH

abacus books

ABACUS

First published in Great Britain in 2024 by Abacus
This paperback edition published in 2025 by Abacus

1 3 5 7 9 10 8 6 4 2

A CIP catalogue record for this book is available from the British Library.

ISBN 978-0-349-14598-3

Typeset in Galliard by MRules
Printed and bound in Great Britain by
Clays Ltd, Elcograf S.p.A

Papers used by Abacus are from well-managed forests and other responsible sources.

MIX
Paper | Supporting responsible forestry
FSC® C104740
FSC www.fsc.org

Abacus
An imprint of
Little, Brown Book Group
Carmelite House
50 Victoria Embankment
London EC4Y 0DZ

The authorised representative
in the EEA is
Hachette Ireland
8 Castlecourt Centre
Dublin 15, D15 XTP3, Ireland
(email: info@hbgi.ie)

An Hachette UK Company
www.hachette.co.uk

www.littlebrown.co.uk

Welcome to the No. 1 Ladies' Detective Agency

The story so far . . .

Precious Ramotswe, founder and Managing Director of the No. 1 Ladies' Detective Agency, takes on a quest to find the relatives of a man who, many years ago, left the country for the uncertainties and dangers of a distant conflict. Meanwhile, a club that calls itself the Cool Singles Evening Club is encouraging married men to pretend to be single and meet women under false pretences. Who can be behind such a distasteful venture? Mma Ramotswe and her assistant, Grace Makutsi, will need all their tact, affability and good sense to disentangle such delicate disputes.

By Alexander McCall Smith

THE NO. 1 LADIES' DETECTIVE AGENCY SERIES

The No. 1 Ladies' Detective Agency
Tears of the Giraffe
Morality for Beautiful Girls
The Kalahari Typing School for Men
The Full Cupboard of Life
In the Company of Cheerful Ladies
Blue Shoes and Happiness
The Good Husband of Zebra Drive
The Miracle at Speedy Motors
Tea Time for the Traditionally Built
The Double Comfort Safari Club
The Saturday Big Tent Wedding Party
The Limpopo Academy of Private Detection
The Minor Adjustment Beauty Salon
The Handsome Man's De Luxe Café
The Woman Who Walked in Sunshine
Precious and Grace
The House of Unexpected Sisters
The Colours of all the Cattle
To the Land of Long Lost Friends
How to Raise an Elephant
The Joy and Light Bus Company
A Song of Comfortable Chairs
From a Far and Lovely Country
The Great Hippopotamus Hotel

THE ISABEL DALHOUSIE NOVELS

The Sunday Philosophy Club
Friends, Lovers, Chocolate
The Right Attitude to Rain
The Careful Use of Compliments
The Comfort of Saturdays
The Lost Art of Gratitude
The Charming Quirks of Others
The Forgotten Affairs of Youth
The Uncommon Appeal of Clouds
The Novel Habits of Happiness
A Distant View of Everything
The Quiet Side of Passion
The Geometry of Holding Hands
The Sweet Remnants of Summer
The Conditions of Unconditional Love

THE 44 SCOTLAND STREET SERIES

44 Scotland Street
Espresso Tales
Love Over Scotland
The World According to Bertie
The Unbearable Lightness of Scones
The Importance of Being Seven
Bertie Plays the Blues
Sunshine on Scotland Street
Bertie's Guide to Life and Mothers
The Revolving Door of Life
The Bertie Project
A Time of Love and Tartan
The Peppermint Tea Chronicles
A Promise of Ankles
Love in the Time of Bertie
The Enigma of Garlic
The Stellar Debut of Galactica MacFee

THE CORDUROY MANSIONS SERIES

Corduroy Mansions
The Dog Who Came in from the Cold
A Conspiracy of Friends

THE VON IGELFELD ENTERTAINMENTS

The 2½ Pillars of Wisdom
Unusual Uses for Olive Oil
Your Inner Hedgehog
The Lost Language of Oysters

THE DETECTIVE VARG NOVELS

The Department of Sensitive Crimes
The Talented Mr Varg
The Man with the Silver Saab
The Discreet Charm of the Big Bad Wolf

La's Orchestra Saves the World
The Forever Girl
My Italian Bulldozer
The Private Life of Spies

This book is for Richard Buccleuch

Chapter One

Life Is Like Peri-peri Chicken

Mma Ramotswe had always understood that people who are one thing may at the same time be another. This insight, although not entirely original, is undoubtedly quite true. Embodying more than one identity is part of being human – and one of the things of which we might be justifiably proud. It would be a dull world, indeed, in which we all had only one role to play, and were unable to choose from time to time to be something different. Life, said Mma Ramotswe, is a bit like peri-peri chicken: it is improved with a pinch of spice – but only within reason, of course. Much as she enjoyed hot dishes, she would certainly not want to eat them every day.

And the same was true of Mr J. L. B. Matekoni, for whom a helping of the spicy Portuguese dish was a treat he could take only about once a month or so, given the delicacy of his stomach.

Plain food was what he wanted, and was what Mma Ramotswe provided for him, with her boiled pumpkin, her Botswana beef stew, and the popular fried doughnuts known locally as *fat cakes.* If her friend Mma Potokwani, redoubtable matron of the Orphan Farm, was widely known for her fruit cake, then Mma Ramotswe enjoyed a similar reputation for her fat cakes, once described by Mma Makutsi as the most delicious fat cakes in all Botswana.

Identity, though, was a fascinating subject, once one came to look at the people one knew. Take Mma Makutsi, for instance, currently sitting at her desk in the office of the No. 1 Ladies' Detective Agency: she could be described in a number of ways. First and foremost, she was Grace Makutsi from Bobonong, a village up in the north of Botswana, a not-particularly-exciting place from which one might not expect all that many remarkable people to emerge. That is not to be dismissive of Bobonong, which, like everywhere, has its finer points – it is simply to be realistic as to what we might expect from a place quite so off the beaten track. The beaten track, after all, is beaten for a reason, as is made clear in *The Principles of Private Detection*, the book from which both Mma Ramotswe and Mma Makutsi had received so much guidance. *Remember*, wrote Clovis Andersen, *that what's out there is out there for a reason. And if it isn't out there, then once again there's a reason why it isn't.* Mma Ramotswe and Mma Makutsi had discussed that particular observation at some length, and were confident that they had reached an understanding of its meaning, or had at least begun to do so.

Had Mma Makutsi stayed in Bobonong, of course, she might have remained simply Mma Makutsi from Bobonong. In all likelihood she would have married a local man – a schoolteacher, perhaps, or a minor government official – and gone on to live a worthy even if entirely local life. But greater things were in store, and by dint of hard work and parsimony, she went on to become Grace Makutsi, graduate *summa cum laude* of the Botswana Secretarial College. She was indeed that, but, most importantly, she was also the graduate with the highest mark ever achieved in the final examinations of that distinguished institution – ninety-seven per cent. Of course, there were those who claimed that a more recent candidate had achieved an even higher mark, but no hard evidence had ever been produced to back up that claim. And even if such evidence were to materialise, it would not weaken Mma Makutsi's status as the holder of the highest mark *at the time at which she graduated*. Old records might be broken by subsequent achievements, but they remained records at the time at which they were chalked up, and could still be considered records even after they had fallen. Glories accrued through diligent study or hard work should not be taken away from those who have achieved them – they remained in memory, their glow increasing with the passage of time.

But there was more. Mma Makutsi was also a wife, a mother, a private detective, an authority on fashionable shoes, a non-executive director of the Double Comfort Furniture Store, and a member of a community advisory panel established by their neighbour, Mr Lebogang Motsumi. Lebogang meant in Setswana 'be thankful', a benign name that certainly suited the mild and affable nature of Mr Motsumi, who was generally viewed by his neighbours as a model citizen.

'Every community needs somebody who will take on the jobs that need to be done,' Mma Makutsi observed to her husband, Mr Phuti Radiphuti. 'There has to be somebody who is prepared to step forward.'

'You're right, Grace,' said Phuti. 'Otherwise, things go to the dogs. That has happened in some places where nobody will take on any of these jobs that have to be done.'

'There are many people who look over their shoulder when they are asked to help out,' said Mma Makutsi. 'They look for somebody who is standing behind them. Then they point to that person and say, "He will be the one to do this thing." That is what happens, I think, Phuti.'

Phuti thought about this and remembered the sign that he had seen by a roadside down near Lobatse. The sign was a large one, the lettering stencilled in black against the light blue that was Botswana's national colour. It proclaimed: 'This improvement project is supported by the Lobatse Improvement Committee.' And underneath that, as a message in smaller letters: 'Look the future in the face with us.'

'There was that sign near Lobatse,' Phuti said. 'I pointed it out to you, Mma. Remember?'

Mma Makutsi did remember.

'We saw it every time we went down there,' she said, smiling at the memory. 'But when we looked for a project, there was nothing to be seen – just empty bush and some goats nibbling at the thorn bushes.'

'Perhaps the goats were the project,' suggested Phuti Radiphuti.

She shook her head. 'No, Rra, I don't think so. I believe that the people who were behind the project forgot about it, or went away and couldn't find anybody to take it over. And then the ants started to eat the sign and it began to look shakier and shakier.'

'It is good that we have Mr Lebogang Motsumi,' mused Phuti. 'He is a real asset to the community.'

Mma Makutsi agreed. She had taken no persuading to be a member of his advisory panel but had never been at all sure what its function was. There had been three meetings so far, each of them held in the living room of Mr Motsumi's house, and the panel members had all gone away at the end of the meetings feeling replete, even if confused as to why they were there. There is a tradition in Botswana that no function is complete without the consumption of food, and the meeting at the Motsumi house had more than honoured this custom. Mma Motsumi, a cheerful, traditionally built lady, had surpassed herself in her baking efforts for the occasion, and the six members of the panel had all eaten far too many of her savoury scones and cheese straws, along with numerous slices of her double-chocolate cake, to feel comfortable when it came to the business of the meeting. It quickly became apparent to Mr Motsumi, who was occupying the chair, that there was no heart for business, which did not matter too much, as it happened, because there was little of substance on the agenda. Nobody had asked for any advice apart from the university, which had requested the community's views on the possible construction of a residential building for students one block away from a road of large prosperous-looking houses.

'We do not want any students round here,' said one of the members. 'They are always making a noise.'

'And they drink all the time,' said another. 'They have very little time to study, with all the parties they have.'

'They are studying for a Bachelor of Parties degree,' suggested a third member. 'That is a very popular degree these days, I think.'

Even the mild Mr Lebogang Motsumi expressed misgivings about the proposal. 'Students should go away,' he said – a comment that brought a general nodding of heads.

And that was all the discussion there was, although the tenor of the views expressed by the members was treated by Mr Lebogang Motsumi as justification for a stiff letter to the university saying that the community had been widely consulted and was of the unanimous view that the area was completely unsuitable for student accommodation. When nothing more was heard of the proposal, the panel took it as an indication of the weight that its views might carry in the wider community.

'They listen to committees,' observed Grace, 'even if they will not listen to individual people. They forget that committees are made up of people.'

Phuti smiled. He thought she was quite right. He was usually proud of his wife, but when she made observations like this, he was even prouder. He had made a great choice, marrying a woman with her style, confidence, and ability to get right to the heart of things. He had never regretted that choice – not for one moment.

Those were the various aspects of the woman who was Mma Makutsi. What of Mma Ramotswe herself – who, exactly, was she? If you asked her, she would undoubtedly say that before anything else she was a citizen of Botswana. She was proud of her country, and what it represented in a world that was full of conflict and confrontation. Botswana was a peaceful country, and its people were quiet and unostentatious. To be a citizen of such a country had always meant much to her, and sat proud among the other ways in which she might be described. And there were many of these, just as there were in the case of Mma Makutsi. She was the founder of the No. 1 Ladies' Detective Agency; she was the wife of that great mechanic, Mr J. L. B. Matekoni; she was the foster mother of two children, Puso and Motholeli; and, very importantly, she was the daughter of the late Obed Ramotswe, the man whom she spoke of as her 'late Daddy', that fine, kind man who knew so much about cattle and the ways of cattle; who taught her what it was to lead a good life and to do so discreetly.

Not a day went past but that she thought of her father, and of how he had supported and encouraged her in all that she did. If she closed her eyes, she could hear him; she could hear him calling her 'My Precious' as he always did, and the memory brought tears, not so much of sadness – for he had been gone a long time now – but of pride and joy that Obed Ramotswe had been her father. To be the daughter of such a man, she felt, was the greatest possible good fortune, especially when there are so many other, lesser men of whom one might have been the daughter, had things been different.

But perhaps the best known of Mma Ramotswe's roles was that of helper of others. Right from the beginning, the No. 1 Ladies' Detective Agency had been about helping people with the problems in their lives. When she had first set up the agency, she had very little idea of what it would be called upon to do. She knew nothing about being a private investigator, and Mma Makutsi knew even less – although strictly speaking it might not be possible to know less than nothing. But word gets round in a place like Gaborone, where people know the business of others, and within a few days she realised that the people who had need of the services of such an agency were those who had very ordinary problems in their lives. There had been some who thought that a detective agency would be involved in solving crimes, but that was far from the case. 'I do not investigate crimes,' she said to a friend. 'I help people with things that are worrying them. And there are many such things, Mma – oh yes, people have many problems, and it is my job to sort them out.'

In doing that, she did not need to resort to complex methods; all she had to do was to use common sense and, if she did not know the answer to something, to ask somebody. Most people, she found, were only too ready to talk to you, particularly if that gave them the chance to air their personal views. Taking advantage of that readiness usually unearthed facts that otherwise might take a long time to elicit. The best line of all, in initiating such a conversation, was simply to say, 'Tell me about yourself.' That always led to immediate and fulsome disclosures.

Those, then, were the two ladies who were sitting in the office of the No. 1 Ladies' Detective Agency on that warm morning in October, when people were looking forward to the first of the rains, and hoping that they would be heavy enough to give the parched ground the soaking for which it yearned. They had dealt with the morning mail, and Mma Makutsi had done a certain amount of filing – the office task at which she excelled, even to the point of wondering whether one day she might write a helpful book on the subject. *The Principles of Filing* was not a title she had ever come across in a bookshop or library, but she was in no doubt that there was a call for such a work. She could just imagine it – a handsomely bound edition with a picture of the author – herself – on the back cover. Underneath her photograph there would be helpful text along these lines: 'The author, Grace Makutsi, was born in Bobonong, an important city in Botswana. She was educated there and in Gaborone, where she attended the Botswana Secretarial College. At college she was awarded the Principal's Prize for Filing prior to graduating with close to one hundred per cent in the final examinations. She is the joint managing director of the No. 1 Ladies' Detective Agency, of which she was the co-founder. She is currently working on her second book.'

There were several examples in this brief note of the creative presentation of facts – something that in less sympathetic days used to be called lies. It was true that she had graduated with a mark that was close to one hundred per cent, but it was possible that the reader might imagine that the actual mark was ninety-eight or ninety-nine per cent, or even ninety-nine-and-a-half per cent, which was as close to one hundred per cent that anybody could realistically get. But authors are not always strictly accurate when it comes to describing themselves on the covers of their books, and a little leeway is surely permissible. Bobonong is not a city, not legally, nor indeed any other way, but the word city may be used in a general sense to describe any collection of houses and other buildings and so it was surely permissible to use it here. The claim to be writing a second book was, of course, without foundation, but she had noticed that it was something that one frequently saw on the dust jackets of books, and therefore must be a form of acceptable aspiration. And it is possible to argue that even if one has not set pen to paper, one might be *thinking* of what would go into a second book, and that, surely, could be described as working on it.

But now the morning's filing tasks were completed, the mail dealt with, and the appointments diary for the day ahead was still completely empty. In the circumstances, although it was not strictly tea-time yet, both Mma Ramotswe and Mma Makutsi thought that it was close enough.

'I think we should call Mr J. L. B. Matekoni in for tea,' said Mma Ramotswe. 'And Fanwell and Charlie too. It will be very hot in the garage on a day like this, and we must not let them get dehydrated.'

Mma Makutsi agreed. 'It is a very bad thing for men to become dehydrated,' she said. 'We women must watch out for that. If we see our husbands, or indeed any other men, getting dehydrated, we should act. Men cannot do these things themselves.'

Mma Ramotswe was not sure that this was entirely true. She

knew men who were clearly well hydrated even although they did not appear to have any woman to ensure adequate ingestion of fluids. But she did not argue the point; what Mma Makutsi said was broadly true – men often did not look after themselves properly, although at long last boys were being instructed at an early age in important domestic and personal tasks. There were now men who used scissors, rather than relying on biting to trim their nails. Boys were now being taught in school how to change a baby, clean a bath and bake bread. It was slow work, as it was often convenient for men to forget how to do such things, but education, at least, was going in the right direction.

Mma Makutsi left her desk to go through to the garage and inform the men that tea would be ready in a few minutes. From underneath an arthritic people carrier, an ancient vehicle of uncertain provenance on which the legend *Reliable Minibus* had been painted, Mr J. L. B. Matekoni replied that they would shortly finish the repair on which they were working, and would come through to the office once they had tidied up.

She returned to the office, switched on the kettle, and had tea ready by the time Fanwell announced their arrival with a polite knock on the door.

'It is very hot today,' said Mr J. L. B. Matekoni, as he sat down on the client's chair that Mma Ramotswe always kept facing her desk. Fanwell and Charlie were young men who preferred to lean against things rather than sit in them, it being, in Charlie's opinion, more interesting for women if men leaned against the furniture rather than sat on it. Fanwell expressed no such view. 'I am not so cool as my friend Charlie,' he was known to say, but his working clothes were a bit greasy, and he did not want to leave his mark on the office chairs.

After remarking on the heat, Mr J. L. B. Matekoni nodded in

the direction of the garage and went on to say, 'We're working on a minibus through there. It's owned by a man who has five of them in his fleet.'

'He overloads them all,' Charlie interjected, 'but he makes a lot of money. He has a lot of cattle now.'

Fanwell whistled. 'That's the way to make your dough: buy a minibus and fill it full of people. Put some on the roof if there isn't room inside. Then you become rich.'

'You cannot put people on the roof,' said Mma Makutsi. 'They will fall off if you hit a bump in the road.'

'I've seen it done,' said Charlie. 'I once saw a minibus with a small child on the roof. It was in a chicken coop – you know those cages they use to transport chickens. The child was in one of those, and it was tied to the roof. He was perfectly safe.'

Mma Ramotswe could see that Charlie was winding Mma Makutsi up. Now she intervened. 'That is very funny, Charlie. I know that you do not expect Mma Makutsi to believe that.'

Mma Makutsi gave a short laugh. 'Hah! Charlie thinks I believe the nonsense he talks. But I never do.'

Catching Mma Ramotswe's eye, Mr J. L. B. Matekoni said something more about the owner of the minibus. 'He's called Mr Mo Mo Malala, that man. He is a very small man.'

Charlie smiled. 'Yes, he is an extremely small man. But he is married to a very big lady. Rra Small-Small and Mma Big-Big – hah!'

Mma Ramotswe failed in her attempt to suppress a smile. Mma Makutsi, unwilling though she was to encourage Charlie, struggled too, but eventually gave up and grinned weakly for a moment. 'There are many cases of that sort of thing, Charlie,' she admonished him. 'When you have lived a bit longer you will know that it does not matter what is on the outside – it is what is on the inside that counts.' She turned to Mma Ramotswe. 'Is that not true, Mma Ramotswe?'

Mma Ramotswe inclined her head in agreement. Charlie was a well-meaning young man, if a bit headstrong, and in her view he should not be judged too severely. All young men were like that – to an extent – and it was only if they showed no signs of natural improvement that it was necessary to reproach them. But she had to support Mma Makutsi in this sort of thing, and so she went on to say, 'Mma Makutsi is quite right, Charlie. A small person may be big inside – and a big person may be small inside.'

Charlie frowned. 'But are there not big people who are big inside too?'

'That is possible,' said Mma Ramotswe. 'And there are small people, I think, who are small inside too.'

Charlie looked thoughtful. 'So there may be a big person who is small inside married to a small person who is big inside?'

Mr J. L. B. Matekoni joined in. 'There are many different combinations. You never know what sort of combination is going to turn up.' He paused. 'Anything can happen – that is one lesson you learn in this life – anything.'

Fanwell had been silent until now. 'It's best to be careful,' he said. 'If anything can happen, then you should be very careful – all the time.'

'That is the best policy,' said Mr J. L. B. Matekoni.

Mma Makutsi had been busy pouring the tea. Now she handed a cup to Mma Ramotswe and a mug to Mr J. L. B. Matekoni. He blew across the surface of the hot liquid, causing a small cloud to rise up. In the shaft of sunlight falling from the window behind Mma Ramotswe's desk, the tiny droplets of steam danced briefly before they disappeared. 'This Malala,' he said, 'turned sixty last week. When he brought the minibus in, he said to me, "I had my sixtieth birthday last week, would you believe it?"'

'That is very old,' said Charlie. 'It's amazing that there are people who are sixty and who are still walking about. That is very amazing.'

Mma Makutsi glared at him, but said nothing. Mma Ramotswe felt, though, that she could not let Charlie go unrebuked, even if mildly. 'One day even you will be sixty, Charlie,' she said.

Charlie shook his head and muttered, 'Ow!'

Mr J. L. B. Matekoni had more to say about Mr Malala. 'He mentioned his birthday, and so I asked him whether he had received any presents. He said that his wife had given him a new driver for his set of golf clubs. He said that it would get him closer to the green.'

'He would need very small clubs,' mused Charlie.

Mr J. L. B. Matekoni continued, 'But then he said to me that he was planning to get himself something that he had wanted for a very long time. He asked me to help him.'

There was a short silence, ended when Charlie said, 'A smaller wife?'

'That is very rude,' exploded Mma Makutsi. 'You say some very stupid things, Charlie.'

Charlie defended himself. 'It was a joke, Mma Makutsi. We are allowed to make jokes sometimes.'

Mma Ramotswe turned to Mr J. L. B. Matekoni. 'So he wanted you to help, Rra. That is very interesting. Did he tell you what this present was?'

'He did,' replied Mr J. L. B. Matekoni.

They waited.

Mr J. L. B. Matekoni looked smug. 'You'll never guess,' he said.

'A car?' suggested Mma Makutsi.

Mr J. L. B. Matekoni's disappointment showed. 'As a matter of fact,' he said, 'you're right, Mma.' He rallied. 'But I do not think you will guess what *sort* of car. I think that will come as a big surprise to you.'

Mma Makutsi did not hesitate. 'A sports car?'

Charlie laughed. 'She's right, isn't she, boss?'

Mr J. L. B. Matekoni could not hide his disappointment. 'Yes,' he said, rather lamely. But then he shook his head, to emphasise the unlikelihood of Mr Malala's ambition. 'Can you believe it, everybody? A sports car? When he's sixty-something?'

Charlie made a circular motion at the side of his head. 'Well, Rra, we all know that once you get to forty, things start to go wrong in your head. You forget things. You forget where you live. You . . . '

'Don't be ridiculous, Charlie,' snapped Mma Makutsi. 'You should not joke about these things.'

But Charlie was serious. 'I'm telling you, Mma Ramotswe. I know somebody who started to do very strange things when he was forty-two. He went and bought a saxophone. He had a small general dealer's store – he sold flour, batteries, tea, that sort of thing. He started a rock band. He couldn't play but . . . '

Mma Makutsi sighed loudly. 'That's something quite different, Charlie. That's the mid-life crisis. That's what happens to men on their fortieth birthday. Bang. They do that sort of thing. Every time.'

Mr J. L. B. Matekoni frowned. 'Not all men, Mma,' he protested.

'Well, maybe not one hundred per cent of men,' Mma Makutsi conceded. 'But almost.'

Mma Ramotswe made an effort to bring the conversation back to Mr Malala. 'Are you sure that's the sort of car he wants, Rra?'

Mr J. L. B. Matekoni explained that he had been left in no doubt. 'He showed me a picture from a magazine. It was one of those small Italian sports cars. I know the model. I've never seen one, of course, but I know somebody over the border who can get one. He wants a second-hand model with a low mileage. I know somebody in the trade over in Johannesburg who can get any car you like.'

Fanwell whistled. 'Those South African cars are often stolen, Rra. I wouldn't touch them. South Africans drive round in stolen cars all the time. That is what they do.'

'Not all of them,' said Mma Makutsi. 'I have an aunt over there. She doesn't drive a stolen car.'

'What does she drive?' asked Charlie.

'She doesn't,' answered Mma Makutsi. 'But if she did, it wouldn't be stolen.'

'My friend in the trade over there is honest,' said Mr J. L. B. Matekoni. 'He is a Catholic, and all the cars he sells come from Catholic homes.'

'So, this car will have belonged to a priest?' Charlie challenged. 'Is that what you're saying, boss? Because I don't think priests drive Italian sports cars. The Pope may do – but not ordinary priests.'

Mma Ramotswe looked at Mr J. L. B. Matekoni with concern. 'Are you going to help him, Mr J. L. B. Matekoni? Are you going to help him to do something . . . unwise?'

The question hung in the air for some time before it was answered. 'I feel very uncomfortable about it,' Mr J. L. B. Matekoni said at last. 'You see, I feel responsible for the cars I get for people. I do not like to see people driving the wrong sort of car. I do not like to see them behind the wheel of something they can't manage.'

'Then just say no,' said Mma Makutsi.

Mr J. L. B. Matekoni looked away. 'The problem is, Malala's brother runs the biggest car rental firm in the country. They're very big. And who has the contract to service their cars? We do. Tlokweng Road Speedy Motors.'

Fanwell drew in his breath sharply. 'Those cars, boss? We need those cars. If they take them elsewhere, then we lose twenty-five per cent of our work.'

'Twenty-five per cent less to eat,' remarked Charlie, patting his stomach.

'Exactly,' said Mr J. L. B. Matekoni.

They exchanged glum looks. Mr J. L. B. Matekoni drained the last of his tea. 'Well, it won't help to sit around and talk about it. Time to get back to work.'

He rose to his feet. Charlie and Fanwell finished their tea and put their mugs down on one of the filing cabinets.

'Excuse me,' said Mma Makutsi pointedly. 'Do mugs wash themselves? I don't think they do.'

Mma Ramotswe was first home that evening. While Puso and Motholeli were busy with their homework, she made sure that the stew was simmering gently on the cooker. Then she went out into her garden to check up on her rows of beans and the bed of onions she had planted a month ago, which were developing nicely. They were a variety that produced large bulbs, and there were already signs that this promise would be fulfilled. She inspected the plants, adjusted the drip-watering system, and then stood for a while under the spreading branches of the large jacaranda tree that grew to the side of the house. She looked up at the evening sky, which was pale blue and devoid of cloud. Sometimes she felt dizzy when she looked up at a sky like that. It was so high, so empty, so echoing; the air of which it was composed was so thin.

She closed her eyes, taking a breath that filled her lungs with air. That made her light-headed for a moment. I could faint, she thought, and when Mr J. L. B. Matekoni came home he would find her on the ground, with dust about her, and the ants. That would be such a sad thing, because every married woman – or at least very many of them – fears at some time that she will come home and find her husband collapsed on the ground. Men, for all their strength, were fragile creatures, lent to women by a providence that might at any moment call them back.

When she opened her eyes, it was to see Mr J. L. B. Matekoni's truck nosing its way through the gate and into the yard. A few minutes later, he was at her side, crouching down to take a closer look at the bean plants.

'They are doing very well, I think, Mma,' came his verdict.

'I hope so.'

He scratched the back of his head. 'You know that matter we were discussing this morning? This business of Malala's car?'

'I would like to hear more about that,' she said.

'I didn't tell you,' Mr J. L. B. Matekoni continued, 'about another big, big problem with that car.'

Mma Ramotswe looked anxious. She did not like Mr J. L. B. Matekoni to fret over his work, and it seemed that this Malala business was making him do just that.

'He isn't telling his wife about it,' he said. 'And he made me promise not to let her know in advance about the sort of car he is wanting to buy.'

Mma Ramotswe made a clucking sound. This was her way of communicating disapproval. It was very effective.

'That is very bad,' she said.

'I agree. But I can't break my word to him. I promised him before I thought about it. Then I realised what I'd done.'

'That's often the case,' said Mma Ramotswe. 'We say things and then we come to see what we've said, and we don't always like it.'

'That is very true,' said Mr J. L. B. Matekoni, shaking his head sadly. 'It is very true, Mma.'

They looked at one another. It was clear to Mma Ramotswe that he was relieved at having been able to talk to her about this. It was often the case that the simple act of revealing a problem to another made the problem itself seem so much less serious. Bottling something up within yourself only served to make things worse: she was sure of that. But there was something that puzzled her, and so she asked, 'He may not be proposing to tell his wife that he is planning to buy a sports car, Rra, but won't she find out eventually – when she looks out of the front window and sees the new car parked in the drive? Won't that give the game away, Mr J. L. B. Matekoni?'

It was a good question, he thought, and he had himself asked it of Mr Malala when he had first revealed his plan. It had been quickly answered, though. 'He told me that he would be parking this new car at a friend's place. He would keep it there and in that way his wife would never know about it. Then he would be free to drive around in it whenever he wished.'

It took Mma Ramotswe some time to gather her thoughts after this disclosure. In one sense, this was ridiculous. For a grown man to behave in this way was absurd – it was the sort of subterfuge to which a sixteen-year-old boy might resort, but for a man at Mr Malala's stage of life to be planning to do such a thing was almost unbelievable. But then she reminded herself that there were many men who behaved like young boys, and in some cases such behaviour became more common the older a man became.

She sighed at the thought. Poor men: how sad it was that

something as unimportant as a sports car could turn a man's head in this way. Why, she wondered, would a man like him set such store by driving a sports car? Was it simply the attraction of fast, responsive machinery, or ... It came to her. Men drove showy cars to attract women. Mr Malala would not be planning to drive around in his sports car by himself – he would be envisioning company. She sighed again. There was nothing unusual here: this was male behaviour of a sort that she had seen time and time again in the course of her work in the No. 1 Ladies' Detective Agency.

Clovis Andersen's words came back to her. As usual, Clovis Andersen, in a few well-chosen words in *The Principles of Private Detection*, put his finger on the nub of the matter. *Men do things to attract the attention of women. Once you understand that, you will begin to understand men.*

Chapter Two

Oh Dear, Here Is an Elephant

The following day, Mma Ramotswe went to the Riverwalk shops to buy three new pairs of men's socks. Socks were a constant problem for Mr J. L. B. Matekoni, as they never seemed to last long. Many socks have a vulnerable spot at the place where the foot becomes the ankle, and that is why you see so many men with a patch of bare skin showing just above the heel of the shoe. In the days when people bothered to mend their clothes, it was not uncommon to see darning in that part of the sock, but now, in the days of plentiful socks, distressed socks were quickly abandoned. And the same applied to shirts; the turning of a collar, which Mma Ramotswe had learned from an aunt, was now a dying skill, although Mma Ramotswe knew that her friend Mma Potokwani was still a believer in making shirts, and other clothes, last longer through a bit of judicious repair work. She had seen the matron's husband with extra cloth sewn onto the seams of his trousers, to conceal edges that had become frayed through long use; she had seen him with collars that had been skilfully turned, but which were still recognisably the original. Mma Makutsi had tut-tutted about the parsimony that such things revealed, and had suggested that the Potokwani family could surely afford at least the occasional new shirt, but Mma Ramotswe had been more understanding. Mma Potokwani was a conservationist at heart, and liked to avoid buying new things if serviceable older items were available. That spirit was admirable, Mma Ramotswe thought, in a world where we were only too ready to buy new things, in spite of the rate at which we were depleting the world's resources.

'There is only so much Botswana,' Mma Potokwani had once said to her, 'and when we use that one up, where will we find another Botswana? You tell me that, Mma.'

She had considered darning Mr J. L. B. Matekoni's socks, and had indeed succeeded in bringing about a repair to the toes of one pair, where both the left and right socks had been affected. It had taken some hours, though, and the repair had lasted a very short time, with holes reappearing exactly where they had been before.

It was Mma Potokwani who had explained the cause. 'I have had exactly the same problem with my husband,' she said. 'His toes are always coming out of his socks. He said that the reason for this is that socks are badly made these days – that the people who make socks are no longer taking pride in what they do. He said that he was sure that this was the reason, Mma, but I don't think it is. No, I have discovered that there is another reason – and that is to do with the fact that men do not bother to cut their toenails.'

Mma Potokwani had gone on to confirm this by examining her husband's toes. 'He did not like it, Mma,' she told Mma Ramotswe. 'Men can be embarrassed by these things. But I told him that I was not going to laugh at his toes, and eventually I had a good look. And do you know what, Mma? I found that his toenails were very sharp at the very point where the holes appeared. That was what was happening. The material was being cut by the toenails and holes were the result.'

'Hah!' said Mma Ramotswe. 'That must be the problem with Mr J. L. B. Matekoni too. That is very interesting, Mma.' She paused. 'So, what did you do, Mma?'

'I cut them for him and told him that I would deal with them every month – at the end of the month. That way we shall not forget to keep the nails under control.'

Mma Ramotswe considered this. 'I shall have to speak to Mr J. L. B. Matekoni,' she said. And then she added, 'It may not be easy, Mma. I have never talked to him about his toes before.'

'It is the only way of dealing with holes in socks,' said Mma Potokwani.

That conversation had not taken place by the time that Mma Ramotswe made her way to *Smart Man Outfitters.* She had decided that the easiest way of introducing the subject would be to say something when she presented him with new socks. It would be natural then, and not at all embarrassing, for her to say something like, 'Let's keep these socks in good order, Mr J. L. B. Matekoni. Let's do something about your toenails so they do not ruin them. As you know, sharp toenails cause such damage . . . I'm sure I don't have to tell you that.'

A tactful approach like that was, of course, recommended by Clovis Andersen when he said, *People do not always like to be told things. It is best, then, to suggest that they already know what you want to tell them. They don't know it, of course, but they will like you to think that they do.*

The young saleswoman working in the outfitters' showed

her various socks with specially reinforced toes and heels. 'As I'm sure you know,' she said, giving her a sideways look, 'men's toenails are always going through the end of their socks. And holes in the heel are caused by shoes that are too tight. A man's clothes – and shoes – should not pinch against the man himself. Men do not like to be pinched, you see. Of course, you know that, Mma.'

Mma Ramotswe was momentarily taken aback that this young woman should know something like that. Was there, perhaps, a book similar to *The Principles of Private Detection* that was used by people in the clothing trade? That was possible, she supposed: every trade or profession must have its manual.

While Mma Ramotswe examined the socks, the saleswoman continued, her voice lowered as if to impart a secret. 'The truth of the matter, Mma,' she continued, 'is that many men are the wrong shape. That makes it very difficult for us in this business. You should see some of the men we get coming in here, Mma – you should just see them.' The saleswoman rolled her eyes. It was a moment of shared understanding between women.

Mma Ramotswe smiled. 'Poor men,' she said. 'They do their best, I think, but, as you say . . . '

The young woman glanced over her shoulder. 'Men have many problems with their stomachs, Mma. Have you noticed that? This happens at thirty-five, I've noticed.'

Mma Ramotswe waited.

'You see,' the saleswoman continued, 'men drink beer and eat sausages – they are all a bit like that – and then after a while their stomachs say, *No more room for all this beer and all these sausages* – and they start to spread in the only direction possible – which is to the front. This thing they develop, Mma, is called a paunch – and all men have it, although many claim they do not. Many men see their paunch developing and they start holding in their stomachs. They breathe in a lot, although it is very important, if you breathe in, to remember to breathe out as well.' She paused. 'In and out should be equal, Mma.'

Mma Ramotswe smiled again. 'That is very true, Mma.'

'I have seen men walking around in great discomfort, Mma – very great discomfort – because they are holding in their paunch. They do this when they are trying to impress ladies. And while they are doing it, they cannot say very much, in case their paunch pops out. Oh dear, Mma, it is very hard for those men.'

Mma Ramotswe felt that she should speak up for men. It was easy to run men down, but it was important to remember that we were all in this life together and we should be tolerant of one another's failings. The Bishop himself had said something about that not all that long ago at Gaborone Cathedral, and the congregation had all looked around at one another, presumably trying to ascertain what failings others had. Some had shifted in their seats – a sure sign, somebody later observed over congregational tea, that they had major failings. 'Not that we should gloat,' the same person had said. 'But at least we know.'

The saleswoman had a few final observations to make. 'Once they get a paunch,' she went on, 'men have to do something about their belt. It is no good wearing the belt above the paunch, as that will not hold up your trousers. So, what you have to do is transfer the belt to your new waist line, which is *below* the paunch. The belt then prevents further slippage of the paunch towards the ground.' She paused. 'That is what I recommend, Mma.'

Mma Ramotswe nodded. 'I'm sure you are right, Mma. However, I am happy to say that my husband does not have a paunch. He is in very good shape. His stomach is very flat.'

The saleswoman pondered this. 'Is he eating enough, Mma?

Sometimes when men do not get enough food, their stomach stays flat. That can happen when their wives . . . '

She stopped. She had not intended to imply that Mma Ramotswe was not feeding her husband adequately.

'I am sure that you are a very good cook, Mma,' she said hurriedly. 'And I can see that you yourself are not going hungry, because . . . '

Once again, the sentence was left unfinished.

Mma Ramotswe did not mind. 'Yes, I am a traditionally built lady, Mma. I am not ashamed of that. This is how ladies have always looked and I do not think that we should change these things.'

The saleswoman was relieved not to have caused offence. 'Yes, Mma,' she enthused. 'And I am sure that I shall look like you in a few years' time. I am sure that will happen.'

Mma Ramotswe glanced at her watch. Botswana was a country with few, if any, failings, but sometimes an ordinary transaction, such as the purchase of a few pairs of socks, could turn into rather a long conversation if one was not careful. But was that a failing? In a world in which people seemed to have less and less time for others, she was not sure that exchanging views was something to be discouraged. A few kind words, a few remarks about this and that, could make a village of a city – and that was no bad thing, she felt.

She pointed to the socks. 'I think these socks will be ideal, Mma,' she said.

Mma Ramotswe did not notice it, but while she had been talking to the saleswoman, a man at the other end of the shop – a man looking at a display of men's sportswear – had been glancing across the room. And his glances had been directed at her. Now, as she left the shop, package in hand, this man came up to her and addressed her.

'*Dumela*, Mma,' he began, observing the necessary formalities.

She stopped and replied accordingly.

'You do not know me, I think,' he said.

She gave him a searching look. She had a good memory for faces, but she couldn't identify this neatly dressed man of about forty who was standing before her. Her eyes slipped down to his stomach – she did not mean them to, but the conversation that she had just had with the saleswoman made that more or less inevitable. And she noticed that this man did not have a paunch – not even the first signs of one.

'No, I don't think we have met,' said Mma Ramotswe. 'But now we have.'

The man laughed. 'And since we have not met you will not know my name. It is Quick Babusi. I am usually called just Babusi. I do not mind the Quick part, but people seem not to bother with it. I am happy with Babusi.'

'And my name . . . ' began Mma Ramotswe.

'I think I know who you are,' said Babusi. 'I think that you are Mma Ramotswe. I think that you are that lady who helps people. You work with that lady who's married to Phuti Radiphuti. She is called Grace Makutsi, I believe. Phuti used to know a cousin of mine because that cousin is a carpenter and he made some tables for his shop. He has gone to live in Francistown now, because they needed a carpenter up there and he had met a lady whose people lived up at Masunga. It would be easier for him to move up there rather than bring all her people down here – what with the cost of housing.'

Mma Ramotswe nodded. Such connections, distant and attenuated in many cases, lay at the heart of the community that was

Botswana. Nobody was a stranger; everybody had some link with others, and all that people had to do was talk to one another for a few minutes to discover it.

'That Makutsi woman,' Babusi continued, 'is a very intelligent lady, they say. I have heard people say that she knows a great deal.'

Mma Ramotswe agreed. 'She is very smart,' she said. 'She knows a lot about many things.'

Babusi shifted from foot to foot. 'I hope you don't mind my talking to you like this, Mma. I saw you in the shop back there. I had heard of you, you see, and I knew who you were. I thought that you looked like a kind lady. I decided that you might not mind if I spoke to you about something that is troubling me.'

Mma Ramotswe hesitated. She had more shopping to do. She needed to buy vegetables for dinner that night; there was virtually no toothpaste left in the house; and supplies of cleaning liquid needed to be replenished. But those were everyday matters, and she did not think that everyday matters should take precedence over things that troubled others.

'You may talk to me, Rra,' she said. 'I am always happy to listen.' And then she added, 'I am sorry if you are troubled by something.'

Babusi gave her a grateful look. 'They all say that you are kind, Mma – and now I see that what they say is true.'

Mma Ramotswe pointed to the café at the end of the mall. 'We could go to that place, Rra,' she said. 'It is a good place to talk.'

'I will buy you tea, Mma.'

'Then let us go, Rra.'

They walked together in a silence that lasted until a few moments before they reached the café. Then Babusi said, 'I am very unhappy with something that is happening, Mma. I am very unhappy.'

'Then you must tell me,' Mma Ramotswe said, reaching out to touch his arm gently, in a gesture of both solidarity and solace.

The waitress said, 'So there you are, Mma Ramotswe. I have been waiting for you to drop in for tea. Every day I have been saying to myself, *Where is Mma Ramotswe these days?* And now here you are, Mma.'

Mma Ramotswe sat down and gestured to Babusi to do the same. She smiled at the waitress. 'Well, now I am here, Mma.'

The waitress looked at Babusi. 'I know you, Rra,' she said. 'You are Babusi, aren't you?'

For a few moments, Babusi looked confused. Then he brightened. 'Ah yes, Mma. You're Dolly, aren't you?'

The waitress nodded. 'That is me, Rra. I worked in the hotel – remember?'

'Then you had a baby. Of course, I remember.' He smiled. 'I hope you are well, Mma – and the baby . . . '

'She is three now, Rra. She is very well.'

Babusi turned to Mma Ramotswe. 'I am the manager of a hotel, Mma. Dolly was one of the best of our waitresses – if not *the* best.'

Dolly beamed under the warmth of the compliment. Seeing this, Mma Ramotswe smiled too, and Babusi immediately rose in her estimation. She had not yet been able to form an impression of this man, but this was as clear an indication as one might want of his character. It was not hard to praise others, but so few people did it with readiness and grace. A few words about how people have done their jobs, a verbal pat on the back following some achievement, a reference to a good quality a person might have – all of these could boost another in an immediate and visible way, thought Mma Ramotswe; you could see them increase in stature, fill out, hold their heads high. It was so easy to do, but it seemed to require a generosity of spirit that not everybody possessed.

'Oh, Rra,' said Dolly, 'there were many others. I was only doing my job.'

Mma Ramotswe decided to intervene. 'But you obviously did it very well, Mma,' she said. 'That is a good thing, I think.'

Babusi shook his head ruefully. 'If only everybody did that,' he said. 'Life would be much easier for all of us.' He paused, and then shook his head again. 'I went into a post office the other day, you know, and there were people sitting about on the other side of the counter. There were five or six of them, and they were sitting there drinking tea. One was having her hair braided, would you believe it, Mma? Having your hair braided on government time?'

Dolly made a disapproving face. 'They need to spend a little time in the private sector,' she said. 'Cafés are in the private sector, Mma – you know that? There are no long lunch breaks in the private sector. You can't sit around and drink tea in the private sector, I can tell you.'

Mma Ramotswe felt a momentary embarrassment. The No. 1 Ladies' Detective Agency was clearly part of the private sector, and yet she and Mma Makutsi *did* sit about and drink rather a lot of tea – almost every day, in fact. And when it came to lunch breaks, the duration of these was entirely flexible, depending on whether there was any pressing work to be done, which there often was not. Mma Makutsi sometimes went off for lunch at twelve and did not return to the office until half-past-three, only to leave again at four. Mma Ramotswe did not enquire as to where she went, although she knew that her colleague enjoyed the lunch served each day on the veranda of the President Hotel, where she met a number of friends in a club that they had started a few years previously. This club, she had announced proudly, was a service club, set up to allow publicly spirited women to assist the less fortunate. They played a major part, she said, in the winter-blanket relief project, and in the funding of a women's shelter. These were undoubtedly good causes, even if their planning seemed to require rather long lunches for the committee, of which Mma Makutsi had been the chair ever since its inception.

'I do not like to talk about these good works the group does,' Mma Makutsi said modestly. 'But one day I shall write down a list for you, Mma Ramotswe. Then you can see all that we do and how much we help other people. I do not like to mention it too much, though.'

Now, after Dolly had singled out tea and long lunches for attention, Mma Ramotswe said that she thought that tea breaks were important for staff morale, but should, of course, not be drawn out too long. 'Certainly, when there are customers waiting there is no excuse for drinking tea,' she said. 'In a post office, for example. If you work in a post office and you want to drink tea, then you should do it in a back room. You can't have people waiting to buy stamps or whatever while these idle employees take their time with their tea.'

Dolly nodded her agreement. Then she asked them for their orders.

'Tea,' said Mma Ramotswe.

Babusi grinned. 'We are not on duty, you see, Dolly. And this is not a post office.'

'I will fetch tea for both of you,' said Dolly, noting the order down on a pad. 'Two teas, then. And some cake, perhaps?' This was aimed at Mma Ramotswe. 'You should have some cake, Mma. There is no reason not to have cake.'

Mma Ramotswe acceded. 'That would be very good,' she said. 'A small slice, perhaps.' She hesitated. 'Or two small slices.'

Dolly made a note on her pad of paper. 'Both for you, Mma?'

Babusi came to her rescue. 'Yes, Dolly, two slices for Mma Ramotswe, and two small ones for me. Four slices altogether.'

With the waitress away, Babusi leaned across the table and said to Mma Ramotswe, 'She really was first class, that young woman. Married to the wrong man, though. She married him at eighteen.' He shook his head ruefully. 'Marry in haste, repent at leisure – have you heard that saying, Mma? I think it is one of those sayings that are only too true.'

Mma Ramotswe was silent. She did not disagree, because that, after all, had been her own experience. She had married the jazz musician Note Mokoti when she was young, blinded by his glamour. Her father, Obed Ramotswe, who was as good a judge of men as he was of cattle, had known that Note would bring only unhappiness to the marriage, but had not tried to stop her. Nor had he ever reproached her for her impetuosity, but had taken her back under his wing with the silence and unconditional support of a good parent. She had eventually forgiven Note when he had returned, long after the end of the marriage, to extract money from her; she had forgiven him and told him that there was no hate in her heart because she knew that you only lengthened the shadow of a bad marriage if you withheld forgiveness and nurtured hate.

Babusi was waiting for a response to his question, and so eventually she said, 'I have heard that said, Rra – and I think it is definitely true. It is not a good idea to get married too early – or to make up your mind about anything too quickly – especially marriage.'

'Her husband is going to end up in prison, Mma,' Babusi went on. 'He sells people worthless insurance policies. Or that is what the police say he does, because they came to ask me about him. They would like to arrest him, but there is always a difficulty with proof. When they question him, he is always Mr Clean-Clean who is just a businessman. Many policemen end up grinding their teeth over that man, Mma.'

'Poor Dolly,' said Mma Ramotswe.

'Yes. She is innocent. She has tried to get her husband to find an honest job, but I think she has failed. She will have to leave him, I think.' He paused. 'There are quite a few good women who are married to bad men, aren't there, Mma?'

Mma Ramotswe agreed. 'Women seem to think that they can change men for the better. I'm not sure that this is very easy. Sometimes it happens, but most of the time it fails.'

Their conversation now came to an end, as Dolly had arrived with their tea and cake. She served them, and then left.

Mma Ramotswe gave Babusi an enquiring look. 'You wanted to talk to me about something that was worrying you, Rra. If you would like to tell me . . . '

Babusi cut her short. 'I would like that, Mma – as long as you don't mind.'

She told him that he should go on.

'As you've just found out, Mma – from what Dolly said – I am the manager of a hotel. It is down that way, past Mokolodi, near a small river. It is called the Great Hippopotamus Hotel.'

Mma Ramotswe looked up from her teacup. 'Oh, that hotel, Rra. I have seen the signs on the main road – the signs for the road to the hotel. I have often wondered what it is like.'

'But you have never been?' asked Babusi.

'No, I have not. But I have heard that it is a very good hotel. I have heard that from people who have been.'

This pleased Babusi, who smiled appreciatively. But then his face dropped. '*Was* a good hotel, Mma. It *was*, but now . . . Oh dear, Mma, it is a very sad story.'

Mma Ramotswe made a sympathetic sound – something rather like a sigh. 'Hotels go up and down, I think. Sometimes they are very good, and then . . . '

'Then things go wrong,' supplied Babusi. 'Just like that.' He clicked his fingers. 'Things start to go badly wrong.'

Mma Ramotswe shook her head. 'That can happen to any business. One minute you have a good business, and then the next you are staring bankruptcy in the face. That happens, Rra.'

Babusi looked miserable. 'Bankruptcy is not a word that I like to hear, Mma. When people talk of bankruptcy, my heart becomes a stone inside me. Bankruptcy is a very bad thing.' He paused and crossed himself.

Mma Ramotswe had not expected this. 'You are a Catholic, Rra?' she asked.

He inclined his head. 'Yes, Mma, I am a Catholic. I make the sign of the cross because I think that God sees these things and knows when we are worrying about things like bankruptcy. God does not want people to go bankrupt, Mma.'

She neither confirmed nor challenged this proposition. 'Perhaps you should tell me a bit about the hotel, Rra. Perhaps you should tell me why you are so worried.'

Babusi sat back in his chair. 'I have worked there for ten years, Mma. When I started, I was a junior member of staff. I was in charge of kitchen supplies. I bought what the chef said we needed. I made inventories of the liquor stocks. That sort of thing. I think I was good at my job, and I was soon promoted.'

'Within four years I was assistant manager. Sometimes, when the manager went off to the other hotel that the owner had – he would go away for three or four weeks at a time to a place up in Maun – I was in charge of the hotel. I liked that, because I could run the hotel the way I wanted to.'

'So, when he became ill and had to retire, I was the obvious person to take over. The owner was a man called Mr Goodman Tsholofelo. He lives in Gaborone. He is very keen on cactuses. That is his hobby, and he spends all his time on it. He likes the hotel, but is not interested in running it. He has always left that to the manager.'

'He appointed me, and I took over the manager's office. I was very happy, Mma. I had always wanted to be a manager – of anything, as long as I was the manager. Now I was manager of the Great Hippopotamus Hotel that the newspaper had described as one of the best small hotels in southern Africa. They really called it that, Mma – and I was the manager. That was a big thing for me. I had prayed and prayed for that to happen, and now my prayers were answered.'

Mma Ramotswe smiled encouragingly. 'You must have been very pleased, Rra. Some people pray for a long time and nothing happens. No result. Nothing.'

Babusi considered this. 'Perhaps that is because they are not Catholic, Mma.'

Mma Ramotswe looked at him in astonishment. 'That does not matter, Rra. In fact, that is a very unkind thing to say. It does not matter who you are, Rra – or what church you go to. We are all the same.'

Babusi backtracked rapidly. 'Oh, you're right, Mma. I am not thinking about what I am saying. I am very upset, you see.'

Mma Ramotswe took a sip of her tea. 'You should go on with your story, Rra. And you should drink some more tea – it is very good for you to drink tea if you are upset.'

Babusi hesitated. He had felt the reproach that Mma Ramotswe had voiced, and now he apologised. 'I'm very sorry, Mma Ramotswe. I am not saying that I am any better than anybody else.'

'Just carry on, Rra,' she said. 'I have already forgotten that unkind thing you said.'

Babusi reached for his teacup. 'I was very happy to be working for the owner, for Mr Goodman Tsholofelo. He has been kind to me in many ways, Mma – but not just to me: he has been kind to everyone. He paid the school fees for the cook's son. He helped me pay the deposit on the first car I bought. He was always buying this thing and that thing for members of staff. He did not like to turn anybody away.'

Mma Ramotswe listened to that with interest – and a certain amount of concern. There was always need, whatever the economic climate. Botswana was a prosperous country by African standards. Since independence, since that windy night all those years ago when the Bechuanaland Protectorate had come to the end of its days and the new state had come into existence, people had built up their country, brick by brick, mile by mile of newly laid road, pula by pula of money put back into the bank, carefully husbanding the resources of this vast, empty land until the foundations had become a building of which they all could be so proud. They had wasted nothing, and so many of their wise leaders, from Seretse Khama onwards, had turned their face against the corruption that had so sapped the strength of other parts of Africa. The country that she loved so much had succeeded, and the wealth that the diamonds gave them had been used for the clinics and the schools and the irrigation schemes that people needed. That had all worked, but there was still need – just as there was everywhere in the world. There was, quite simply, never enough, and life for many people was still a battle. It was like that even in rich countries abroad; with all that glittering wealth, there were many people down at the bottom who could not see a doctor because they did not have the money to pay. How could that be?

How could that be? How could anybody let their fellow citizens die because they could not afford the medicines they needed? She could not understand that. In Botswana, even with its limited resources, you could go to a government clinic, and you would not be turned away.

But in spite of the fact that the Government did its best to make sure that people had the basic things they needed, there were still those whose lives seemed always to be on an economic knife-edge. Mma Makutsi had been one of those: when she first came to work for the No. 1 Ladies' Detective Agency – when she invited herself to do so – she had very little money. Mma Ramotswe had not been in a position to pay her much of a salary in those early days because there had been few clients – and few receipts. Mma Makutsi had lived in cramped, crowded accommodation. She had shared a water tap. She had had no curtain for her tiny window; she had owned only one pair of shoes – now, of course, she had far too many, but that was a personal issue for Mma Makutsi, and Mma Ramotswe would never make mention of that. Her circumstances had changed dramatically when she had married Phuti Radiphuti, who had the Double Comfort Furniture Store behind him, as well as a substantial herd of cattle, but there were still many people in the position that she used to be in. They struggled to make ends meet, and every time prices rose, every time it cost them more to make their journey to work or to pay the electricity bill, or to buy a pound of sugar or a bag of sorghum meal, it hurt. That was the lot of so many, and it meant that anybody who was willing to help could quickly become inundated with requests. A hungry man has only one question to ask, the saying went. And that question was: where is my next meal coming from?

So Mma Ramotswe could imagine that Mr Goodman Tsholofelo would have faced many demands from his staff, let alone others around him who might know of his generosity. She raised this with Babusi. She said, 'He must have been asked for things all the time, Rra. People like that get very little peace, I think.'

Babusi agreed. 'Oh, you are right, Mma. People took advantage of him whenever he came down here to see how things were going. Sometimes I found myself getting cross with them because they kept asking him for things. There was a man who looked after the hotel gardens, Mma – he was one of the worst, if not the worst. He was always asking Mr Tsholofelo to help him with something or other. One day it would be his sister's baby needed something for its stomach, or his aunt needed new glasses because she could not see where she was going and had recently nearly walked into an elephant. I ask you, Mma Ramotswe – an elephant? How do you miss an elephant, even if you can't see very well?'

'It's possible,' mused Mma Ramotswe. 'Those people up in the north have a lot of elephants walking around their villages. They go out to their fields and they find elephants tramping around. They have to be careful. The elephant hides in the trees and then he comes out and waves his trunk at you and makes that noise that elephants make. And you think: *Oh dear, here is an elephant.*'

'Yes,' said Babusi. 'But I happened to know, Mma, that this aunt of his did not live up north. He had told me about his aunt before, and he had said that she lived in Tlokweng. There are no elephants in Tlokweng. Maybe one hundred years ago, but not now. There are no elephants in Gaborone or Lobatse. That is one thing you will not see, Mma.'

Mma Ramotswe laughed. 'You are right, Rra. He did not need to make up a story like that. Even if this aunt had never walked into an elephant, she still needed glasses. He should have been truthful.'

'Well, he wasn't,' said Babusi. 'And even if Mr Tsholofelo did not believe that story, he still gave him money for the glasses. And there were other requests – not involving elephants – that were genuine enough. He was just a kind man, Mma. That's all there was to it – he was kind.'

Mma Ramotswe saw that Babusi's teacup was empty, and she filled it from the teapot that Dolly had brought them. Then she filled her own. There were some stories that were two-cup stories, and some that were three. This might be one of those, she thought. It might be three cups before Babusi got to the point and told her what was worrying him. She looked at her watch, discreetly. She had the time – and she could always order more tea, if necessary. As long as supplies of tea hold out, there is time to listen. That is well known, she thought.

Chapter Three

I See You, Dear Friend

The following day was a Saturday, and with the No. 1 Ladies' Detective Agency closed for the weekend, Mma Ramotswe was able to drive out to Tlokweng to visit her old friend, Mma Silvia Potokwani, redoubtable matron, fierce defender of orphans, and liberal dispenser of home-baked fruit cake described by Mr J. L. B. Matekoni as the finest cake he had ever tasted. It was not this fruit cake that enticed Mma Ramotswe out to the Orphan Farm – although, admittedly, it was one of the reasons why Mr J. L. B. Matekoni needed no encouragement to make that trip himself; Mma Ramotswe made the journey sometimes as frequently as once a week for the sheer pleasure of the matron's company. In Mma Ramotswe's view, Mma Potokwani was the embodiment of the qualities anyone would want in a friend: loyalty, good humour and a willingness to listen. There were many people, she felt, who were simply not interested in what their friends had to say; indeed, some did not even notice that their friends were talking, and took in little or nothing of what was said. That was unusual, but it did occur, and Mma Ramotswe always found it a most trying characteristic.

It was the opposite with Mma Potokwani: she was always eager to hear what her visitors had been doing; to learn where they had been and what they had seen; and to elicit their views on the issues of the day. In return, she was always willing to give a frank account of recent developments at the Orphan Farm, or of debates at the local *kgotla*, or council, where people would go to air their grievances or make suggestions as to how the community should respond to things that might affect it. You could speak your mind at a *kgotla*, without fear of being gagged because what you said was unpopular. It was the same at a funeral – by ancient tradition in Botswana, you could say what you felt needed to be said at a funeral without having to be too worried about possible repercussions.

Mma Ramotswe was expected, and a battered red and white traffic-cone, holed at the top and leaning to port, had been placed exactly where she liked to park her tiny white van, reserving the place for her. It was a shady spot, protected by the wide branches of an acacia tree, and it was therefore often occupied by another vehicle when Mma Ramotswe arrived. The traffic cone had been placed there on the orders of Mma Potokwani, who had told the groundsman that her friend Mma Ramotswe was arriving from Gaborone and would not expect to have to park out in the sun. If delivery vehicles came, they would have to park elsewhere: Mma Ramotswe was not just any member of the public, Mma Potokwani explained – she was an old friend of the Orphan Farm and a well-known member of the community. You could not expect well-known members of the community to park just anywhere, she pointed out; and the groundsman agreed. He knew and respected Mma Ramotswe; his father had bought cattle from her father, and he was hoping one day to ask Mma Ramotswe to track down a man who had owed him fifteen hundred pula for eleven months.

Standing on the veranda of her office, Mma Potokwani waved to her friend as she climbed out of the tiny white van, straightened her dress, and looked up at the sky.

'I see you, Mma Ramotswe,' the matron called.

'And I see you, dear friend,' replied Mma Ramotswe, using the words that they had always used over the long course of their friendship.

They shook hands – they had never embraced, as some friends do – not because they were more formal with one another, but because they had passed beyond that. Their handshake was far from perfunctory, and resulted in a linking of fingers that persisted as they went into the office, holding hands as might two children, naturally, in the innocence of friendship and alliance.

The office was untidy, with papers stacked on the large desk under the window, some of which had drifted to the floor.

'I have been sorting things out,' said Mma Potokwani. 'Sometimes I do that on a Saturday because there is nothing else going on. The problem with having other people working around you is that they distract you. *Please can I have this or that, Mma.* Or, *Where is the money for this thing or that thing*? You must know how it is, Mma Ramotswe.'

'Oh, I do, Mma. That is an office for you.' She paused. 'You need Mma Makutsi to come here and fix your filing system. She is the big filing lady, you know.'

Mma Potokwani smiled. Her relationship with Mma Makutsi was much easier than it had been in the past – she had always been slightly wary of the younger woman's manner. It was those glasses, she had told herself; and then she had thought that perhaps it was the way in which Mma Makutsi could be so certain about things, laying down the law, almost, and going on about that secretarial college she had attended as if it were some big university or whatever. It was not that at all – it looked rather like a run-down office block, Mma Potokwani thought, although she had never dared say that to Mma Makutsi. But these were small things, and over the years Mma Potokwani had developed considerable admiration for Mma Makutsi, seeing beyond the intimidating glasses and the slightly prickly manner, to the determined, competent woman who had achieved so much after a difficult start. Mma Potokwani knew all about starting with nothing: that was the position of the children she looked after, and she was fierce in her defence of their right to make something of their young lives.

But it was one thing to enjoy cordial relations with Mma Makutsi; it was quite another to let her come into the office and tell her where papers should be put. Mma Potokwani had her own filing system, and that would do perfectly well, she felt, even if she was the only one who understood exactly how it worked. And that was, she felt, rational enough if you bothered to look closely enough. Papers relating to matters that *had* to be dealt with were placed in the top drawer of the cabinet; papers that could be left for the time being were placed in the drawer below, and those that you were not at all sure about were tucked into the bottommost drawer. What could be more straightforward and practical than that?

And interspersed among the sheafs of papers were the odd crumbs of fruit cake – the result of their crossing the matron's desk at the same time that cake happened to be served to a visitor, or indulged in during a working cup of tea. Not that Mma Potokwani noticed these crumbs, but her secretary had, and always smiled at the sight.

'We can come back here for tea later on,' Mma Potokwani said. 'There is a new housemother I would like you to meet – Mma Oteng. She has taken over from Mma Kenosi. You remember her? Mma Kenosi is late now, I'm afraid.' She paused. 'But we all become late, don't we, Mma?'

'We do,' said Mma Ramotswe. 'Most people want to become late later rather than sooner, I think.'

The humour took the edge off the note of seriousness that had crept in.

'Mma Kenosi knew that she did not have much time,' said Mma Potokwani. 'She was very brave about it. But it was hard for the children in her house. Like all the ladies we employ here, Mma, she was the closest thing they had to a mother.'

Mma Ramotswe inclined her head. She had come across the phrase *the valiant dead* in a picture of a war memorial somewhere far way – in Cape Town, she thought – and it had resonated with her. The ranks of late people, as she called them, might be large ones, and most of them might be filled with those who had not done very much with their lives. But at their head there would be the gloriously lit throng of those who had led good lives in the service of others: Seretse Khama, Nelson Mandela, Mother Teresa of Calcutta, and lesser people, but still heroes and heroines, like Mma Kenosi and Obed Ramotswe. These were the valiant dead she thought about.

'Still,' continued Mma Potokwani, 'children are resilient, as we all know, and they bounced back soon enough, particularly when Mma Oteng took over as their new housemother.'

As they left the office to walk through the grounds to the small bungalow presided over by Mma Oteng, Mma Potokwani described how the new housemother had been recruited.

'I very rarely have to advertise for staff,' she said. 'People just appear.'

Mma Ramotswe thought of the staff of the No. 1 Ladies' Detective Agency, such as it was. She had never advertised for anybody either. Mma Makutsi had appointed herself – more or less; Charlie, who was now a part-time employee of the agency, while remaining a part-time (unqualified) mechanic with Tlokweng Road Speedy Motors, had been taken on as an act of charity; and there was nobody else. If she were ever to need more staff, then she could always put an advertisement in the newspapers, but she imagined that such an appeal would attract entirely the wrong sort of person. Private detective agencies did not need fantasists, but that was just the sort of person who would beat a path to her door were she to advertise. *Be very careful when you employ somebody,* Clovis Andersen wrote. *Remember that the public has an entirely unrealistic idea of what a private investigation business does. Ideally, you need to hire former policemen or women, or experienced service personnel. Be very wary of anybody else.* There might be a lot of truth in that – Clovis Andersen generally knew what he was talking about – but at the same time neither she, Mma Makutsi, nor Charlie would have satisfied those criteria. She herself had no formal qualifications and had done only small jobs, such as helping out in a local store; Mma Makutsi was a qualified secretary, admittedly with ninety-seven per cent in the final examinations, but with no experience, even of office work; and Charlie was a mechanic – of sorts – who would never be considered suitable for the police or the Botswana Defence Force. So, all of them would be turned down by Clovis Andersen, were they ever to seek employment with him. That was a sobering thought.

'No,' continued Mma Potokwani, 'most of the people who work here come by personal recommendation. All I have to do is to let it be known among the staff that there is a vacancy, and I do not have to wait long before somebody comes to the office to tell me that they have a sister, a cousin or a friend who has just the right qualifications for the job.'

'And is that how you found Mma Oteng?'

'Yes. The woman who is in charge of the laundry came to see me. She said that there was a lady from her home village. She came from Kanye.'

Mma Ramotswe nodded. 'Bangwaketse. They are strong people.'

Mma Potokwani agreed. 'They have done very well over the years, those people. They had very good leaders. People like Bathoen II built lots of good things. It is helpful if a people's leaders build things, rather than knock them down.'

'It is,' said Mma Ramotswe. 'And this lady, Mma – what about her?'

'The laundry lady said that she was not related to her in any way, but that she knew she was a hard worker. She also said that she felt very sorry for her because she had no husband and not much of an income. She said that she looked after a young boy who was handicapped, Mma – one of his legs was very thin – like a stick, really. People in the village had found him when he was just a few months old. Somebody had wrapped him in newspaper and left him by the side of the road. Anything could have happened if a man from the village had not been going that way on his bicycle. There are jackals, and once they sniff out a baby, he will have no chance. Or vultures, Mma. You lie down on the ground down there – even over at Kgale Hill – and close your eyes for a while. Then you open them and you will see a vulture sitting in a tree looking at you, Mma. That is not a good feeling, I think.'

'That poor boy,' said Mma Ramotswe. 'Left on the roadside like that.'

'Yes,' said Mma Potokwani. 'He can walk now – not very

fast – but he can walk. He has another problem, though. He will not speak to adults. He speaks to Mma Oteng, but says hardly anything to others. Just silence.'

'Still,' remarked Mma Ramotswe, 'he is lucky that he has that kind lady to be his mother.'

Mma Potokwani said that she was of the same view. Over the years she had dealt with a number of children who had been abandoned – it was not all that unusual – and she knew of a number of cases where the child had not had the good fortune to be found. 'But, of course, Mma Ramotswe,' she went on, 'my ears pricked up when I heard that this woman was looking after an abandoned child. I wanted to help, and so I went down there to Kanye and I found the woman whom the laundry lady had told me about. This was Mma Oteng.'

'I went to her house, which was a very small one, in a part of the village where there were still traditional buildings. Those houses can still be comfortable, Mma, even if they are a bit dark inside. They are often cooler in the hot weather than these modern houses made of breeze blocks. Cement can get hot, and a tin roof draws the heat in like a magnet. Thatch is what you need, Mma Ramotswe, to stay cool. And a floor of stamped-down cattle dung is a very good floor if you want to escape the heat outside. Not being modern is not always uncomfortable, Mma, as I am sure you will agree. Modern people think they are the only ones who are comfortable – but are they?'

Mma Ramotswe laughed. 'Modern people often have to starve themselves – to look modern. That is not very comfortable.'

Mma Potokwani was delighted by that. She, like Mma Ramotswe, was traditionally built – and proud of the fact.

'I could tell,' Mma Potokwani continued, 'that Mma Oteng was very poor. There was very little food in the house, although she insisted on giving me a slice of bread and jam with the tea that she made. It would have been rude not to accept, but I could see the boy looking at the bread with hungry eyes, Mma. That was what made me decide, right there and then. I said to her, "I have come to offer you a job at my place over in Tlokweng. It is a job that starts right away – tomorrow, if you are free. There is a salary and you will live in a small house looking after children. There is plenty of good food, which it will be your job to cook for the children."

'I could see her hesitate, and I knew at once why she was hesitating. It was the little boy – the boy who could not speak. She looked at him, and I knew that she felt that she could not take him back to Kanye – I could see that very easily, Mma. So I said at once that he was welcome to come with her, because our place here was intended for children who had no real mother or father and that was what our farm was all about.

'When she heard this, she looked at me and she started to cry, Mma Ramotswe. I put my arms about her while she cried. That is what you must do if somebody cries. You must never stand and look at them – you must put your arms about them.'

'And when she had finished crying, she said, 'Mma, I will come tomorrow. I will come on the bus . . . ' She stopped, and I realised that she would not have money for the bus fare, and so I gave her some, and she promised that she would arrive in Gaborone the next day – which she did. I went in to fetch her from the bus station and brought her out here. That is how it happened, Mma.'

They were approaching Mma Oteng's house, and Mma Potokwani finished her tale. 'She is expecting us,' she said. 'And there she is, Mma – at the window.'

Mma Ramotswe saw a face appear briefly at the window. Then the front door of the house was opened and Mma Oteng was standing there, dusting her hands on a kitchen towel.

'I have been baking, Mma Potokwani,' she said. 'Flour gets everywhere when you're baking.'

'Mma Oteng makes all the bread that her house uses,' explained Mma Potokwani, as she introduced the two women. 'And for some of the other houses too. Her baking is very popular with the housemothers.'

Mma Oteng dismissed the praise. 'You are the best baker, Mma Potokwani.'

'Certainly, when it comes to fruit cake,' interjected Mma Ramotswe.

'Ow!' exclaimed Mma Oteng. 'That is very famous fruit cake. I could never make anything half as good as that.'

They went inside. In a small parlour, three chairs had been set around a table covered with a gingham cloth. Cups and saucers, along with a large metal teapot, were ready for the visitors.

The conversation was easy; Mma Ramotswe took immediately to Mma Oteng, responding to her easy warmth. There was much to talk about, beginning with the affairs of Kanye, where Mma Ramotswe had spent several months staying with a relative many years ago. It was not hard to establish the existence of several mutual acquaintances – it was easy to do that in Botswana, with its relatively small population. Everybody, Mma Ramotswe was fond of saying, shares an ancestor if one is prepared to go far enough back. There is nobody without ancestors, and in Botswana people were prepared to remember these late people who had lived all those years ago. How could one forget about them when their faces were written in our faces; when the words we used were the words they invented a long time ago; when the sky under which they led their lives was exactly the same sky as that under which we lead ours?

'And how is Khumo?' asked Mma Potokwani during a lull

in the conversation, turning to Mma Ramotswe to explain that Khumo was the young boy whom Mma Oteng had brought with her.

Mma Oteng gestured towards the inside of the house. 'He is in there. He is a bit shy.'

'Mma Ramotswe would like to meet him,' said Mma Potokwani. 'As long as it doesn't distress him.'

Mma Oteng rose to her feet. 'He must learn to be with people,' she said. 'He is getting better at that as he settles here.' And to Mma Ramotswe, she said, 'Khumo does not speak to other people, Mma. He speaks to me, though, although his voice is not strong. It is soft like the wind in the trees. Like that – but I can understand what he is saying.'

Mma Ramotswe lowered her eyes. 'That is very sad, Mma. I am sorry to hear that.'

Mma Oteng sighed. 'They looked at him at a government clinic in Kanye. They said they could not find any physical reason why he could not speak. They said that sometimes children will not speak because they have suffered something very bad. I do not know of anything like that with this boy.'

Mma Potokwani said that she had encountered this issue before. 'There was that child some time ago, Mma Ramotswe – do you remember?'

Mma Ramotswe did.

'And now here it is again,' said Mma Potokwani.

Mma Ramotswe looked at her friend. Mma Potokwani was immensely competent, and she was not one to be defeated by the trials and misfortunes that were an inevitable part of life. But every so often the suffering of others appeared to weigh so heavily upon her that even her broad shoulders seemed close to buckling under the strain. Yet they never did, and she cheerfully tackled whatever was sent in her direction. Mma Ramotswe admired that so much, and now she saw it happening again, as Mma Potokwani made an effort to look on the positive side of things.

'He is such a good child,' she said, reaching out to lay her hand briefly on Mma Oteng's forearm. 'He is very bright, I think. And he is kind to smaller children – one of the other housemothers noticed that the other day, Mma. She said he was very gentle with the little boy who has fits – you know the one.'

'Thank you, Mma,' said Mma Oteng. 'I am proud of him. One day perhaps he will be able to speak properly.'

'I'm sure he will,' said Mma Potokwani.

Mma Oteng went off into the back of the house, to reappear with a boy of about eight. This was Khumo.

'This lady is a friend of Mma Potokwani,' said Mma Oteng. 'This is Mma Ramotswe, Khumo.'

Khumo glanced at Mma Ramotswe, and then looked away. His gaze seemed attached to the floor.

'Khumo is very interested in insects,' Mma Oteng offered. 'He is always catching things. And lizards too. Geckos. He has two chameleons at the moment.'

Mma Ramotswe gave an involuntary shudder. 'Not for me,' she said. 'I do not like these creepy-crawly things. Even a dung beetle makes me go cold. And when it comes to scorpions . . . ' The mere mention of these led to a further shudder, more marked this time.

'Khumo caught a couple of scorpions yesterday,' said Mma Oteng. 'He has them in one of his boxes.'

Mma Potokwani looked concerned. 'You must not let the other children touch these things,' she said. And then, to Mma Oteng, 'Do you think he understands what I've just said?'

Mma Oteng assured her that there was nothing wrong with

Khumo's understanding. He grasped everything that was said to him – it was responding to speech that was the difficulty.

Khumo looked up at Mma Oteng and tugged at her hand.

'I think that he wants to go now,' the housemother said. 'He's making something with a wooden box that somebody gave him.'

Khumo left.

'He is a lovely boy,' Mma Ramotswe said. 'You are doing a very good thing in looking after him, Mma Oteng.'

'I am very fond of him,' said Mma Oteng.

As Mma Oteng topped up their teacups, Mma Ramotswe asked her how she was settling in. 'If your family is all over in Kanye, you must be missing them,' she said.

'I do miss them,' came the reply. 'But I have relatives not far from where we are here. I have a sister and a cousin. And they each have friends who have been very good to me. My sister has come to see me here many times already.'

'So, she lives locally?' asked Mma Ramotswe.

Mma Oteng nodded. 'She works in a hotel not all that far away. She is a cook – not the main cook, not the chef, but somebody who makes the breakfasts and so on.' She paused. 'She is also a big help with Khumo. She often comes over from the hotel to collect him for the weekend. He stays with her in the staff quarters there. It gives me a bit of a break.' She gave Mma Ramotswe an apologetic look. 'Sometimes I feel that my life is just a bit too full of children, Mma.'

Mma Ramotswe understood. 'I can imagine that, Mma Khumo – Mother of Khumo. You will need some rest.' She addressed her in the customary manner, in which a woman is spoken of as the mother of a named first-born child.

Mma Ramotswe asked about the hotel. 'This hotel place is in Gaborone?' she asked.

'No, it is a hotel out that way.' Mma Oteng pointed to the south. 'Not as far as Lobatse, but in the Lobatse direction.'

Mma Ramotswe frowned. 'What is the name of the hotel?' she asked.

'It is the Hippopotamus Hotel,' said Mma Oteng. 'It is not a big hotel. There are twenty rooms, I think, but it is well known. People come from far away because they have read about it. Foreign people come – and some Batswana. But mostly well-off people who can afford to travel. They like going to that hotel.'

'The Great Hippopotamus Hotel?' asked Mma Ramotswe.

'That is the one,' said Mma Oteng.

Mma Ramotswe shook her head in wonderment. 'That is amazing, Mma. I was talking to somebody about this hotel just yesterday. I was speaking to the manager. He was in Gaborone, and I met him when I was out shopping.'

Mma Oteng clapped her hands together. 'That sort of thing is always happening,' she said. 'You think of something and then the next day you see the thing you were thinking about. It is very strange.' She paused. 'What did the manager say, Mma? What did he say about the hotel?'

Mma Ramotswe was on the point of giving her the gist of what Babusi had told her, but something within stopped her. 'Oh, this and that,' she said.

'I have not met that man,' Mma Oteng continued. 'But my sister said that he has been very good to her. Sometimes people who work in hotels are not very well paid. Sometimes managers bully the people under them.'

'There is plenty of that,' interjected Mma Potokwani. 'Some people let power go to their heads.'

'Or they are small people inside,' added Mma Ramotswe. 'They are small people inside and they think that they will become bigger if they humiliate or bully others. You see that time and time again.'

'That manager is not like that at all,' said Mma Oteng. 'My sister says that he is the best manager she has ever worked with. He never shows it if he gets upset. He does not shout and wave his hands about – like some people do these days. He does not do that. And if you make a mistake, he makes sure that you don't feel too bad. He says things like "We all make mistakes – and I make some of the biggest ones around." Isn't that a kind thing to say, Mma Potokwani, even if it is not true – even if he never makes mistakes himself? He just wants people to feel good about themselves.'

'I am glad that your sister likes him,' said Mma Ramotswe. 'It is never easy to work with people you don't like for one reason or another.'

'She is very happy with him.'

Mma Ramotswe hesitated. She still felt that she should be careful, but she wanted to know a bit more about the Great Hippopotamus Hotel, and it occurred to her that the sister of one of the cooks would be as good a source as any.

'Is the business doing well?' she asked. 'Do you think that this Great Hippopotamus Hotel is in good shape?'

There was a momentary hesitation on Mma Oteng's part. Then she said, 'Every business has its problems, Mma. No business is perfect.'

'That's true,' said Mma Ramotswe.

She waited, but Mma Oteng seemed not to have anything to add to what she had to say.

'I think Mma Ramotswe and I should leave you to get on with your work, Mma Oteng,' said Mma Potokwani.

'I am making a beef stew for the children,' said Mma Oteng. 'They love stew, and I try to give it to them every Saturday.'

'To have beef stew every Saturday is very good for children,' said Mma Ramotswe. 'It is a good start in their lives.'

'They deserve it,' said Mma Potokwani. 'Even if they do not have much else, they have that to look forward to.'

'And love,' said Mma Ramotswe. 'The children here get a lot of love. That is the thing that children want, Mma.' She paused. 'That is the thing that we all want.'

Mma Potokwani looked at her friend. Mma Ramotswe was better than she was, she felt, at expressing the truths that she, and others, could see in the world about them. Perhaps Mma Ramotswe had the time to ponder these things, and to find just the right words, while it was difficult, if you were a matron with responsibility for so many children, to sit down and think quite as much as you might wish to. What she had just said was an example of that. We all knew that what people yearned for was love, but how often did we actually say that? How often did we look at the fights and arguments that disfigured this world and say to ourselves – or to anybody else who might be listening – 'What those people want to do is to *love* one another.' Because that was what so many wars and conflicts were about – at heart. They were about a failure of love. One set of people were deprived of love and turned to hate as a result. And those whom they hated responded with hate, while all the time they should respond with love.

Then there were those who had forgotten altogether how to love, because they had been consumed with greed, or pride, and these things were like a drought falling upon the land, stopping the growth of love.

'You are thinking of something, Mma Potokwani?' asked Mma Ramotswe.

Mma Potokwani ended her reverie. She had not done so much deliberate thinking for some time, and she had rather enjoyed it.

Perhaps, she told herself, I should spend fifteen minutes when I get up each morning just thinking. And then I could get on with the day's work without thinking about how little time I have to do the thinking that I need to do . . .

'Yes,' she replied to Mma Ramotswe. 'I was thinking, but now I shall stop thinking because we have to get along and Mma Oteng will be wondering: *Why is this lady standing there thinking like that when I have stew to prepare for the children?*'

Mma Oteng laughed. 'I often think myself,' she said. 'In fact, Mma Potokwani, making a stew is a very good time for thinking. I think many things while I am doing it.'

As they made their way back to Mma Potokwani's office where, Mma Ramotswe hoped, there was the possibility of fruit cake, they talked about Mma Oteng, about how she had fitted in so well, and about how she was such a positive addition to the Orphan Farm staff.

'Such ladies are one in a hundred,' observed Mma Potokwani. 'They are the people who keep everything going, Mma Ramotswe. They are the ones.'

Mma Ramotswe agreed. No programme of training, no system of education, could be relied upon to produce somebody like Mma Oteng. Such people were born; they were endowed with character and gifts that no amount of effort on the part of others could create. They were who they were *because* they were who they were. Did that make sense? Mma Ramotswe was not sure, but it sounded right, she thought.

'About that hotel, Mma Potokwani,' she said.

'What hotel, Mma?'

'That hotel that Mma Oteng mentioned. The Great Hippopotamus Hotel.'

Mma Potokwani smiled. 'I drive past that sign whenever I go down to Lobatse,' she said. 'I have never turned off along that road. I have never seen the hotel.'

'Neither have I,' said Mma Ramotswe. 'The sign always makes me smile. The children sometimes say: "Is that a hotel for hippopotamuses to go on their holidays?" They like that idea.'

'What about it, Mma?'

Mma Ramotswe explained that she had been intending to mention the hotel to Mma Potokwani, even before its name came up. 'The manager came to see me,' she said. 'In fact, he didn't come to see me in the office. He saw me at a shop, and he asked to talk to me. We had tea together.'

Mma Potokwani encouraged her to continue.

'He said there were issues with the hotel. He was keen for me to look into something."

They had almost reached the office. 'You should tell me about this over a slice of cake,' said Mma Potokwani. 'You would like some cake, I assume, Mma Ramotswe?'

'I would.'

'Good. Then we shall sit down and have a slice – a large slice.' She paused, and then added, 'Perhaps even two, Mma.'

'You are a very generous person,' said Mma Ramotswe.

'I am a very weak person,' Mma Potokwani corrected her. 'When it comes to cake, I am very weak, Mma.'

'We all are,' said Mma Ramotswe, adding, 'In that department.' And then, as an afterthought to that afterthought, 'As in others, Mma.'

'Oh well,' said Mma Potokwani.

Chapter Four

Some Men Are Weak All the Time

While Mma Ramotswe was visiting Mma Potokwani, Mma Makutsi and her husband, Phuti Radiphuti, were out at Block 8, at his uncle's house on Mmaleso Road. This uncle, a legendary figure in Botswana furniture circles, had always taken a close interest in Phuti. Phuti's own father, who was asthmatic, did not respond well to the dust and pollen of the bush, and tended to stay in town if he possibly could. Uncle Phomolo Radiphuti – his full name was Phomolo Itumelang Radiphuti – had enjoyed getting out of town with his nephew, and had taught him many of the Setswana names for plants and for the creatures that lived their small lives under leaves and bushes. So many of these words were being lost, particularly to children brought up in the towns, that the old people in the villages and at the lands found their grandchildren sometimes looking at them in incomprehension – as if they came from a different country. So that black beetle that people might see marching stoically across the sand might just be referred to as a black beetle, or a *gogga*, that imported guttural generic for anything that crept or crawled, rather than called by its local name. And even a locust, a common enough insect, might find itself called a locust rather than a *segongwane*, which somehow seemed to suit it much better. Uncle Phomolo did his best to preserve the language, and Phuti, with his acute memory for detail, proved to be a good learner, even when he was very young. But when a language needed effort, then the writing was on the wall, at least for its more specialist reaches, and now Uncle Phomolo simply shook his head and sighed when he heard the way people spoke on the radio or in the supermarket. They spoke a language, he said, out of which the dignity had been stripped.

He had long since retired from the family furniture business in which Phuti's father had also been a partner, and devoted his time to growing traditional medicinal herbs under shade-netting in the back of his yard on Mmaleso Road. He knew all the Setswana names for these, of course, and provided supplies to the herbalists who still used them. That kept him busy enough, although he also served on the committees of several welfare organisations, and the boy scouts, for whom he had once been a district commissioner. His wife divided her time between a village where they kept a small house, this larger house in Gaborone, and the remote lands where her family had cultivated its crops for generations. Her sadness was their childlessness – a state which to her was the greatest of all possible misfortunes – but she successfully concealed this beneath a cheerful exterior.

The visits to Uncle Phomolo had become a venture of the Radiphuti household's Saturday. On most visits, they all went – Phuti, Grace and young Itumelang – although on occasion Phuti would go by himself, if Mma Makutsi had commitments elsewhere and took Itumelang with her. On this Saturday, they were all there, and while Itumelang investigated a box of children's toys, Mma Makutsi stood in the kitchen while Uncle Phomolo made them tea. It was in the kitchen, against the innocent backdrop of the preparation of tea, that Uncle Phomolo dropped his bombshell news about a new appointment that was about to be made. Being ignorant of the reputation of the main protagonist in the story, he was surprised by Mma Makutsi's reaction to what he said.

'Who?' she asked, her voice rising sharply. 'Who did you say they have chosen, Uncle?'

'A woman called Violet Sephotho,' said Uncle Phomolo. 'I think that was the name my friend mentioned.'

Mma Makutsi shot a glance in Phuti's direction. It was a look that was half disbelief, half outrage. With his usual mildness, Phuti said, 'It could be somebody else altogether, Grace. Sephotho is a common enough name.'

Mma Makutsi would have none of it. 'There is only one Violet Sephotho as far as I am concerned, Phuti,' she retorted. 'And that Violet Sephotho is the Violet Sephotho I met on my very first day at the Botswana Secretarial College.'

'But it's always possible . . . ' Phuti began, to be brushed aside by Mma Makutsi, who said, 'There she was, on that very first day, when the rest of us were noting down our timetable and the subjects we were going to be studying; there she was, talking about men she had met the previous night at some dance somewhere or other – talking about men as if they were breeding cattle – sorry, uncle, I do not wish to be crude, but that is what Violet is like. Men are like cattle to her – specimens to be judged as if they are in the show ring.'

'Oh, my goodness,' said Uncle Phomolo. 'That is a very bad way to judge other people. That is not good at all.'

'It certainly is not,' said Mma Makutsi. 'And all the way through the course, from start to finish, who was the one always talking in the back row, or painting her nails with bright, bright nail polish? I can tell you that, Uncle – it was Violet Sephotho. And at the end of the course, in the final examinations, what mark do you think she got?'

Uncle Phomolo shrugged. 'Not very much, I imagine, Mma. If you spend all your time talking about men and painting your nails, you cannot expect to do very well in any examination.' He paused. 'I am not an expert in examinations, but that is what I would have thought, anyway.'

'And you are quite right, Uncle,' said Mma Makutsi. 'Violet Sephotho got barely over fifty per cent in the final examinations. Anybody would think it was hard to get such a low mark, but she did. Technically, it was a pass, because fifty per cent has always been the pass mark at the college. I think they should have raised it to sixty per cent at least. Or they should have seen what mark she actually got, and then declared that the pass mark was five per cent above that. That would have meant that everyone would have passed except Violet, because hers was the lowest mark of any.'

Mma Makutsi seethed as she spoke, prompting Phuti to make an attempt to lower the temperature. 'What did your friend say about this lady, Uncle?' he asked.

The answer did little to calm Mma Makutsi. 'He says that she is in line for the important job he was talking about.'

'What exactly is this job?' exploded Mma Makutsi.

Uncle Phomolo was taken aback by the force of the reaction. 'It's nothing definite yet,' he said. 'My friend is on the board of something called the Botswana Inward Investment Council. The council is thinking of appointing a new director. They would like it to be a lady, I think, and he said that this lady's name has come up . . . '

Phuti had been silent. Now he asked, 'Why does it have to be a lady, Uncle?'

'I didn't say that it has to be a lady,' Uncle Phomolo replied. 'I said that they would like that – or that is what my friend said.' He shrugged. 'Anyway, they are appointing ladies to most things these days. And I think they're doing a very good job. There are many ladies . . . '

He trailed off. Mma Makutsi was glaring at him.

'Phuti would never deny that ladies are very good in these jobs they are doing, Uncle. You would never say that. Would you, Phuti?'

Phuti shook his head. 'I am very much in favour of ladies,' he said quickly. 'All that I wondered was whether there would be any jobs for men. Not too many – just one or two.'

Mma Makutsi shook a finger at him. 'Men used to take all the jobs, Phuti. You know that as well as I do. All the best jobs went to men, and women got the rubbish jobs at the end. That was how things were for a long, long time.'

Uncle Phomolo looked thoughtful. 'I remember those days,' he said. 'Everywhere you looked in business, there were men at the top. And in the government too. Everywhere. It was very easy being a man in those days.'

'And it was hard to be a woman,' said Mma Makutsi. 'Men said: jobs are given out on merit, but, surprise surprise, it is men who turn out to have the most merit.'

Phuti winced. 'That was very unfair to women. It must have been hard to bear.'

'It was,' said Mma Makutsi. 'But now that has changed – not

entirely, because there are still places where women are not treated fairly. But it's certainly much better.' She paused. 'And when people say that they would like a woman to be appointed to a job, they are usually just trying to make up for the fact that women did not get their fair share in the past.'

She gave Phuti a searching look, as if to detect whether there might be any smouldering embers of resistance to this entirely necessary adjustment of life's playing field. But Phuti did not dissent, and Mma Makutsi brought the conversation to the subject of Violet Sephotho.

'Have these people, the Botswana . . . '

'Inward Investment Council,' supplied Uncle Phomolo. 'The Botswana Inward Investment Council.'

'Yes, those people – do they know what she's like, do you think?'

'They can't do,' said Phuti. 'If they did, they wouldn't be thinking of appointing her.'

Uncle Phomolo looked thoughtful. 'My friend said that the person who is speaking in her favour on the council board is a businessman called Mr H. J. Morapedi. He is one of those people who uses his initials – like Mma Ramotswe's husband, Mma Makutsi . . . What is he called again?'

'He is Mr J. L. B. Matekoni,' she said.

'Mr J. L. B. Matekoni?' repeated Uncle Phomolo. 'Why is he called that?'

'That is his name, Uncle,' said Phuti. 'We are given our names, you see . . . '

Mma Makutsi cut him short. 'Uncle knows that, Phuti. He is asking why he uses his initials. That is what he wants to find out.'

Uncle Phomolo, however, was keen to find out what the initials stood for.

Mma Makutsi frowned. This had always been a bit of a mystery to her. Had she ever been told? She felt that she might have been, but could not now recall. 'I am not sure that anybody knows,' she answered. 'We've always called him Mr J. L. B. Matekoni – even Mma Ramotswe calls him that. Nobody ever uses any other names.'

Phuti smiled. 'That is because he is so widely respected,' he said. 'If you respect somebody, it is only natural to use their initials. People are too quick to use first names, in my view. Those should be for close friends and family.'

Uncle Phomolo nodded his head in emphatic agreement. 'You get these young people – sixteen-year-olds – calling you by your first name these days. One of them, not much more than a boy, really, said to me the other day – he was serving in a shop – he said, "Hi, Phomolo, what do you want today?" Can you believe it, Phuti?' This boy – for that was what he was – a mere boy – speaking to me as if I was one of his schoolmates.'

Mma Makutsi remembered something. 'I think I heard that the L stands for Limpopo.'

Uncle Phomolo grinned. 'Perhaps he is embarrassed. People give their children such odd names, forgetting that the poor child is going to have to live with it for the rest of his life.'

Mma Makutsi was keen to hear more about Mr H. J. Morapedi. 'Why do you think this Morapedi person is so keen to appoint Violet Sephotho, Uncle?'

Uncle Phomolo looked thoughtful. 'I don't like to say bad things about people I don't know, Mma. There are too many people these days running round saying bad things about all sorts of people – people whom they haven't met, and never will. Suddenly everybody is an expert and can talk about all the bad things that other people do.'

Phuti glanced at his watch. Much as he loved his uncle, the

retired furniture dealer could go on at excessive length. He had never been known for his brevity, and it seemed to Phuti that his tendency to take a long time to say very little was only getting worse as each year passed.

They waited.

Uncle Phomolo sounded uncomfortable. He was not one to engage in this sort of tittle-tattle, but he had started this conversation, and he could hardly decline to conclude it. 'I believe that Mr H. J. Morapedi is a man with an eye for the ladies. He is married, but some men cannot help themselves if an attractive lady comes along. They fall. They cannot help themselves.'

Mma Makutsi let out a shriek of triumph. 'I thought so!' she exclaimed. 'I thought that there would be something like this going on. The moment you mentioned Violet Sephotho's name, Uncle, I thought: this is going to end up with something like this.' She paused, enjoying the satisfaction of having had her suspicions confirmed. 'There are so many men who have fallen because of that woman. This Mr H. J. Morapedi will not be the first man to make a fool of himself over Violet Sephotho – oh no.'

Phuti looked doubtful. 'We don't know the whole story, Mma. We can't assume that . . . '

He did not finish. 'Phuti,' said Mma Makutsi, 'remember what I am by profession. I am an investigator of the problems of other people. I am specially trained to look at a situation and work out what is going on. That is what I do. And when I look at what we have here – Violet Sephotho about to be appointed to an important job by a man who has a reputation as a ladies' man – well, what could anybody possibly conclude other than that Violet is using this poor weak man . . . '

'But we do not know that,' protested Phuti. 'We do not know that this man is weak.'

Mma Makutsi answered in measured tones, as if explaining a point of great complexity. 'We must assume, Phuti, that all men are *sometimes* weak, and that some men are weak all the time. We may also assume that some men are weak about *some* things, while other men are weak about *everything*.' She paused. 'I am not passing judgement here. But it seems to me that if people are saying that this Mr J. H. Morapedi . . . '

'H. J.,' interrupted Uncle Phomolo.

'Thank you, Uncle. If this Mr H. J. Morapedi is known to have a weakness for attractive ladies, and if his name is mentioned alongside that of . . . ' She struggled with herself. Even to utter the name of Violet Sephotho required effort on her part. But uncomfortable truths have to be spelled out, and so she continued, 'alongside that of Violet Sephotho, then there is only one conclusion we can reach, Phuti, and that is that Violet has recognised this man's weakness and has seen in it a chance to get a highly paid job with the Inward Investment Council. He is going to appoint her because that is what men like that do with their lady friends. They appoint them to important jobs. There are hundreds of examples of that. Wherever you look, you will see girlfriends in highly paid jobs with very few duties.'

Uncle Phomolo shook his head. 'That is very bad, Mma. But then . . . ' He looked thoughtful. 'But then, do women not do the same thing? Do they not appoint their men-friends to highly paid jobs?'

Mma Makutsi dismissed this out of hand. 'I do not think so, Uncle. It doesn't work that way.'

'They appoint other women, I think,' ventured Phuti.

Mma Makutsi gave him a discouraging look. 'There is no evidence of that, Phuti. Women are very fair in these matters.'

Phuti knew not to pursue the issue. He glanced at his uncle, who returned his glance in silent assent. They both knew that there were some subjects on which it was best to remain silent, and this was one of them. But although they both believed that there were occasions on which Mma Makutsi was perhaps a bit rigid, there were reasons why she should feel passionate about the position of women. She had struggled against male assumptions of superiority, as so many women of her background had been obliged to do, and she had made a success of herself. She knew what it was like to be on the receiving end of condescension and discrimination, and if she sometimes appeared outspoken on these issues, this was the result of personal experience more than anything else. So neither of them said anything for a few moments. Eventually, Uncle Phomolo rose to his feet and proposed that he show Phuti a new power saw that he had bought and had recently installed in his garage workshop. That ended the discussion of Violet Sephotho and her machinations, at least for the moment.

In the car, on the way home, though, Mma Makutsi said, 'What do we do about Violet, Phuti? Have you any ideas?'

Phuti was not sure that Violet was any of their business. 'Do we need to do anything, Grace?'

Mma Makutsi seemed taken aback. 'Do you mean that we should stand by and let that woman carry on with her tricks? Do you want her to get away with it?'

Phuti refuted the suggestion. 'Of course not, Mma. I don't want Violet – or anybody, for that matter – to get away with anything. But the world is full of things that I would prefer not to be happening, and we can't stop everything, Mma.'

'But we can stop her. We can stop Violet.'

He seemed unconvinced. 'How can we do that, Mma?'

'By finding out who is at the head of this council or whatever. By going to that person and saying, 'Look, there is this job being given to this woman who is not qualified for it at all and who is only getting it because your Mr H. J. Morapedi is having an affair with her.'

Phuti saw an obvious difficulty with this. 'But what if the head of the council *is* Mr H. J. Morapedi? Do we go to him and say, "We would like to report you to yourself for giving a job to somebody with whom you yourself are having an affair"? Is that what we do, Grace?'

Mma Makutsi bristled. 'This is a serious matter, Phuti, and it does not help if you make jokes about it.'

Phuti was apologetic. 'I'm sorry, Mma. I should not make light of this heavy thing.'

'No,' she said, her tone becoming conciliatory. 'I know that you do not mean it, Phuti. I know that you agree with me on all these things. I know that.'

Phuti drove on in silence. Did he agree with his wife on everything? It was a question that he felt many men preferred not to ask – in case the answer was not what they – or their wives – wanted it to be.

'I am going to have to go and see this Mr H. J. Morapedi,' Mma Makutsi announced. 'It will not be easy, but I think it is my duty to go.'

Phuti remained silent.

'I will save him,' Mma Makutsi continued. 'Sometimes people need to be saved from their own stupidity, Phuti – they just do.'

'I'd be very careful, Grace,' Phuti said. 'That woman will not thank you for interfering in her private affairs. And I can imagine that she can be violet.'

'Violet?'

'I meant *violent*.'

Mma Makutsi laughed. 'A funny mistake,' she said.

Chapter Five

Look, Mma, Look at the Hills

Mma Ramotswe drove down to the Great Hippopotamus Hotel the following Tuesday, a day she had planned to take off to attend to various tasks around the house. Those tasks would remain undone, although none of them was so urgent as to require immediate attention. If a cupboard had been full to overflowing and in dire need of clearing out, the fact that it had been like that for at least two years meant that a further delay of a couple of days, or indeed weeks, would make no difference. Nor did a persistent tide line on the bath – caused by the children's failure to remember that they should always wipe the bath clean after use – need to be removed as a matter of urgency. And if Mma Ramotswe was free to do the trip that Tuesday, so too were Mma Makutsi and Mma Potokwani, both of whom had expressed an interest in seeing a hotel they had heard about but never visited.

The expansion of the party to three was not without its problems. The tiny white van could manage three people in the front – it had an old-fashioned bench seat – but such passengers would need to be on the small side, and neither Mma Potokwani nor Mma Ramotswe could, by any stretch of the imagination, be called small. Mma Makutsi had always claimed to be of average size, but Charlie had once pointed out that the concept of 'average size' depended on where you were at the time. If you were out in the Kalahari, mingling with a San community, for instance, a person of average size would be much smaller than if you were in some village in the far north, where tallness, traceable, so people said, to ancient ancestry from further north, was much more in evidence. Mma Makutsi, Charlie said, was large by most modern standards, and should not claim to be anything else. 'There is no disgrace in having large feet and hands,' he said. 'Large hands are useful.'

When Mma Makutsi heard that Mma Ramotswe was planning to take Mma Potokwani on the trip, she offered to drive them all down in her car, which was bigger and, moreover, had firmer suspension. 'You never know with some of those roads down there,' she said. 'They are not good for car springs. Your springs, Mma, are very old now and they may give out. You never know, Mma. You have to be careful.'

Mma Ramotswe was happy to agree. The engine of her tiny white van was in good health, but the rest of the vehicle – the coachwork, the suspension, and what Mr J. L. B. Matekoni called the 'nervous system' – the wiring – had been showing its age for some time. Nowadays, she restricted herself to routes that were familiar to herself – and the van – and avoided roads on which a breakdown would be awkward. Trips to Mochudi were no problem, nor were outings to Tlokweng to visit Mma Potokwani: in either case she could be easily rescued were anything untoward to occur.

'That is very kind of you, Mma Makutsi,' she said. 'And perhaps we can have lunch in the hotel, if they are serving it.'

Mma Makutsi asked if this was an official enquiry now, and whether she should open a file. Mma Ramotswe hesitated. She had not discussed this with Mr Babusi when he had spoken to her in the café. He had known, of course, exactly who she was, and that she ran the No. 1 Ladies' Detective Agency, but it was not clear that he had been consulting her professionally.

Mma Makutsi noticed the hesitation. 'You did not say anything to him about our terms, Mma?'

Mma Ramotswe looked away. Mma Makutsi had spoken to her on several occasions about the need to make it clear to people that they could not expect free help with all their problems. 'If you allow that, Mma,' she had said, 'then there will be no limit to the requests that people will make of you. Soon you will be sorting out all of Botswana's problems. Everybody will think they can come up to you and say, "Help me with this problem, Mma Ramotswe," and because you are so kind you will say yes, and they will think that you are doing it out of the kindness of your heart and that there will be no bill at the end of the day. You cannot run a business on that basis, Mma. We learned that more or less on the first day of our training at the Botswana Secretarial College. The lecturer said: "A business must always charge for its time. A business is not a charity."'

She fixed Mma Ramotswe with a reproachful stare as she continued, 'That is what he said, Mma, and he was right, you know. Look at Phuti's furniture store. If somebody comes into the store, Phuti doesn't give them a table or a chair, even if they need it badly and cannot afford to pay for it. He has to say, "Put down your deposit first and then we can talk about tables and chairs." He *has* to say that, Mma Ramotswe, because otherwise we would have no money and there would be no food on our tables – and we wouldn't have a table, anyway, to put the food on it that we do not have, because we would have had to sell it. This is all true, Mma, and you must remember it.'

There was more to come. 'You just have to be firm, Mma. You are a kind lady – you are the kindest lady in Botswana, I think, but you have to be firm with people. You have to say to people, "If you want me to help you, then you must pay money in advance to cover the first few hours of our work." Then you must say, "Give your details to my colleague, Mma Makutsi, who is in charge of bills. She will send you a bill so that you can transfer money into our bank account." And I will then open a file, with a time sheet so that you can put down the hours that you spend on a case and we can then charge the client for that time. That is the only way.'

And now Mma Makutsi sighed as she realised that the matter of the Great Hippopotamus Hotel was not yet on a formal footing. 'I shall start a file,' she said. 'I will not charge Babusi for that first conversation you had with him over tea. But when we go down to see him at his hotel, you must make it clear to him that there will be a fee for everything we do.' She paused. 'Is that agreed, Mma?'

Mma Ramotswe had to give her assent. Mma Makutsi was right: they had to charge fees, because if they did not, she would be unable to pay Charlie for the work he did; nor would there be funds to cover the office electricity bill, or postage charges, or any of the overheads that seemed to get bigger and bigger each year, even as fee income remained the same, or even shrank.

'I shall speak to Babusi,' she assured Mma Makutsi.

'Good.'

There was something else – a more sensitive issue to deal with, and now was the moment. 'I am very happy that Mma Potokwani is coming with us, Mma Ramotswe,' she began. 'She is always very good at seeing things. She is what I would call an observant lady.'

'That comes from being the matron of the Orphan Farm for so long,' said Mma Ramotswe. 'She sees so many people and has to deal with many different situations. Every day there is something happening at that place.'

'Oh, I can imagine that,' said Mma Makutsi. And then, rather sniffily, 'Mind you, Mma, many of us have a lot happening in our lives and have to deal with all types of people. Phuti runs a big store, as you know, and I am involved in that to some extent. We see many different types coming into the store to try out our furniture.'

Mma Ramotswe assured her that she had never doubted the variety and demands of the Radiphuti lifestyle. 'You are very experienced, Mma Makutsi,' she said. 'And, of course, at the Botswana Secretarial College you studied . . . '

'Human psychology,' supplied Mma Makutsi. 'Yes, we did, Mma. It was a very popular course. We had ten lectures on it over ten weeks. One lecture a week, every Thursday morning. I often think of human psychology on Thursday mornings – even today.'

'There is much to think about in that department,' mused Mma Ramotswe. 'People are very complex. They are always doing surprising things, and then you look behind the things they do, and you see the reason for it. There is always a reason for what people do, Mma Makutsi. That is well known, I think.'

Clovis Andersen said something about that, thought Mma Makutsi, although she could not remember exactly what it was or where he said it. And if he did not say it, it was certainly the sort of thing that he *should* have said, not that it was appropriate for her to put words into Clovis Andersen's mouth.

'Mma Potokwani,' said Mma Makutsi. 'Yes, she is observant, but . . . But, Mma, if Mma Potokwani has any faults – and we all have faults Mma, myself included – if she has any faults, one of them is *taking over*. I am not saying that she is bossy – that is not a word that I would use for Mma Potokwani – I would not say that, Mma, and I am not saying it now. No. But there are some people, I think, who might say that. I am not saying who these people are, but there are definitely some people who would say that the trouble with Mma Potokwani is that she tells people what to do – all the time.'

Mma Makutsi, the allegation made and out in the open, stared at Mma Ramotswe, as if challenging her to refute it.

But Mma Ramotswe did not intend to argue. Mma Makutsi was right: Mma Potokwani *was* bossy. She had always seemed bossy, right from the time that Mma Ramotswe had first met her, and there was no sign that anything had changed. But if it was bossiness, then it was a very special sort of bossiness. It was a good-hearted, loving bossiness; it was the bossiness of one who was simply trying to get things done, when inertia or active opposition might otherwise prevent something positive and necessary from happening. We needed people like that, thought Mma Ramotswe, and if they occasionally ruffled feathers because they were thought to be overbearing, then that was a small price to pay for what they achieved at the end of the day.

In the face of Mma Ramotswe's silence, Mma Makutsi continued, 'So, I think it will be important, Mma, that you don't allow her to interfere too much in our *professional* investigation.' She stressed the word *professional*; Mma Potokwani might well be observant; she might well have a sound intuitive grasp of human nature; but she was not a professional detective – and that made all the difference.

Mma Ramotswe smiled. 'Don't worry, Mma Makutsi,' she said reassuringly. 'I shall make sure that Mma Potokwani does not overstep the mark.'

Mma Makutsi liked that expression. *Overstep the mark* ... That was what so many people did – they overstepped the mark and, to continue in terms of feet, they then ended up treading on toes.

With those preliminary matters sorted out, Mma Ramotswe and Mma Makutsi set off for Tlokweng, where they would pick up Mma Potokwani and then double back towards Kgale Hill and the Lobatse Road. Mma Potokwani was in a talkative mood, and kept them both entertained with Tlokweng gossip as, with Mma Makutsi at the wheel, they negotiated the roads and roundabouts on the way out of town. At the turn-off to Kgale, the traffic thinned, and by the time they reached the Mokolodi Road, the bustle of Gaborone was well behind them and the land was opening up under the wide skies of the south. And it was not long then before they saw the sign in its position just off the road: *The Great Hippopotamus Hotel.* Underneath the large lettering was painted an old-fashioned hand, complete with white cuff, pointing off to the east. In smaller letters underneath were the assurances that any traveller might be looking for: *Clean rooms, all with baths; world-renowned dining room; parking to rear; seating.*

Mma Potokwani read out these attributes as they turned off the main road and drove past the sign. 'That is everything you might need,' she said. 'Including seating, it seems. I wonder why they have to say something about that. Are there any hotels where there is no seating? Where the guests have to stand?'

'They would not be in business for long,' observed Mma Ramotswe. 'Sitting down is important. We all need to sit down.'

Mma Makutsi wondered about the world-renowned dining

room. 'Can that be true?' she asked. 'Are there people all over the world talking about the dining room of the Great Hippopotamus Hotel? I do not think so.'

'Perhaps they mean world-class,' suggested Mma Potokwani. 'People are always talking about things being world-class. Those words are being used too much these days.'

Mma Ramotswe considered this. She rather liked the expression *world class*, and had been tempted, when drafting the wording for an advertisement for the agency, to claim that it offered *world-class services to the Botswana community*. She had liked the sound of that, but had refrained, at the end, from using the expression because she was not sure that it was quite true. The No. 1 Ladies' Detective Agency was good – there were few who would dispute that – but was it world-class? Perhaps it would be more modest to claim that their services were as good as one could ever expect on a *national* level. That would make them Botswana-class, which unfortunately did not have quite the same ring to it.

'We shall see,' said Mma Ramotswe.

She looked out over the bush that spread out on either side of the narrow, unpaved road along which they were travelling. There was little variety: on the horizon there was a low range of hills, blue at this distance, but, for the rest, the land was without salience, a vast stretch of acacia scrub, grey-green vegetation on red-brown earth, presided over by a dome of empty sky. There were those who would see nothing in such a landscape, but for Mma Ramotswe, this was a distillation of the immense, brooding spirit of her country. It was a song for which you needed to have the right ear, but if you were attuned to it, it was a melody of peace and calm and abiding love. She glanced at Mma Potokwani, who was looking out of the window in the same direction as she was, and she waved a hand in the direction of the hills, as if to say, *Look, Mma, look at the hills*, and Mma Potokwani understood her gesture, and smiled in recognition of what it was that Mma Ramotswe wanted to say. There were no words that would express this effect that the land had upon her, but they both felt it, and knew what it meant.

Suddenly the road veered off to the right. As they made the turn, the hotel came into view – a small cluster of buildings, sheltering in a ring of trees that were considerably taller than the ordinary acacia that covered the surrounding plains. The foliage of these trees was of a darker green, and bent in a gust of wind that had sprung up from the south, but that passed quickly off to the interior, towards the Kalahari, warm breath from the Cape of Good Hope, from somewhere far away towards the very tip of Africa.

They approached the hotel. It was typical of the country's older buildings, relics of the later days of the Bechuanaland Protectorate or the first decades as the new state of Botswana. Buildings of that time were modest in their ambitions, reflecting the quiet mood of a culture that had no desire to prove anything to anybody, and that eschewed any form of show. They were times, too, when people appreciated dark interiors and the importance of cool verandas. It was a comfortable architecture, happy with nooks and niches and permissive towards plants, which were allowed to cover structures if they so desired. It was an architecture that preferred wood and brick and tin to expanses of smooth concrete and glass.

'So,' said Mma Makutsi, as she switched off the engine. 'This is the hotel.'

They sat in the car for a few moments, looking at the building before them. Among the pillars of the veranda running along the front of the building grew a riot of bougainvillea, red and purple and somewhere in between. Behind this, shaded by the foliage and flowers, were a few chairs of the sort to be found on any hotel veranda, comfortable with their faded cushions, placed around low tables, ready for tea or other drinks. Then came the open entrance, affording a view of the hotel lobby beyond. A guest's suitcase stood just inside the door, and behind it a receptacle for walking sticks. There was no sign of anybody being about, although from a chimney on the side of the roof a small wisp of smoke curled skywards from a cooking range within.

There were several other vehicles parked nearby, one by the side of a tennis court that abutted upon a small patch of lawn. The court looked playable, but only just; the net, strung between two green-painted wooden posts, sagged badly in the middle, and would allow even the weakest serve past. The white marking lines were still discernible, but had cracked and powdered in several places.

'I don't think anybody has played tennis recently,' observed Mma Potokwani as she stepped out of the car. And to Mma Makutsi she said, 'I don't suppose you play tennis, Mma.'

Mma Makutsi was guarded. 'I have not played that game, Mma.'

Mma Ramotswe picked up the note of tension in this response. Mma Makutsi was sensitive to slight, and might see this as a veiled criticism. 'I think that Mma Makutsi would be very good at tennis,' she said quickly. 'A champion, in fact – if she played.'

This discussion of tennis was cut short by the appearance of Babusi on the veranda. 'Mma Ramotswe,' he called out. 'Here you are. I did not hear you arrive.'

The manager bounded down the steps to welcome them. He shook hands with Mma Ramotswe and was introduced to Mma Potokwani and Mma Makutsi, who were introduced by Mma Ramotswe as a friend and colleague respectively.

Babusi fixed his gaze on Mma Makutsi. 'I know exactly who

you are, Mma,' he said. 'We have never met, but I know that you are the wife of Phuti Radiphuti. That is correct, isn't it?'

Mma Makutsi inclined her head. 'That is who I am, Rra.'

'My cousin knows your husband – or used to know him. He has gone up north now.'

Nobody was surprised by this connection, remote though it was. This was Botswana, and it would have been unusual if there had been no link of some sort.

He transferred his gaze to Mma Potokwani. 'I think I know who you are, Mma. I think that you have given a job to the sister of one of the ladies who works here – a cook. You are the matron in charge of that children's place, aren't you?'

Mma Potokwani nodded. 'Mma Oteng has spoken of her sister. I think the sister has been very helpful to her.'

'People are,' said Babusi. 'As a general rule, people look after one another.' He paused. 'I heard that that lady, that Mma Oteng, had had a bit of a struggle. There is a boy she looks after all by herself. I don't think there was much money.'

'She is much better off now,' said Mma Potokwani. 'We pay our housemothers quite well and they have a comfortable place to stay.'

'Then they should be happy,' said Babusi. 'A salary and a roof over your head – what more does anybody need?'

Mma Makutsi had been quiet during this exchange. Now she said, 'Shoes. You need shoes.'

Babusi laughed. 'Of course, Mma. I was just making a general observation. There are many other small things that you need apart from a salary and somewhere to live. And you're right, we all need shoes, don't we? And some of us . . . ' He gave Mma Ramotswe a playful look. 'And some of us, particularly if we are ladies, need more than one pair of shoes.'

Mma Ramotswe tried not to catch Mma Makutsi's eye. Mma Makutsi was unquestionably one of those who seemed to need more than one pair of shoes, but that was territory into which it would be unwise for Babusi to venture. She might have said to Babusi, 'Men can be fashion-conscious too, Rra,' but instead she said, 'We have come all the way from Gaborone, Rra. I am feeling a bit thirsty after the journey . . . '

Babusi clapped his hands together. 'Tea, Mma – of course, of course. What am I thinking of? We can have tea up there on the veranda. We can talk there, where nobody can hear us.'

Mma Ramotswe looked up at the bougainvillea. It was a useful plant in any garden, as it needed little encouragement. But its thick growth, its tangle of winding branches and flowers, was a favourite place for arboreal snakes, for the thin, lethal green snakes that avoided the ground and twisted themselves along twigs and sprigs, watching and waiting. A small bird might alight, momentarily unwary, or a gecko, or some other innocent morsel, and die there among the flowers. She looked away.

Chapter Six

My Tears Have Been Wiped

They sat on the veranda, a pot of tea before them.

'I have already told Mma Ramotswe about the person who owned this hotel,' Babusi said. 'But just so that you know, Mma Potokwani and Mma Makutsi, he is called Mr Goodman Tsholofelo, and he lives in Gaborone. But he is getting on a bit now, and he very rarely visits the hotel, as he used to do. We miss him, because he was always so kind to everybody.'

'He has retired?' asked Mma Makutsi.

'More or less,' said Babusi. 'He has one or two businesses that still belong to him, but he decided about six months ago to pass the hotel on to his family. He is no longer the owner of the Great Hippopotamus Hotel.'

'He has children?' asked Mma Potokwani.

Babusi shook his head. 'Mr Tsholofelo was married to a lady

who was never very well. It was very sad. He nursed her himself for many years until she became late two years ago. They never had children.'

'I think I heard of that lady,' said Mma Potokwani. 'She gave some money to the Orphan Farm.'

Babusi said that he was not surprised by this. 'They have always been kind like that. They have helped so many.' He sighed. 'It is sad that there were no children, but if that is the Lord's will, then that is the Lord's will. And it was the Lord's will that he should have two nephews and a niece. They are the people who now own the hotel. They are my new employers.'

He stopped to take a sip of tea. Mma Ramotswe noticed that while he had been animated when talking about Mr Goodman Tsholofelo, a note of resignation crept into his voice when he talked about the new owners. 'Perhaps you should tell us about these people,' she prompted.

Babusi put down his cup. 'Yes, well, the new owners . . . ' He trailed off.

Mma Potokwani cleared her throat. 'They are his nephews and niece, you say, Rra. What are their names?'

Mma Makutsi shot Mma Potokwani a glance. 'He was just about to tell us, I think, Mma.'

Babusi sighed again. 'There are two nephews who are brothers. They are the sons of Mr Goodman Tsholofelo's late sister, Kaboentle. They are called Morapedi.'

It took Mma Makutsi a moment or two to react. But then she stiffened. 'Morapedi, Rra? They are called Morapedi?'

'There are many Morapedis,' Mma Potokwani interjected. 'It is a common name. I am friendly with a Morapedi who works in the Department of Water Affairs. And there is one at the airport, in the café there. And now I come to think of it, I know a

Sergeant Morapedi in the police. He is a big football man in his spare time . . .'

Mma Makutsi took control. 'These Morapedis,' she said. 'What are their first names?'

Babusi hesitated. 'One is called Pardon. It is an odd name, but that is what he is: Pardon Morapedi. Then the other one, the younger brother: I am not sure what the initials stand for, but everyone calls him Mr H. J. Morapedi.'

Mma Makutsi froze.

'You know him, Mma?' asked Babusi.

Mma Ramotswe was puzzled. She had never heard of Mr H. J. Morapedi, but clearly the name meant something to Mma Makutsi.

'I have come across that name very recently,' said Mma Makutsi, struggling to keep her voice even.

When she did not venture any further information, though, Babusi continued, 'The niece is by a different sister of Goodman's, one who is not late but who went off when she was young with a man who was a prospector. They lived up in Angola, I think, until something happened to him – I'm not sure what. But he became late a long time ago. The sister came back and set up a shop selling clothes – mostly ladies' clothes now, I think. You may know the place, Mma: *Select Fashions.* She did that for a long time and then passed the business over to her daughter, who is the niece who is now one of the owners of hotel. She is called Diphimotswe.' He smiled. 'I have always liked that name. *My tears have been wiped.* That is a lovely meaning for a name.'

Mma Ramotswe glanced at Mma Makutsi. It was clear that she was not going to say anything further about Mr H. J. Morapedi – that would come later, she assumed. What interested her now was the crisis the hotel was facing. Babusi had alluded to that when they first met, when he had first asked for her help, but had not gone into any detail. Now she felt she should ask him to explain.

Mma Makutsi caught her eye. 'Mma Ramotswe would like to clarify one thing before we go any further, Rra,' she said. 'You do know, do you, that we carry out investigations for people as our business? Mma Ramotswe would like to confirm that you understand you will need to pay a fee.'

'But of course I do,' said Babusi quickly. 'I do not expect people to work for nothing.'

'We do take on cases for nothing if people cannot afford . . . '

Mma Makutsi interrupted her with a discouraging look. 'So, there will be a bill,' she said in a raised voice.

'I will pay your bill the day I receive it,' Babusi continued, looking slightly offended at any suggestion to the contrary. 'I do not like to let bills sit there.'

'I'm sure you don't, Rra,' said Mma Ramotswe. 'And we are not expensive.'

'Nor are we cheap,' said Mma Makutsi quickly. 'We are in the middle.'

'That is a good place to be,' said Mma Potokwani. 'If everybody was in the middle, for everything, then would we have problems in this life? We would not, I can tell you. The world would not be full of conflict and strife and people getting at one another.'

'I think that is true,' said Mma Ramotswe. 'But tell me, Rra: what has been going wrong in this place? You told me that you were very concerned. You said the hotel faced problems.'

Babusi sat back in his chair. 'It is a very worrying story,' he said. 'Not just for me, Mma Ramotswe, but for other people who do not have what I have. It is easy for a manager – I can always get another job, but some of my staff cannot. If this hotel goes out of business, then that is the end for them, Mma. It is that serious.'

'You must tell us, Rra,' said Mma Ramotswe. 'We are all listening.'

It had begun a few months ago, Babusi told them. It was shortly after the change of ownership, when the nephews and niece had taken over from Mr Goodman Tsholofelo. The handover had been uneventful and went unnoticed by most of the staff. Babusi himself had received a letter from Mr Tsholofelo's lawyers telling him that his contract of employment had been transferred to a new partnership consisting of Pardon Morapedi, his brother, Mr H. J. Morapedi, and their cousin, Diphimotswe. The lawyers said that nothing would change other than that Babusi, as manager, would be expected to attend a monthly meeting with the three new owners. Prior to that, Goodman Tsholofelo had largely left matters to his manager and had only given the broadest of guidance.

The new arrangement worked well. The two brothers seemed less engaged with the business than Diphimotswe, who settled into a routine of spending two days a week in the hotel, driving down from Gaborone on Friday afternoons and returning to town on Monday morning. Although she still ran her clothing business, Babusi explained, she had time to give to the Great Hippopotamus Hotel. He got on well with her as in his view she understood what it was that guests were looking for in a small hotel like theirs. What was most important, he said, was that things should run smoothly, and that guests should get no unwelcome surprises.

But unwelcome surprises began to occur – and did so quite frequently, the first being an episode of food poisoning that befell the hotel at the worst possible moment – during the stay of a group of travel agents, touring Botswana to assess the destinations they would be recommending. The timing, he said, could not have been more unfortunate; nobody ended up in hospital, but everybody who had dinner on that Friday night experienced more than a day of distress.

There had been intense discussion about the source. The ingredients used to make the courses for the meal were scrutinised and appeared blameless. Everything, it seemed, had been bought within the last few days, kept under refrigeration, and seemed quite fresh. Ice cream had been served for dessert, and ice cream, as everybody knew, could be a good place for bacteria to breed, but once again this ice cream came from a reliable source and was well within date.

Mma Potokwani had been listening closely. Now she interrupted Babusi to ask if everybody had been affected. 'Sometimes some people eat this thing and others eat that thing,' she said. 'It is important to know who had what.'

Mma Makutsi frowned. She had been about to ask that precise question, which she thought was more the preserve of a member of the enquiry team – which was, of course, made up of her and Mma Ramotswe – and no business of *lay people*, of whom Mma Potokwani was a representative. 'Let me rephrase the question put by my friend, Mma Potokwani,' she announced. 'Did everybody have the same food?'

Mma Potokwani smiled. 'That's what I just asked, Mma.'

Mma Makutsi brushed aside the protest. 'You asked who had what. I want to know if that *what* was the same thing,' adding, after a moment's thought, 'as the other *what*, that is,' and concluding, 'Mma.'

Mma Ramotswe thought it was much the same question, but did not say so.

'Everybody had the same courses,' said Babusi. 'We believe

in a narrow menu because that allows the cooks the chance to put a lot into each dish. Narrow range, high quality – that's the way to go.'

'So, there was no choice?' asked Mma Makutsi.

'Yes, there was no choice. Unless . . . '

'Yes, Rra?'

'Unless you chose the vegetarian option. You always have to have that choice these days now that so many people have stopped eating meat.'

Mma Potokwani shook her head. 'Those people will become very weak. If the whole country stopped eating meat, we would all be very weak indeed. Meat contains iron, and we need iron. Children, in particular, must have iron every day. I have always said that.'

'There are other sources,' said Mma Makutsi, sounding slightly irritated. 'You can get iron from many places, Mma Potokwani. Perhaps you should read up about it. Eggs, for instance: did you know that eggs contain iron? And spinach has it too. Beans and nuts. Everywhere there is iron.'

Mma Potokwani defended herself. 'I am not saying that you cannot find iron. I am just saying that if you do not eat meat, then you must be careful about getting iron elsewhere. That is all, Mma Makutsi.' She paused, and then added, 'I have plenty of iron myself – I am satisfied that I do not need more iron.'

Mma Makutsi bit her lip. There were many grounds on which to take issue with Mma Potokwani, and dietary iron was clearly one of them. But they were with a client, and she did not want to end up disagreeing with colleagues (or even with adjuncts) in the presence of the client.

Mma Ramotswe turned to Babusi. 'But were they *all* sick, Rra? Was everyone ill, Rra – all the guests?'

Babusi looked thoughtful. 'Yes, they were all sick. But not everyone.'

This answer hung in the air.

'You mean . . . ' began Mma Makutsi.

'I mean all the guests,' Babusi clarified. 'All the guests who had dinner. One or two did not want to have dinner because they had eaten too much at lunch.'

Mma Ramotswe encouraged him to explain further. 'So they were not sick? Those who did not have dinner?'

'No,' said Babusi. 'They were not sick that night. They were sick the next day, though.'

Mma Potokwani looked puzzled. 'After breakfast?'

'They did not eat breakfast,' said Babusi. 'There was no breakfast, because the kitchen staff – there are three ladies who work in the kitchen – they were not at work. One of them had run away.'

They waited for further explanation.

Babusi looked at them with a certain weariness. 'People are always running away,' he said. 'The young man who helps the gardener with the garden – he is only seventeen – he ran away last week.' He paused. 'But that was because he had got a girl in his village into trouble. She did not want to have a baby.'

Mma Makutsi looked disapproving; Mma Potokwani rolled her eyes. Mma Ramotswe, though, did not show a reaction to this. This was what happened. It should not happen, but it did, and she still loved the young people who made it happen because . . . well, because they were young people, and young people did these things all the time, and it did not help to shake one's head too much.

Now Mma Ramotswe said, 'That is a separate matter, I think. There is not much you can do about young people doing that sort of thing.'

Mma Makutsi glowered, 'But there is, Mma – there is. You can say to young men: if you do these things, then you are not to run away, because the young woman can't run away, can she? You are to stay and face the consequences. You are to get a job and give the money to the young woman and the baby. That is what you must do.'

Babusi nodded. 'I cannot disagree with that, Mma. There is too much of that going on these days. I am surprised that there are any young men left. They are all running away all the time.'

Mma Ramotswe tried to steer the conversation back from matters of social policy to the tale of the food poisoning. So, there had been no breakfast because there had been no kitchen staff, one of whom had run away. The obvious question was why that member of staff had run away. That was the question she now asked.

Babusi nodded to indicate that this was an issue that he, too, thought needed to be addressed. He looked away for a moment. When he turned back to face her, Mma Ramotswe could see that he was embarrassed. 'That lady was bad trouble, Mma,' he said. 'She was one of those ladies who think that they can become friendly-friendly with the husbands of other ladies. You know the type, Mma.'

Mma Makutsi thought, *I know the type all right. Violet Sephotho – that is the type.*

'So, she had been found out?' asked Mma Ramotswe.

Babusi nodded. 'One of the other kitchen ladies had found out that she was seeing her husband. There was a very big row in the kitchen. Plates were thrown, Mma. And pans too.'

Mma Ramotswe shook her head. 'That is not the way people should behave.'

'There is no excuse for throwing things,' said Mma Makutsi.

'Well, that's what happened,' Babusi continued. 'So, we were one short in the kitchen anyway, and then the other ladies did not turn up. They said that they had overslept, but why should two of them oversleep on the same morning? That is a question that I asked them, and they could come up with no explanation. They just shrugged. You know how kitchen ladies can sometimes just shrug? That is what they did.' He paused and gave Mma Ramotswe a meaningful look. 'I think they were ashamed. They thought I would blame them for what happened.'

'That would not be surprising,' said Mma Potokwani. 'After all, it was food poisoning – and they were the ones who prepared the food.'

Mma Ramotswe asked Babusi whether he trusted the kitchen staff. He replied that he did: apart from the woman who had run away – the woman with an eye for men – they were, he said, completely reliable. One had been with the hotel for five years, and the other for seven. 'One thing you should know, Mma,' he said, 'is that both of these ladies are in the ZCC.'

'Ah.'

The Zion Christian Church was a popular church, the members of which wore brightly coloured uniforms and were often to be seen marching along the roadside, singing hymns. Even in a country with a strong choral tradition, as Botswana was, their singing stood out.

'So, I think we can immediately rule out suspecting them of anything,' Babusi went on. 'ZCC people don't do that sort of thing. They are good people, Mma Ramotswe.'

'You are right, Rra,' she said. 'It is unlikely.' And yet, she thought, unlikely people did unlikely things all the time – while likely people might do nothing at all. *Beware of stereotypes*, Clovis Andersen wrote in *The Principles of Private Detection*. And he went on to say, if she remembered correctly, *People may do the things you expect them to do, or may not. It all depends. That's what most people are like.* It occurred to her, though, that this in itself was stereotyping people – to say that was what most people were like.

There was something she needed to find out: had anybody else not eaten dinner that evening? She now asked Babusi that.

'I didn't,' he said. 'That was why I was all right. I was not ill.' He hesitated. 'I was not hungry, you see, Mma Ramotswe. If I have lunch – and I did have lunch that day – then I often feel that I have no room for dinner. I think I may have a small stomach.'

'And was there anybody else who didn't have dinner?' asked Mma Ramotswe. 'Including the staff.'

Babusi explained that the staff usually ate separately – in the kitchen, after the guests had finished their dinner. They often polished off the leftovers from the guest dining room. That did not happen that night, though, as one of the waiters had absent-mindedly thrown the leftovers away. Sometimes they did that, Babusi said – when they weren't thinking.

Or when they *are* thinking, thought Mma Ramotswe.

'So that was one of the worst things that happened,' said Babusi. 'But there were other things that kept going wrong. There was the occasion when all the guest laundry went missing. We have a member of staff who does the laundry. He is very reliable and never loses anything. Yet a couple of weeks ago, all the laundry disappeared from the drying line. *All* of it, Mma. Nobody had any idea of how that happened. One moment it was there, drying in the wind – the next minute it was gone. I thought that perhaps it had blown away, but it hadn't. I sent a herd-boy out to look through all the bush near here, but he found nothing. And then there was the scorpion found in one of the bedrooms. A guest was stung, and his leg swelled up like a balloon. Then a bathroom flooded and ruined a carpet in the corridor outside. And so on – incident after incident. And word got out. There were bad reviews, and once that starts it's very difficult to stop it.'

'Some of these things seem like little matters, Mma Ramotswe,' Babusi concluded. 'But put them together, and they make a pattern. Somebody is trying to ruin the hotel's reputation. Somebody wants it to fail.'

'It certainly sounds a bit like that,' said Mma Ramotswe.

Mma Potokwani had a question. 'I have been asking myself something,' she said. 'Who is the person most likely to want a business to fail? I can answer that, Rra. It is the competition – the people who would stand to gain the most if you failed.'

Mma Makutsi opened her mouth as if to come up with some refutation of this, but she stopped herself. It was an entirely reasonable suggestion – and she saw from their expression that Mma Ramotswe and Mma Potokwani felt the same way. 'Another hotel?' she asked.

Babusi fixed his gaze on her. 'Precisely, Mma.'

'And do you know which hotel that would be?' asked Mma Ramotswe.

Babusi shrugged. 'It could be anyone.' He frowned, and then, 'There's no obvious competitor, Mma – not around here.'

'Then it must be personal,' Mma Makutsi interjected. 'Forgive me for asking this, Rra, but is there anybody who really dislikes you?'

Mma Ramotswe was taken aback by the directness of the question. 'I think that what Mme Makutsi means is . . . '

She was not allowed to finish. 'What I mean,' insisted Mma Makutsi, 'is this: are you on anybody's enemies list? I mean *you*, Rra – not the hotel.'

Babusi shifted in his seat. 'I don't think so. I try not to make too many enemies.'

Mma Makutsi smiled. 'We all do that, Rra – unless we are very foolish. But do we always succeed? That, I think, is the real question.'

Mma Ramotswe felt it was time to bring this exchange to an end. 'I think we shall have to make further enquiries,' she said. 'We need to think about what we have heard, and then, once we have done that, we can decide what to do next.'

Mma Makutsi nodded her head in agreement. 'Mma Ramotswe and I will confer, Rra,' she said. 'Then we shall revert.'

We shall revert . . . It was a phrase that Mma Ramotswe had heard Mma Makutsi use from time to time. She had learned it at the Botswana Secretarial College, reference having been made to it in the business correspondence course. Reverting was getting back to somebody about something. It had a ring about it, and a certain finality too. Perhaps we should all do a bit more reverting, she thought.

'Yes,' said Babusi, rising to his feet. 'Please revert at any time.'

Chapter Seven

Young Men and Sports Cars

That evening Mma Ramotswe sat on the veranda of the house in Zebra Drive in that precious half-hour before dinner, that time of half-light, when the last birds of the day made their way back to their trees, when the air was still and our human work was done. At her side, in the chair he habitually occupied and whose rickety legs he tolerated, sat Mr J. L. B. Matekoni, her husband, her lover, her greatest friend (along with Mma Potokwani), her confidant. They were talking, as they always did every evening, about the events of the day.

'So, I am listening, Mma Ramotswe,' began Mr J. L. B. Matekoni. 'Tell me about the Great Hippopotamus Hotel now that you have been there at long last. It was just a sign, and now it is a place that you have seen.'

'It is very beautiful,' said Mma Ramotswe. 'If there are hotels in heaven, then they will be like that place. There are flowers under the eaves of the veranda. It is shaded and cool. There are trees around it that make the noise of the sea when there is a breeze. There is even a tennis court.'

'Hah!' exclaimed Mr J. L. B. Matekoni. 'I do not think there will be tennis courts in heaven, Mma.'

'Perhaps not.'

He waited for her to say more, but she needed prompting. 'So, Mma Ramotswe, you said that they were having difficulties. They told you that things were going wrong.'

She told him about the incidents that Babusi had described. 'He said that it was more than just a run of bad luck. He said that too many things had been happening.'

Mr J. L. B. Matekoni frowned. 'I can see why he thought that. And food poisoning, Mma? That is very bad. People can die from food poisoning. There is something called salmonella. If you have that in food, then you can be very ill. You can become late, I think.'

'You can,' confirmed Mma Ramotswe. 'I remember Dr Moffat telling me about how careful you had to be about water in the old days.'

Mr J. L. B. Matekoni said that he was still careful. 'People say that borehole water's safe,' he said. 'But sometimes it isn't, Mma. It can be contaminated. You can't be too careful.' He paused. 'They must have borehole water out there. They'd be far too far away to get it from any town supply.'

Mma Ramotswe had not enquired, but she assumed that the hotel had its own borehole supply. But if the water supply were the cause, then that would have been a persistent problem – this outbreak of poisoning had been a one-off event. She pointed this out to Mr J. L. B. Matekoni, who agreed. 'Somebody must have put something in the food,' he said. 'Or – and you should think about this possibility, Mma Ramotswe – or, it is just a coincidence. You get a bit of fish that has gone off, or some meat, and before you know it, everybody's sick. It happens all the time – no matter how careful people are.'

She agreed that this was possible. And yet, when considered alongside all the other things that had happened, it was easy to see how one might be suspicious.

'Of course,' she continued, 'the real question is *who*, rather than *how*. At the moment we have no idea of who might want to damage the hotel. A disgruntled employee? That's always a possibility, I suppose.'

'A big possibility,' said Mr J. L. B. Matekoni. 'I remember hearing Phuti say that he had to settle a big phone bill run up by somebody who worked for him in the store. He had been obliged to give this person a rap over the knuckles for some reason – rudeness to a client, I think he said – and the employee did not like it one little bit. He got his own back on Phuti by calling Nairobi on one of the furniture-store phones and leaving the line open all day. He got through to a recorded message line in Nairobi and left it speaking to Gaborone for eight hours. You can imagine what that cost.'

'It cost him his job, I imagine,' said Mma Ramotswe.

'It did. But not before Phuti had to pay a bill of over one thousand pula for the call. Over one thousand, Mma!'

Mma Ramotswe shuddered. We were all at the mercy of malevolent people if they really decided to target us – that came with the technology that we thought would make our lives easier and better. It could do that – to an extent – but it could also do the opposite if it was used by the ill-disposed.

'One interesting thing, Mr J. L. B. Matekoni,' she said. 'Babusi told us about the people who own the hotel now. They are the niece and nephews of the former owner, Mr Goodman Tsholofelo. And one of them has a connection with somebody we all know.'

Mr J. L. B. Matekoni waited.

'Violet Sephotho,' said Mma Ramotswe.

For a few moments nothing was said. Mma Ramotswe heard Mr J. L. B. Matekoni draw in his breath. She saw his eyes narrow slightly as he considered this disclosure. Then he said, 'Hah!'

That was comment enough, but he had more to add. 'Ah!' he said.

'Yes,' said Mma Ramotswe. 'When this man was first mentioned by Babusi, I could tell that the name had a big effect on Mma Makutsi. She did not say anything, though, and it was only when we were in the car on the way back that she told me about something she had heard from Phuti's uncle – you know, the one who lives over on Block 8 – the one who used to be involved with the furniture business. That one. He said that he thought this person, the nephew who is now one of the owners of the hotel, Mr H. J. Morapedi, was involved with Violet Sephotho.' She paused. There had been an additional disclosure – one that seemed to complicate matters further. 'Mma Makutsi said that this Morapedi was appointing Violet to some sort of influential job.'

'That's interesting,' said Mr J. L. B. Matekoni. 'But I don't know if it really means anything. The fact that this Mr H. J. Morapedi may – and I say *may*, Mma – be having an affair with Violet doesn't mean that she has anything to do with this hotel of his. I do not think there is necessarily a connection, Mma.'

Mma Ramotswe had reached that conclusion herself. 'Mma Makutsi is very suspicious, though. In the car on the way back, she went on and on about it. She said that anybody who is involved with Violet is automatically suspect, and that if there is anybody up to no good in that group, then it will be the person who has the Violet Sephotho connection.'

'I see.'

'But that, Rra, is too far-fetched,' said Mma Ramotswe. 'I think it is irrelevant to the issue that we are looking into. Even if Violet is involved with one of the new owners, why would she have anything to do with the difficulties that the hotel is facing? Why would she do anything to harm it? It does not add up, Mr J. L. B. Matekoni.'

'You are probably right, Mma Ramotswe,' said Mr J. L. B. Matekoni. 'But you know what Mma Makutsi is like. She gets an idea in her head and it is very difficult to get it out again. I don't think it is an easy task to change Mma Makutsi's mind – about anything.'

For a few minutes they sat in silence. Each guessed – and guessed correctly – what the other was thinking – an ability that many couples develop after years of marriage. This had its uses, as it was possible, in some cases, for people to have a perfectly good and useful conversation without actually saying anything. So, this evening, after an elapse of time suited to the complexity and gravity of the subject, Mr J. L. B. Matekoni was able to mutter 'Violet Sephotho' and Mma Ramotswe, in response, was able simply to sigh, which was enough to constitute a meaningful exchange and, for the time being at least, to put the troublesome issue to bed. There would be time to consider the matter later – tomorrow perhaps, or the day after that; for the time being they could move on to the next subject, which was Mr J. L. B. Matekoni's day.

'And you, Rra? What about you? What happened today?'

That was the way Mma Ramotswe always put it when she enquired about what Mr J. L. B. Matekoni had done, and he replied in his own time-honoured way, 'This and that, you know.' That would usually be followed by an explanation of what this and that entailed, which on that particular day had included the difficulty of obtaining a spare part for a car belonging to an old client, Mr Seaka Keabetswe, generally known by his nickname of Special.

'Special Keabetswe brought his car in,' he told Mma Ramotswe. 'You know the one maybe – that blue and white Ford with the red stripe down the side. A very natty car – on the outside, that is.'

Mma Ramotswe smiled. 'And on the inside?'

Mr J. L. B. Matekoni made a face. 'I have told Special time and time again. That car may look good, but mechanically, oh dear, oh dear.'

Mma Ramotswe pointed out that people liked their cars. She did not say it, but she was thinking of her own tiny white van, which, like Special Keabetswe's car, had caused Mr J. L. B. Matekoni to shake his head in despair.

'Oh, I'm well aware of that, Mma,' he said. 'I know why Special likes that car of his, with the job that he does. That car is good for his image.'

Special Keabetswe owned a dance studio, the *Smart Steps Studio*, and dressed appropriately. He always wore tight-fitting trousers and two-tone shoes, and a jacket that showed his slightly portly frame to best advantage. He was a striking figure and the blue and white car completed the picture.

'He had to leave the car with me,' Mr J. L. B. Matekoni went on, 'because it was making a bad sound. Cars give you warning, you know, Mma. People say that cars can't talk, but they can – if you are prepared to listen to them. And this car was making its feelings as obvious as can be. It was saying, *Oh, my automatic transmission is causing me big problems, oh, oh.* That was what it was saying loud and clear.'

'Oh dear, Rra. So, what happened?'

'He had to leave the car with me and walk off to his studio. He had to walk in those two-tone dancing shoes of his – you've seen them, I think. It was very sad to see a man like that having to pick his way along the side of the road in two-tone shoes. Very sad.'

Mma Ramotswe tried not to smile. There was something about male vanity that touched her. She was all in favour of men taking care with their appearance and trying to look reasonably well-groomed. She was very much in favour of clean clothes for men, in spite of the indifference that many men seemed to show on that issue, preferring, as they tended to do, shirts that were generally grubby and unironed, indeed sometimes fraying round the collar or trousers on which oil or paint stains had been ignored for days. Mma Ramotswe thought that the least a man could do was ensure that his clothes were not dirty, and yet so many men failed to do even that. These were men who got dressed in clothes like that and left the house in the morning before their wives had time to inspect them and insist on the donning of something cleaner.

Mma Ramotswe prided herself on being what she described as 'an up-to-date lady', which meant, in her view, that she was aware of the changing roles of men and women in modern society. She understood, and had consistently supported, the cause of women's equality, and had no time for men who tried to perpetuate old notions of a subsidiary role for women. At the same time, though, she saw that there were certain things that women generally did better than men or that they cared about more. More and more men were learning how to cook – that was true – and some of these male cooks were known for their creativity in the kitchen. But when it came to the mundane task of feeding a family day after day, women tended to be better at that, she thought. And they were better at getting the children to bed in the evening and up in the morning and dealing with all the small tasks of keeping a household going. One of these tasks was making sure that men were clean and tidy and that was something that women did very well, and should do, if they were in a position to do it.

Men could dress themselves, of course, although many did not. There were many men who expected their wives to find their clothes for them when they were getting ready for work in the morning. 'Where are my socks?' or 'Is there a clean shirt for me?' were questions that were often asked of women in the morning. The answer might well be, 'If you put your socks away in your drawer after you washed them you would be able to find them', but such answers were rarely given.

She thought of this now, briefly, and then went on to think about men who took a lot of care with their appearance. The image of poor Special, picking his way along the edge of the road in his unsuitable two-tone shoes and tight trousers, prompted these thoughts of male dressiness. There was something sad about it. She was not sure why there should be that sadness, but there it was. Mutton dressed up as lamb, perhaps? Was that it? Women could wear attractive clothes because . . . well, why did women look better in such clothes? Was it because men were somehow *plainer*? Was that it? Were men more functional-looking? Were they *rougher*? And because they looked the way they did, was there something sad in their trying to brighten themselves up, to look more appealing, when they were, when all was said and done, just *men*? Perhaps it was like painting a tractor. You did not bother to paint a tractor an attractive colour because a tractor could never be anything but a lump of functional machinery. Were men like that? Were men just *lumps*? Were men *tractors*?

She suddenly felt guilty. This was not the way in which one should think of men. This was not the way in which one should think of *anybody*. And Mma Ramotswe did not think of men in a disparaging way. She liked men. She liked everybody, really. Men had their little ways – they could be difficult at times – but then so could women. And if men made themselves seem a bit ridiculous if they dressed themselves up excessively, then that was nothing to be bothered about. There was always room for hopeless ambition.

Mr J. L. B. Matekoni was saying something.

'Mma? Are you thinking? You are smiling about something.'

She admitted that she was. 'I was thinking about Special in his shoes. I hope that the part arrives for his car soon.'

'I have asked them to hurry,' said Mr J. L. B. Matekoni. 'And also . . . '

'Something else happened today?' she asked. 'Did Fanwell and Charlie get up to some mischief?'

He shook his head. 'No, it was not that. It was another matter altogether. It's that Malala business.'

Mma Ramotswe looked at him. He was clearly unhappy. As well he might be, she thought. 'Oh, Rra,' she said. 'That is not a good business. Malala should not be making these demands of you. You should stand up to him. You told me he wanted you to find him some sort of ridiculous sports car. Tell him to go away and find it himself – if he wants to drive around like a twenty-year-old or whatever.'

It was the wrong thing to say, and she realised that immediately; Mr J. L. B. Matekoni's face fell and he looked, more than anything else, like a man in real distress. And his response to her outburst confirmed this. 'But I am caught now, Mma Ramotswe,' he said. 'I had told him that I would get hold of such a car, and I have done that. It is now here in Gaborone . . . '

Mma Ramotswe interrupted him. 'Here? At Tlokweng Road Speedy Motors?'

He shook his head. 'No. I have had it delivered to Charlie's place. Charlie is looking after it until I deliver it to Malala himself.'

Mr J. L. B. Matekoni delivered this bombshell with a voice that faded noticeably towards the end of the message; so might one who did not believe in what he was saying trail off through lack of conviction.

Mma Ramotswe might have looked disapproving, but she did not. Rather, she spoke with solicitude, asking him whether it was altogether wise to leave Charlie, of all people, in charge of a high-powered sports car. 'I know that he's more responsible these days, Mr J. L. B. Matekoni,' she said, 'but he's still a young man, and young men and sports cars don't always mix.'

Mr J. L. B. Matekoni looked miserable. 'I had to, Mma. Malala's wife drives past here every day – you must have seen her, Mma. It would be too risky to keep the car here. If she saw it . . . '

He saw that Mma Ramotswe was shaking her head. 'Mr J. L. B. Matekoni,' she began, 'I find it hard to believe my ears. Here you are hiding something away as if you were a naughty schoolboy. You are covering up for a man who's going through some sort of mid-life crisis. I cannot believe it, Rra. You are the former president of the Motor Trade Association, and you are doing such a thing.'

The response that this brought forth was an abject one. 'I know, Mma,' he said. 'All you say is true. I am caught.' He paused. 'If you want to tell her, then that is what I will do. I shall tell her that her husband has bought a sports car and that he is driving it without her knowledge. I shall do that, Mma, if you think that is what I must do.'

Mma Ramotswe hesitated. Honesty, she had been taught, was always the best policy . . . except, perhaps, in those situations where honesty would only make things worse. This, she thought, might be one such situation. If a solution could be found that did not involve telling any direct untruths to anybody, then, in a sense, the requirement of honesty would be met. After all, there was no obligation to tell everybody everything: sometimes, indeed, people had to be left in a state of ignorance because to end that ignorance would cause them too much distress. If Mma Malala never found out about the sports car, and if Mr Malala himself was somehow persuaded to give it up, nobody would have been harmed.

Mma Ramotswe wondered whether a solution along those lines could be found. She decided to think about it, and so she said to Mr J. L. B. Matekoni, 'I do not think it would be a good idea to tell Malala's wife about that car . . . '

His relief was palpable.

' . . . yet.'

His face fell.

'Perhaps she will never need to be told,' Mma Ramotswe continued.

Mr J. L. B. Matekoni looked more hopeful.

'Let me think,' said Mma Ramotswe.

'Oh, Mma Ramotswe,' he said. 'I am so pleased that you are going to think about this. You always find a solution if you think. You have never failed.'

'We shall see,' said Mma Ramotswe. 'This is a very tricky situation, Rra, and the problem with very tricky situations is that they sometimes turn out rather differently from how you want them to turn out.'

'I'm sure that is true,' said Mr J. L. B. Matekoni. 'But we shall see. I am ready to do exactly what you tell me to do. And I am very sorry that I have allowed this situation to develop. It is all my fault.'

'You did what you thought was the right thing,' Mma Ramotswe reassured him. 'You were thinking of it from a male perspective, Rra. That is sometimes not the best angle on these things. It's not your fault that you were completely wrong.'

'Ah,' said Mr J. L. B. Matekoni. He was uncertain what else he could say in response to Mma Ramotswe's judgement, and so he simply said 'Ah' again, and left it at that.

Chapter Eight

Rehydrating Salts

Mma Ramotswe began to feel out of sorts shortly after nine that night. Puso and Motholeli were safely asleep in bed – they had both had exhausting days at friends' houses, engaged in the frantic activity that children enjoy, in between periods of listlessness and boredom, and nothing had been heard from them after an early bedtime. Mr J. L. B. Matekoni had likewise retired to bed, intending to read a copy of yesterday's newspaper, but had been lulled into sleep, with the light still on, by a particularly soporific report on the government's transport policy. He was glad that he had nothing to do with such matters, and he was quite content to leave it to the authorities to decide what to do, but he felt that he at least needed to be informed of what was going on. Yet fatigue, and the pleasant sensation of drifting off to sleep, had won the day, and the newspaper slipped off the bed and onto the floor, largely unread.

That left Mma Ramotswe to satisfy herself that both the front and the back doors were locked, and to turn out the lights before herself going off to bed. She had a well-practised ritual for this, involving the checking of the front door, the extinction of any lights left on in the living room or on the veranda, and then a round of the kitchen, ensuring, among other things, that the fridge door was securely closed – people had a tendency not to shut it properly, in spite of Mma Ramotswe's reminders. Then, before she locked the back door, which led directly out of the kitchen into the yard, she would step outside briefly and look up at the night sky.

It was an important part of the night's ritual, a closing ceremony, as it were, for the end of the day. She had done it from girlhood, inspired by her father, the late Obed Ramotswe, who had never tired of gazing at the night sky. 'It may look the same night after night,' he had said to her, 'but it isn't, you know. Those stars are travelling around up there – they are all on a journey, just like us.'

He liked the Southern Cross, and she did too. Viewed from her house on Zebra Drive, it could be seen hanging in the sky above the dark shapes of the acacia trees and of Kgale Hill beyond. She looked for it each night before she went to bed. It was important, she felt, that we should have in our lives some things that are always there, that are always the same, and this constellation was just that. There was the Southern Cross, dipping and swinging in the vastness of the sky; there was Mochudi, where she was born, and there was the hill above it, where she had gone to school; there was the sound of cattle bells in the morning as the sun floated up over the horizon to the east; there was Botswana.

She looked up at the sky and turned round to go back into the house and closed the kitchen door behind her. And it was at that moment that she realised that she was not feeling well. Once back inside, she helped herself to a glass of water. On occasion she suffered from mild heartburn, and she found that water helped, but tonight it seemed to have the opposite effect. Rather than make her feel better, she felt even worse – sufficiently uncomfortable to sit down at the kitchen table and wonder what was happening to her. There were, as usual, various infections doing the rounds: people were always complaining that there was a rampant cold, sometimes even flu, that was taking its toll, and that the only thing to do was . . . and here they would propose their personal way of avoiding infection, none of which, including social isolation, seemed to make much difference.

Was that what she was feeling? She felt her brow to see if she had an obvious high temperature, but her skin was cool, and she did not feel feverish. But then, just as she had reached that conclusion, she started to shiver, and her shivering lasted for a good four or five minutes.

She stood up, and for a few seconds she wondered whether she was going to collapse. She felt nauseous, but that sensation persisted for only a few moments, and was followed by a slightly more settled feeling. She decided that a couple of aspirin and a cup of redbush tea would be the best treatment for whatever was brewing, and that with any luck she would feel better after a good night's sleep. Redbush tea was wonderful that way, she felt: it was free of caffeine, but it still refreshed you when you wanted to be lively, even as it was immediately soothing if you wanted to calm down. So, with a mug of redbush in her hand, she made her way along the corridor that led to the bedroom. There she picked the newspaper up from the floor, switched off Mr J. L. B. Matekoni's bedside light, and changed into the loose-fitting white nightgown in which she slept.

She lay down. The aspirin she had swallowed with the first sip of tea had yet to have any effect, but she was confident that it would. She never needed to take anything stronger – aspirin always seemed to work for her. But that night it did not, and by the time morning dawned, Mma Ramotswe, having had very little sleep, realised that she had eaten something that disagreed with her. Her diagnosis was firm: she had food poisoning – and it seemed to be a particularly uncomfortable form of that common condition.

Mr J. L. B. Matekoni was always very solicitous when Mma Ramotswe felt below par.

'I shall take you to the doctor,' he said. 'His place will be open at nine. He will give you something.'

Mma Ramotswe protested that she did not feel all that bad, and that these things passed with time, even if one took nothing to hasten the natural process of recovery. But Mr J. L. B. Matekoni was insistent, and after he had seen Puso and Motholeli safely off to school he returned to the house and escorted a reluctant Mma Ramotswe to his truck.

'I do not need to bother the doctor,' Mma Ramotswe said as she climbed into the cab of the vehicle. 'There are many people who are far more ill than I am, Rra.'

'That may be so, Mma,' he said. 'But if you have eaten something bad, then he might want to give you an antibiotic to deal with it. Then you will get better quicker.'

'But I will get better,' she said, somewhat weakly, since she could feel, as she spoke, her stomach churning within her. 'And people are taking too many antibiotics. That is not a good thing.'

He was adamant. 'When did *you* last take an antibiotic, Mma Ramotswe? I cannot remember. Maybe four years ago – maybe five. You are not sitting there swallowing antibiotics all the time, like some people. Swallowing them with their morning tea. Inviting their friends to come round to their house to have a few antibiotics. You do not do any of that, Mma: you are entitled to the occasional antibiotic.'

She did not argue further – she did not feel that she had the strength to do so. The infection, she thought, has taken all her reserves away; it was as if a plug had been pulled and all her energy, all her vigour had drained away. And her muscles ached; walking – even a few short steps – made her legs feel as if she had just climbed a lengthy and demanding flight of stairs.

There had been a cancelled appointment, and their doctor was able to see them quickly at his small clinic behind the museum. Dr Phiri was a young man, a graduate of the medical school in Lusaka, whose father had known Obed Ramotswe, and whose car was regularly serviced by Mr J. L. B. Matekoni. He greeted Mma Ramotswe with concern, and listened sympathetically to her description of her symptoms.

'I am not feeling too bad, doctor,' she said. 'I should not be troubling you, you know.'

The doctor held up a hand. 'I must be the judge of that, Mma Ramotswe. And I can see that you are not well at all.'

'She is not,' echoed Mr J. L. B. Matekoni, who had accompanied her into the consulting room. 'Mma Ramotswe is never ill – but now she is.'

The doctor nodded. 'Many of the people who come in here are what we call the worried well. They are people who are not ill at all, but who are worried in case they are sick. They spend much of their time worrying about things they should not be worried about.'

'And taking antibiotics too,' said Mr J. L. B. Matekoni.

'Oh, they love antibiotics,' said the doctor. 'I try not to hand them out except when necessary, but I come under a lot of pressure. And they love injections. Give them an injection, and they couldn't be happier.'

'It might be better to give them a good kick in the pants,' muttered Mr J. L. B. Matekoni. 'Sometimes that is the best medicine for people who are always complaining.'

Mma Ramotswe looked at him in astonishment. 'You must not say that, Mr J. L. B. Matekoni. That is not very kind.' She glanced at the doctor. 'And what will Dr Phiri think of you if you say that sort of thing?'

Mr J. L. B. Matekoni looked sheepish. 'I did not really . . . ' he began.

Dr Phiri's face, though, was covered with a broad smile. He said, 'I know what you mean, Rra. You don't need to apologise. What you say is quite true: a kick in the pants is a very good treatment for many conditions – not that the Medical Association would let me say such a thing.' He paused. 'There are many things that we are not allowed to say these days that are nonetheless true.'

He took Mma Ramotswe's wrist to feel for her pulse. He shone a small torch in her eyes. He asked her to open her mouth so he could inspect the state of her throat. He invited her to lie down on a couch while he felt her stomach. At the end of this brief examination, he sat back in his chair and reached for a prescription pad.

'From what you tell me, Mma Ramotswe,' he began, 'and from what I see from my examination, it is most likely that you have eaten something highly toxic to your system. I have recently had a couple of cases of E. coli poisoning. In this hot weather, we have to be very careful about food going off.'

'She is always careful,' said Mr J. L. B. Matekoni. 'She is always reminding us to keep the fridge door closed.'

'Yes,' said Dr Phiri. 'That is very important.'

He wrote on his pad. 'I am going to give you some rehydrating salts. They should keep you safe while your system is dealing with whatever it is that you have ingested.' He passed her the slip of paper. 'But what I must advise is that you take at least three days off. Four or five would be better. Stay in the house and rest. Drink fluids and then take food when your appetite returns. This is very important. Your system has taken a bit of a knock with this infection, and you must give yourself time to recover properly.'

He looked at Mr J. L. B. Matekoni for support. 'You see that she takes the time off, Rra,' he said. 'Spoil her. Make sure that people don't persuade her to do things. I know how people take advantage of good ladies like Mma Ramotswe.'

In the truck on the way home, Mr J. L. B. Matekoni admonished her on the need to take Dr Phiri's advice seriously. 'You are not to lift a finger, Mma,' he said. 'I shall do everything. I shall make dinner tonight for us – if you feel like eating anything – and for the children too.'

'That is kind of you,' said Mma Ramotswe. 'What will you make, Rra?'

There was a brief silence. 'Pumpkin,' he replied at last. 'I shall cook some pumpkin – and some meat.'

'That is a very good idea,' she said. Had she felt better, she would have smiled at his response. But she did not feel better at all and was now thinking of how much she wanted to be back in bed, making up for the sleepless night, safe in the embrace of the medicine that Dr Phiri had prescribed for her. She did not like to think of pumpkin – not with her stomach in the state it was – rehydrating salts were much easier to contemplate.

*

Mma Makutsi heard the news of Mma Ramotswe's misfortune from Mr J. L. B. Matekoni when she turned up for work that morning, later than usual. She had guessed that something was wrong, as on most mornings Mma Ramotswe was first to arrive in the office. She had thought of calling her to find out whether anything was amiss, but had decided against it. Very occasionally, if she had a disturbed night's sleep, Mma Ramotswe would allow herself a lie-in until almost nine o'clock, and if this was one of those mornings she would not want to be woken up by the telephone.

Hearing Mr J. L. B. Matekoni at work in the garage next to the agency's office, she peered through the workshop door. From underneath a car she saw a pair of legs protruding, and it was to these legs that she addressed the customary morning greeting. The legs replied with the prescribed words, and shortly afterwards Mr J. L. B. Matekoni emerged, wiping his hands on a piece of the blue paper towelling he used for such purposes.

'This car is always going wrong,' he muttered, casting a regretful eye over the vehicle behind him. 'I think the owner drives it badly – without consideration.'

Mma Makutsi nodded. 'Phuti says that there are some people with no respect for machinery,' she said.

'Phuti is right,' agreed Mr J. L. B. Matekoni, adding, 'although it is also that there is some machinery with no respect for people.'

Mma Makutsi gestured towards the office door. 'Where is Mma Ramotswe?' she asked. 'I don't see her van outside.'

Mr J. L. B. Matekoni crumpled up the blue paper, now marked by greasy fingerprints, and tossed it into a cut-off oil drum used for waste paper and other unwanted garage detritus. 'I was going to come and tell you,' he said. 'Mma Ramotswe is feeling unwell. She has been told by the doctor to have a few days' rest. I have said to her it must be five days. She wanted to come into the office, but I have told her to listen to what the doctor says.'

'Quite right,' agreed Mma Makutsi. She hesitated. One had to be careful about asking for details of another's illness – there were some things that people might not wish to talk about. 'I hope she's not too unwell,' she continued, leaving the question in the air, but clear enough even as it hung there.

Mr J. L. B. Matekoni assured her that it was nothing to worry about. 'Just a stomach thing,' he said. 'She must have eaten something that disagreed with her. That happens sometimes, no matter how careful you are.'

'Oh, we all go down with something like that from time to time,' she said. 'But it can be nasty. A few months ago, Phuti . . . '

She was about to tell the story of Phuti's experience on a business trip to Maun when he had experienced a painful attack of stomach cramps after eating a meat pie bought from a roadside café. But she stopped herself. Food poisoning? It was almost too much of a coincidence that they should have been talking about the food poisoning outbreak at the hotel only yesterday and then Mma Ramotswe should experience an episode of it so soon after their discussion. But when did she succumb to it? She asked Mr J. L. B. Matekoni this question and he replied, 'Last night. She started feeling queasy just before going to bed. I took her to the doctor this morning, first thing. Dr Phiri – you know him, of course. He is very highly qualified. He has given her rehydrating salts. She went back to bed and I imagine she's fast asleep now.' He looked at Mma Makutsi and smiled. 'She said that she would call you later, Mma, and that you wouldn't mind being in charge for a few days.'

Mma Makutsi would not mind. In fact, she rather enjoyed being in sole charge of the No. 1 Ladies' Detective Agency, and she liked the idea of five days at the helm. At the back of her mind, though, there was a nagging question: had this problem been triggered by something that Mma Ramotswe had eaten on their visit to the Great Hippopotamus Hotel? Babusi had given them a light lunch, taken in the hotel's dining room, among the handful of guests staying at that time. What had been on Mma Ramotswe's plate – and was it any different from what she herself had eaten?

She asked Mr J. L. B. Matekoni whether Mma Ramotswe would like a visit. 'I could go round and cheer her up a bit,' she offered.

Mr J. L. B. Matekoni shifted his weight from foot to foot: this was awkward. It was kind of Mma Makutsi to offer, but he was determined to follow Dr Phiri's instructions. If Mma Makutsi were to visit Mma Ramotswe then there was a good chance that she might get her involved in some case or other at the very time at which she should be having a complete rest.

'It's very good of you, Mma Makutsi,' he said. 'But the doctor has ordered strict rest and I think Mma Ramotswe should not be seeing anybody – even her very closest friends, such as you or Mma Potokwani.'

To his relief, Mma Makutsi seemed to agree. 'It is always best to have a complete break,' she said. 'Please tell her that I shall look after everything until she comes back. She has nothing to worry about. I won't even bother her on the phone – you just pass that message on, Rra.'

It was in a thoughtful mood that Mma Makutsi made her way into the office. Without Mma Ramotswe, everything was quiet, the only sound being that made by a large fly trapped against a window. After a while that ceased, as the fly found some egress from the room. Now, in complete silence, she sat at her desk, not doing anything in particular until Charlie arrived some twenty minutes later. His week was divided now between his garage duties and his part-time role as an apprentice investigator – or apprentice trainee investigator, as Mma Makutsi insisted he be called. This was one of his agency days, and he had been allocated to routine surveillance work within a warehouse. The owner of the warehouse, a major roofing contractor, was concerned about the high level of stock losses and was convinced that one or more of his employees were diverting supplies for their own use. Charlie was watching under the guise of being a temporary shelf-stacker in the warehouse. So far, he had seen nothing suspicious, but he was getting to know his fellow employees and was confident that sooner or later something would be said to allow him to identify the person responsible.

Mma Makutsi discussed the case with him. Charlie was pleased to be complimented on what he had achieved so far. 'You are doing well, Charlie,' she said. 'I must say that. I think there will be a satisfactory result quite soon.'

'I hope so, Mma,' he said. 'I shall go back there now. Maybe I shall find out something today.'

'Possibly,' said Mma Makutsi. 'But remember: be patient. Everything takes time, Charlie. Remember that.'

He nodded sagely. 'And what about you, Mma? What will you be doing today?'

Mma Makutsi thought for a moment. 'I think I shall go out to see Mma Potokwani. There is something that I want to ask her.'

'What is that, Mma?' asked Charlie, adding, 'If you don't mind my asking.'

Mma Makutsi hesitated. She did not want to involve Charlie in this – perhaps she would at some stage in the future, when the case had developed a bit further, but for the moment there was no need for him to know.

She smiled. 'I want to enquire about the state of her stomach,' she answered.

Charlie took this at face value, and nodded. Mma Makutsi was distinctly odd, he had always thought, and this did not surprise him in the least. 'I suppose all information is useful,' he observed. 'You can never know too much, can you?'

Mma Makutsi shrugged. 'You can certainly know too little,' she said. 'And, unfortunately, there are many people in that position, I think.'

Chapter Nine

Listen to Your Shoes

Mma Makutsi drove along the road leading from the Orphan Farm gate to the cluster of buildings in which Mma Potokwani's office was set alongside the hall, the children's *kgotla*, or meeting place, and the workshop that housed the various bits and pieces of equipment used by the farm's odd-job man. He was a retired railwayman who was something of a miracle-worker when it came to fixing things with pieces of string and wire and whatever else came to hand. Then, dotted about the surrounding acres, were the small houses in which the children lived, each presided over by a housemother. The housemothers made meals for the children, attended to the laundry and repair of their clothes, and provided their eight or so young charges with all the other things that a child needed, including love. That, Mma Potokwani always stressed to a new housemother taking on the job for the first time, was the most important thing of all. 'It doesn't matter,' she said, 'if you forget to repair a tear in a child's clothes, as long as you remember to give that child love. That is something you must never forget.' And most of them, she was happy to discover, did just that: they did not forget.

Mma Potokwani saw her car approaching. To begin with she did not recognise it, and it was only after Mma Makutsi had parked and stepped out of the car that the matron realised who it was who had come to visit her.

She greeted her on the veranda of her office. 'Well, Mma Makutsi,' she called out. 'This is a surprise.'

'I hope that it is not an inconvenient time to call,' said Mma Makutsi, making her way up the steps to the veranda. 'I know how busy you are.'

Mma Potokwani laughed. 'Busy? Who isn't busy, Mma? Do you know anybody who says *I am not busy*? I do not. Everyone is busy now – or at least they think they are.'

She ushered Mma Makutsi into her office. As Mma Potokwani did so, Mma Makutsi enquired after her health. 'I hope that you are well,' she said. 'I hope you are not ill.'

Mma Potokwani seemed to be surprised. 'It's funny you should say that, Mma,' she said. 'I was a bit unwell last night. Then this morning, when I got up, I felt fine again. I think I must have . . .'

Mma Makutsi did not allow her to finish. 'You must have eaten something that disagreed with you.'

Mma Potokwani was puzzled. 'How did you know it was my stomach, Mma?'

'Because Mma Ramotswe felt exactly the same thing, Mma. She has a touch of food poisoning. Mr J. L. B. Matekoni told me all about it. He took her to see the doctor.'

Mma Potokwani's expression turned from puzzlement to

alarm. 'Mma Ramotswe was at the doctor's place? Oh no, Mma. That must be serious. She does not like to trouble the doctor. She has always been like that.'

Mma Makutsi assured her that it was not serious – as least, as far as she knew. 'The doctor has said that she must take a rest,' she said. 'She is doing nothing and seeing nobody for five days.'

Mma Potokwani rolled her eyes. 'She is very lucky. I wish I could do that. I wish I could just put up a sign saying, *Please don't bother me for five days – by order.* Something like that.'

Mma Makutsi now asked when it was that Mma Potokwani had first started feeling unwell.

'It was just after dinner,' she said. 'About seven o'clock, I think.'

Mma Makutsi clapped her hands. 'There you are – exactly the same time as Mma Ramotswe.'

Mma Potokwani thought about this. 'Are you suggesting that we both ate something bad? Are you suggesting it was at the Great Hippopotamus Hotel?'

'I am,' said Mma Makutsi. 'It is too much of a coincidence, Mma, that you should both get an upset stomach so soon after having lunch together. It must have been that lunch.'

'But you had lunch there, too,' said Mma Potokwani. 'Did you feel odd too?'

Mma Makutsi shook her head. 'I have had no stomach trouble,' she said. 'And I haven't been feeling at all strange.'

Mma Potokwani suggested that this might prove that the fact that she and Mma Ramotswe had become ill was nothing to do with having eaten lunch at the Great Hippopotamus Hotel. But Mma Makutsi was adamant. 'Do you remember what you ate, Mma?'

Mma Potokwani frowned. 'I thought we all ate the same thing.'

'But can you remember what that was?' pressed Mma Makutsi.

'Let me see,' began Mma Potokwani. 'I had soup, I think. Yes, I had soup. Did we not all have soup – including Babusi?'

Mma Makutsi thought for a moment. 'I think so. Yes, I think we did. Mushroom soup.'

'And then I had cold meats and potatoes and ...' Mma Potokwani broke off as she tried to remember. 'Yes, and salad. That was what I had. And didn't you have the same thing, Mma Makutsi?'

'Yes,' said Mma Makutsi. 'I had cold meats and potatoes – but I did not have any salad, Mma.' She paused. 'Mma Ramotswe had salad. The two of you had salad – Babusi and I had none. I remember that very clearly because I looked at everybody's plate. We had been talking about food poisoning – remember – and so I found myself looking at everybody's plate.'

Mma Potokwani was tight-lipped. Then she said, 'You think it was that?'

Mma Makutsi's tone became earnest. 'Salad is a very good way of getting food poisoning, Mma. Uncooked food is more dangerous than cooked food. Ask any of your housemothers here – they have training in cookery, don't they? They will tell you the same thing. They will say: be careful to wash vegetables; be careful to refrigerate meat; be careful not to let rice sit about in the open once you've cooked it. They will say all these things – if you ask them.'

Mma Potokwani shrugged. 'Well, Mma,' she said, 'even if there was something wrong with the salad, I'm not sure whether that we can read anything into it. I can't see why anybody on the staff of the hotel would wish to harm us – I really can't.'

Mma Makutsi looked doubtful. 'To warn us off, Mma Potokwani? Don't you think that's possible?'

Mma Potokwani shook her head. 'Frankly, Mma Makutsi, I do not. I think that the fact that we became ill is entirely coincidental. Maybe standards of hygiene in the hotel kitchens are not all they might be.'

Mma Makutsi pointed out that Babusi had assured them that the kitchens were spotless. 'He said that very specifically, Mma Potokwani. I still feel there are grounds for suspicion. In particular, the fact that Violet Sephotho is involved with one of the owners. That sets many alarm bells ringing, in my view.' She paused. 'In fact, I am deafened by them, Mma. I can hear nothing else.'

Mma Potokwani wondered what proof there might be of Violet's influence. She did not think there was any, and it was a mistake, she felt, to jump to conclusions. 'It's not for me to tell you how to do your job,' she said. 'I am a matron – and you are a detective. All that I am saying is that we must have grounds for reaching any conclusion that we reach. Surely that's a basic rule to be applied when you are looking into something.'

She had not intended to sound critical, but Mma Makutsi stiffened at this, and Mma Potokwani realised she had probably given offence. Now she hurried to make up for it. 'As I said Mma,' she insisted. 'You are the one who knows about these things. People say that you are very good at being logical – and precise, too. Unlike me . . . Hah! I am one who is always getting in a mix-up over this, that and the next thing.'

Mma Makutsi seemed to be placated. 'I see what you mean, Mma Potokwani,' she said. 'But there are occasions when my nose tells me something. You know how it is.' And here she tapped her nose while, at the same time, giving Mma Potokwani a meaningful look. It was a bit of a feat, and it made her momentarily cross-eyed.

Mma Potokwani suppressed a laugh. 'Your nose,' she said, looking at Mma Makutsi's nose. It was an average nose in its dimensions, but there were signs, she thought, of slightly enlarged pores beside each nostril. Mma Ramotswe had said something about Mma Makutsi's having problematic skin – she remembered that now.

'Yes, my nose, Mma. My nose says: if Violet Sephotho is involved in anything, then there's almost certainly something that's not right.'

Mma Potokwani made a gesture that indicated that she took the advice of Mma Makutsi's nose seriously. 'Well, Mma,' she said, 'let me know how you get on with all this. I had better get on with my work, as there are one hundred and one things to do.'

'We are all busy,' said Mma Makutsi. 'And once you've done one thing, another thing comes along. Have you noticed that, Mma Potokwani?'

'I have indeed,' replied Mma Potokwani, and sighed. 'A woman's work is never done, Mma. I've always thought that.'

'And I have too,' said Mma Makutsi. 'Maybe one day women will find that their work is done, but I don't think I shall ever see that day.'

She made her way back to her car. It was a warm time of year, and the heat of the day had built up since she had left the office of the No. 1 Ladies' Detective Agency an hour or so earlier. Because she had not found any shade under which to park her car, the inside was oven-like when she opened the door, and she had to stand back to allow the temperature to drop. As she did so, she heard a voice, faint and indistinct, but one that she immediately recognised. She stood stock still, hardly daring to look down at her shoes, at the pair of blue patent-leather shoes that she had treated herself to on her last birthday. She wore them infrequently, and they were not yet fully broken in – patent leather could be tighter than its more supple cousins – but that did not prevent them, it seemed, from following a lead established by her more *experienced* shoes.

It's not your nose you should be listening to, Boss, the voice said. *It's us. Listen to your shoes.*

Mma Makutsi took a deep breath. It was some time since she had reccived a message from her shoes and she was ill-prepared for it. Of course, the whole thing was imaginary – she knew that – and the voice that she thought she heard was entirely within her head. At the same time, there was no denying how real it sounded and how it seemed to emanate from down below, exactly where her shoes were.

She looked down, and it seemed that the shoes were looking back up at her, the blue leather bright in the late-morning sun.

Yes, Boss: you listen to what your shoes have to say to you. And we say this: somebody wants to wreck that hotel. You want to know who it is? It's the person who stands to gain – that's who. And that's all for now, Boss.

She waited to see if the shoes had anything else to say, but there was silence. Mma Makutsi stood immobile, and slowly became aware that there was a child standing beside her, looking up at her in that direct manner that children have. This was Mma Oteng's Khumo.

She smiled at him. 'Now, who are you?' she asked.

Khumo fiddled with the hem of his shirt.

'You must have a name,' Mma Makutsi persisted.

The boy continued to stare at her. It was not an insolent stare – but Mma Makutsi considered it impolite for a child of this age to stand and gawp at an adult.

'You should tell me what you are called,' she said. 'How can I speak to you properly if I do not know your name?'

The boy blinked. 'I am not . . . '

His voice was tiny, like a distant recording.

'You are not what?'

'I am not from here.'

She had to strain to catch the words.

'Oh, I see. So where are you from?'

He did not answer the question. Instead, he said, 'I would like to have shoes that talked.'

Mma Makutsi struggled to contain her surprise. The voice of her shoes was something imagined – it had to be. Yet here was this boy claiming that he had heard it.

'I think you may have heard me,' she said quickly. 'Sometimes I talk to myself.'

Khumo shook his head. 'It came from down there.' He pointed to her shoes.

Mma Makutsi shook her head. 'It is easy to hear things that are not there,' she said.

The boy looked unconvinced. His voice was stronger now – more confident. 'I heard something, Mma.'

'Yes,' muttered Mma Makutsi, half to herself. She was not going mad; her shoes really did have something to say. But she was not going to admit it to this child, because even if people thought that children were more likely to believe in talking shoes than adults were, in fact it would be the other way round. Children were the rational ones now – brought up in a world of electronic devices and complicated machinery, they were scientific in their outlook. No self-respecting child would believe that shoes might talk.

She smiled again at the small boy, and asked him his name.

'I am called Khumo, Mma,' he said.

'Khumo. That is a very good name. If you are called Khumo, then there are many things you can do in this life.'

'I know, Mma. I want to be a pilot.'

'That will be very good,' she said.

She looked at him, and wondered about the start he had in life. It would not have been a good one, until, of course, he came here, and fell under the care of Mma Potokwani. That would have been the point at which things became much better.

'You must work hard, Khumo,' she said.

'I am working very hard, Mma. Every day at school, I work hard.'

Good, came a small voice from below.

Khumo looked puzzled. 'Did you say something, Mma?' he asked.

She shook her head. 'I will have to go now, Khumo. I have enjoyed talking to you.'

And so have we, said a voice, now very faint.

Khumo was staring at the blue patent-leather shoes.

'Do your shoes talk to you, Mma?' he asked.

Mma Makutsi hesitated. 'Some people think that is impossible, Khumo,' she said. 'But I'm not so sure.'

'You are very lucky if they do,' said Khumo. 'My shoes say nothing.'

'That may be so,' said Mma Makutsi. 'But you are lucky in other ways, perhaps. You are lucky to live in this place, with Mma Potokwani and your housemother to look after you.'

'Oh, I know that too,' said Khumo.

Goodbye, said a small voice.

'I really must go,' said Mma Makutsi.

*

Had Mma Makutsi's shoes known what was happening at Tlokweng Road Speedy Motors while they, and Mma Makutsi of course, were gingerly getting back into her car – the seats of which were still hot from exposure to the sun – they would undoubtedly have expressed strong disapproval; not that this would have been possible, though, as the sentience of Mma Makutsi's shoes was an impossibility, surely . . . And yet, what shoes allied to the female cause – as most ladies' shoes are – would remain silent in the face of the arrival at the garage of Mr Mo Mo Malala, unashamedly planning to deceive his wife over the not inconsiderable matter of a small but high-powered Italian sports car specially obtained for him by Mr J. L. B. Matekoni, and concealed for the past few days by Charlie, who had now driven it over to the garage to await the arrival of its new owner.

Mr Malala had called Mr J. L. B. Matekoni at the garage shortly after Mma Makutsi had left on her mission to enquire about the state of Mma Potokwani's digestive system. The point of his call was to enquire whether the car had arrived from over the border. The importing of cars was not a simple matter wherever one was, as it was an activity in which bureaucrats appeared to take an inordinate interest. There was a good reason for that, of course: the trade in used cars, or pre-loved cars as they are coyly referred to in some circles, is not one noted for its transparency, and there are some who earn their living in it who find any opportunity to defeat officialdom an irresistible challenge. Mr J. L. B. Matekoni was not like that, of course; he was scrupulously honest, and did not approve of any of the deceptions to which some people in the motor trade might be drawn. He always filled in paperwork exactly as it was meant to be filled in, and paid any duty payable right down to the last thebe. Mr Malala, being the brother of the proprietor of a major car-hire firm, was familiar with the difficulties of moving vehicles over borders, and was pleasantly surprised to hear that his new sports car had surmounted all obstacles and was now licensed, licit and ready to be collected. He would be at the garage, he said, within twenty minutes, and was looking forward to a test drive. It would be helpful, he said, if Mr J. L. B. Matekoni could accompany him on this drive – 'to iron out any little teething troubles', as he put it. *Such as your wife*, Mr J. L. B. Matekoni thought, but of course did not say.

Mr Malala arrived at the garage in his sedate, official car – the car in which his wife saw him drive off to work each morning. It was, Mr J. L. B. Matekoni had to admit, a very dull car, and for a few moments he felt a sneaking sympathy for Mr Malala in his desire to have something with a bit more power to it, and even a different colour – the dull car was an indescribable colour, somewhere between beige and grey, whereas the new car was red of a shade that he had once seen described in an advertisement as *adolescent red*. The official car was Japanese, at least in design, even if it had been made in a motor plant near Johannesburg, where cars of Japanese inspiration were assembled locally for all of southern Africa. The Japanese made perfectly good cars, in Mr J. L. B. Matekoni's view; they were reliable, hard-wearing enough for the dry and dusty conditions of Botswana, and they performed adequately as long as one did not want excessive acceleration. There was no need to get from nought to sixty in ten seconds, he thought, unless one were intent on showing off or escaping from the police after a bank robbery, or something of that sort. Of course, one wanted a certain amount of acceleration capacity, and too little could be a sign that a new car was needed. Mma Ramotswe's tiny white van was a case in point. That took several hours to go from nought to sixty – if it ever arrived at sixty, that is, which, Mr J. L. B. Matekoni jokingly suggested would require a good length of downhill road and even a following wind.

'I am very much looking forward to this new car,' Mr Malala had said over the phone, his voice rising with excitement. 'Oh, we will put it through its paces, won't we, Rra?'

Mr J. L. B. Matekoni swallowed hard. 'Well, we can do that within the speed limits . . . '

Mr Malala had laughed at that. 'Speed limits? They are not for cars like this one, Mr J. L. B. Matekoni. Speed limits? Bang! There goes your speed limit. Sonic boom. Bang.'

Mr J. L. B. Matekoni laughed nervously. Had Mr Malala been an ordinary member of the public, and not the brother of the man whose lucrative servicing contract played a major part in keeping Tlokweng Road Speedy Motors afloat – and therefore provided a job for Fanwell and, in a part-time sense, for Charlie too – had he not been that person he would have received a mild rebuke from Mr J. L. B. Matekoni. The terms of this reproach would have been a reminder of the fact that speed limits had a purpose and that those who ignored them were endangering not only themselves but other, innocent road-users – not to say cattle, too, who were often involved in accidents at night. Cattle blended with the night itself, and with their immediate surroundings – there was a common type of cow that seemed to be exactly the same shade of black as a tarred road at night. Such cows might only be seen by a speeding motorist if their eyes happened to be caught in the headlights – otherwise the first that such a motorist might know of them was the terrible sounds of shattering windscreen glass, and of animal pain.

Mr Malala did not get that admonition, but he did get a disapproving silence, one that lasted long enough for him to enquire as to whether Mr J. L. B. Matekoni was still on the line.

'Yes, I am here, Mr Malala,' came the reply. 'I am here. But I was thinking of road safety. No matter, though, I shall get one of the young men to fetch the car for you. It will be ready.'

The reference to road safety, dropped in with tact, went unnoticed. 'Red and ready!' exclaimed Mr Malala. 'Oh, my goodness, Rra, I am very excited now.' There was a moment's silence, and then he added, 'Wow!'

'Yes,' said Mr J. L. B. Matekoni, trying to sound as unexcited as possible. But, rather against his better judgement, he echoed Mr Malala and said, 'Wow!' This expression of excitement and anticipation sounded unconvincing – even to himself – and he finished the conversation with a mild, 'I am looking forward to seeing you, Rra.'

I'm looking forward to seeing you, Rra ... So might a sombre lawyer, or a cautious dentist, or even a health-conscious personal trainer, have spoken to a client, arranging a routine meeting in the office, the clinic or the gym. So, too, might a responsible mechanic, he thought, have concluded a telephone conversation with a responsible customer about a necessary repair to an entirely responsible car. Instead of which, here he was preparing to introduce a man well into the age of discretion – past it, some might even say – to a vehicle that was far more suited to a young man in his early twenties wishing to make an impression on young women of a similar age – a car that spoke of wild oats yet to be sown, of excessive testosterone, and of seductive Italian engineering. And red, too, as if these other features were already not quite enough ... Oh, shame on you, Mr J. L. B. Matekoni, he said to himself. Oh, shame on you as a merchant of unsuitable dreams ...

With a general sense of foreboding, Mr J. L. B. Matekoni dispatched Charlie to collect the Italian sports car from its temporary abode.

'Go over and fetch that car now, Charlie,' he said. 'Fanwell will drive you over to your place in my truck. Bring the car back here – Mr Mo Mo Malala is coming over to ... to be united with it.'

Charlie smacked his hands together. 'Cool, boss! Old Mo Mo's going to get into the driving seat. Cool! Small man, big engine. Vroom. Dust. Down the road. Action, first class!'

Fanwell looked embarrassed. He was *far* more sensible than Charlie, Mr J. L. B. Matekoni thought, even if Charlie was much less ... well, less *Charlie-ish* than he had been in the past. He was growing up, but, as Mr J. L. B. Matekoni had observed to Mma Ramotswe on more than one occasion, these things could take a long time. Some people seemed grown-up more or less from the start; others took rather longer. Some took a *very* long time, and there were some who never quite made it, fading into retirement with an undented belief they were still somehow eighteen. Was that the trouble with Mr Malala? Was it simply a case of delayed or incomplete maturity, or was it something quite different – the so-called male menopause that people sometimes saw at the heart of otherwise inexplicable middle-aged misbehaviour?

Mr J. L. B. Matekoni cast a stern eye on Charlie. 'This is not something to laugh about, Charlie,' he said. 'This is the brother of the other Mr Malala. And that other Malala is no Mo Mo – as you well know, he is the man whose business contributes to a large part – to a *very* large part – of the profits of Tlokweng Road Speedy Motors. Remember that, Charlie.'

Charlie looked chastened. 'I know, boss. Yes, you're right. I will take this deadly seriously. I will bring that car over here slow-slow, Rra, and I will not laugh when I see that small man get in and set off. I will not laugh, boss. I am already not laughing, you see. I shall think of something else altogether. I shall think of my grandmother, maybe, and the porridge she used to make in the mornings. I will think of that.'

'You can think of whatever you like, Charlie,' retorted Mr J. L. B. Matekoni. 'All I ask is that you don't laugh at this poor man. One day you will be over sixty and you may be driving a red car and you will not want people laughing at you.'

Charlie looked thoughtful. 'I will never be as small as he is, boss,' he said.

'That's neither here nor there, Charlie,' Mr J. L. B. Matekoni retorted. 'You do not judge people by such things. I have told you how many times? One hundred.'

'Two hundred,' said Fanwell, who had overheard the end of this conversation. 'The trouble is that Charlie has a hole in his head, boss. I've seen it. It's at the back of his neck and all the things that people tell him fall out of this hole – all the time. I'm not making this up, Mr J. L. B. Matekoni. This is one hundred per cent true.'

Mr J. L. B. Matekoni sighed. 'Just get going, boys. Mr Malala will be coming here soon, and I want the car to be waiting for him. That will never happen if you stand about talking about holes in heads and so on.'

Chapter Ten

The No. 1 Car in the Country

By the time that Mr Malala arrived at Tlokweng Road Speedy Motors, Charlie and Fanwell had returned from their mission to retrieve the Italian sports car. It was now discreetly parked at the back of the garage, out of sight of passers-by and protected from the sun by the leafy branches of an acacia tree. There was no denying that it was a handsome machine, low-slung and sleek, with gleaming chrome embellishments, and a retractable top allowing the driver, should he wish, to travel in the open, well-placed for the admiring glances of those in more sedate and less expensive-looking vehicles. For any young man interested in machinery, Mr J. L. B. Matekoni thought, it would be a dream come true. For a wife, though, it would be a nightmare, he reminded himself, and for a moment he felt a surge of sympathy for Mma Malala in her ignorance of this singularly unwise purchase made by her husband.

Now they stood in admiration before the car – Mr J. L. B. Matekoni, Charlie, Fanwell, and Mr Malala himself, the latter quivering with excitement at the mechanical masterpiece before them.

'Oh goodness,' muttered Mr Malala, once he had regained the power of speech. 'Look at that, Mr J. L. B. Matekoni. You will have seen many cars in your life, but have you ever seen anything like this? I do not think you will have. I do not think anybody in Botswana will ever have seen a car as beautiful as this one. Never, Rra. Never, in all the history of Botswana.'

Charlie nodded in agreement. 'This is probably the number one car in the country,' he said. 'This car will be in all the history books – one hundred per cent for sure.'

Fanwell was impressed, but more modest in his comment. 'This is a very fast car, Mr Malala. You will be able to go very fast in this one.'

Mr Malala liked that. 'Fast? Yes, like that plane, that Concorde. Just like that.' He paused, and smiled, 'They will call me Concorde Malala, I think.'

Mr J. L. B. Matekoni looked away. It saddened him to hear a mature man speaking like a teenage boy – and a rather foolish teenage boy at that. 'I think you must be a bit careful, Rra,' he said quietly. 'When the traffic police see a car like this, what do you imagine they will think?'

Mr Malala replied quickly. 'They will be very envious. They will think: that man is very lucky.'

Mr J. L. B. Matekoni disagreed. 'No, Rra, traffic police do not think like that. They will think: we will catch that man. They will think: we cannot have people driving round in cars like that – not here in Botswana. They will be rubbing their hands and thinking of the speeding fines they will slap on you.'

'If they catch him,' interjected Charlie. 'And I don't think they will. Mr Malala will put his foot down on the accelerator, and he will be up in Francistown while the traffic police are still trying to reach Mahalapye. That's what will happen, boss.'

Mr Malala beamed with pleasure. 'See?' he crowed. 'They'll have no chance.'

Mr J. L. B. Matekoni sighed. He had done his best to urge caution, and he did not see what more he could do. There came a point, he decided, where our duty to be our brother's keeper ended, and he felt that in this particular situation he had reached it.

'Just be careful,' he said.

Mr Malala laughed. 'I am always careful, Rra. You need not worry about me.'

Mr J. L. B. Matekoni swallowed. 'Would you like me to come with you for a test drive? Just in case there are any issues?'

Mr Malala considered this for a moment before replying, 'That is a good idea, Rra. There are always teething troubles with a new vehicle, aren't there? And you will be able to explain things to me – a car like this will have many buttons to press. It will be a very automatic car, I think.'

Mr J. L. B. Matekoni opened the driver's door and Mr Malala stepped inside. Then with a nod to Charlie and Fanwell he himself walked round to the other side and lowered himself into the passenger seat. He looked to his side: Mr Malala, being so short, could barely see over the car's dashboard and was trying to raise himself up.

'Perhaps you need something to sit on,' Mr J. L. B. Matekoni said. 'It will make the seat higher, and then you will be able to see where you are going. That is always helpful when you are driving.'

Mr Malala scowled. When he replied, it was in a peevish

tone – that of a customer who has bought what he wants, is in possession of it, and feels entitled to use it as he sees fit. Mr J. L. B. Matekoni had seen buyer's remorse before – when it came to cars – but there was no sign of it here. Mr Malala had made his choice and was not prepared to see any problem with his new car. 'This is perfect, Rra,' he replied. 'I will have a very good view of the road ahead. There is no problem.'

Mr J. L. B. Matekoni tried once more. He had never let a customer drive out of Tlokweng Road Speedy Motors with an unresolved mechanical problem, and he felt he owed it to this man to warn him one last time.

'It's not because you're short,' he began. 'Many normal people find they have an impaired view of what's ahead. It's the fault of the people who design car seats. I sometimes wonder what shape those people are themselves . . . '

It was a valiant attempt, but he realised immediately that he had said the wrong thing. It was so difficult – for everyone – to say the right things these days, he thought. You could say things that you had always said, and that *everyone* had always said, and then suddenly there were people who were shaking their fingers at you and saying that what you said was all wrong, and, more than that, that *you* were all wrong. That was hard: when you had gone through life trying to do the right thing, only to discover that inadvertently you were doing quite the wrong thing – that was a bitter pill to swallow. And it seemed to be happening all the time, even if nobody ever consulted him, or anyone he knew, about changes in words and ways of behaving. For example, he had always stepped aside to allow ladies to go through doors first. That, he believed, was now the wrong thing to do, because there were people who did not want other people to let them go through a doorway first. He could not see why this should be so.

He had heard that it was because it implied that women needed to be treated with respect, in the same way as one treated older people with respect. But now that, too, was changing, and there were elders who resented people helping them with things because it suggested that they could not do these things themselves.

Yet in Botswana people had always treated elders with the deference that age seemed so naturally to require. You did not push past elders; you listened politely to what they had to say; you addressed them respectfully, just as people used to address school-teachers, or ministers of religion, or village leaders in a way that showed they were valued. How was it that this was all changing, with the result that nowadays people spoke in an off-hand manner with everybody, no matter who they were? And what was going to happen in doorways when everybody tried to go through at the same time? People would get stuck, sometimes perhaps for hours, because we all know that we cannot go through at the same time. That was why there were rules, or customs perhaps, when it came to going through doorways – and we interfered with those at our peril.

Mr Malala was looking at him resentfully. 'I am not short, Rra,' he said. 'I am average height.'

It took Mr J. L. B. Matekoni a moment to gather his thoughts. He remembered what Mma Ramotswe had once said to him about the way in which people looked at themselves – when they bothered to do so. She had said that from our own point of view we are all entirely reasonable, and that the way we look at the world is just the way the world should be looked at. And now here was an example of precisely that attitude. If you were the centre of everything, as Mr Malala was, you would think that you were neither too tall nor too small.

'I'm sorry, Rra,' he said. 'I did not mean to be rude.'

Mr Malala nodded. This was not a time to object to an ill-thought-out remark; this was a time to celebrate the arrival of a new car. 'We can go for a drive now, Rra,' he said to Mr J. L. B. Matekoni. 'I am ready now.'

'Let us begin,' said Mr J. L. B. Matekoni, adding, 'The engine is meant to make a loud noise, Rra. You must not think there is something wrong.'

Mr Malala busied himself with ignition, and the engine leapt into life with a satisfactory purr. Then, after a certain amount of fumbling with the manual transmission, he nosed the car out of its parking place. 'Listen to that,' he said. 'That's a good sound, isn't it? That's the sound of a good engine, don't you think?'

Mr J. L. B. Matekoni thought that the sound was unnecessarily loud. There was no need, in an age of sophisticated engineering, for any engine to sound much above a murmur. But then he remembered the intended market for this car: those drivers wanted a rumble at the very least; they would be delighted with a growl.

Mr Malala steered the car towards the public road a short distance away. As he did so, he sounded the horn – a loud, braying noise that startled a small flock of chickens pecking in the dirt at the edge of the road. The hens clucked in disapproval as they made off.

'Stupid chickens,' said Mr Malala.

Mr J. L. B. Matekoni was irritated by this remark. It was no fault of the chickens that they were what they were. He wondered whether he should defend them in some way, but his attention was diverted by a manoeuvre that Mr Malala had now begun to effect – the overtaking of a rattling minibus, crammed full of people heading for the centre of town.

'Stupid minibuses,' muttered Mr Malala.

'Be careful, Rra,' said Mr J. L. B. Matekoni. 'There is a speed limit here, and the police are always waiting round the corner. They like to catch motorists and they will be very happy to catch this car.'

'There are no police this morning,' said Mr Malala. 'They are all at the football match they are having against the Botswana Defence Force. This will be a very good day to put a sports car through its paces.'

Mr J. L. B. Matekoni listened to this in silence. All of us had to go sometime, and if he was destined to leave this world in an awful high-speed pile-up while being driven by this small and rather irritating man, then so be it. He would be sorry though – there were still things that he wanted to do in this life; there were still things to be said to people he was close to, particularly to Mma Ramotswe, to whom he needed to say how much he loved her. There were many people, himself included, who forgot to say that, and who then would remember only at the last moment, when it was too late. That must be the worst last thought you could have, he said to himself; to know that you will not have the chance to say the things that have been in your heart and that you have not said, for one reason or another.

They flew round a corner, briefly swerving over the centreline into the lane reserved for traffic travelling in the opposite direction, before returning to their previous trajectory. Instinctively, Mr J. L. B. Matekoni gripped the side of his seat, a gesture that was spotted by Mr Malala, who laughed. 'No need to worry, Mr J. L. B. Matekoni,' he said, 'you are in safe hands with me.'

It was the last thing he said before the accident. And had it not been for the quick reactions of the driver of a car coming down the road towards them, it might have been the last thing he ever said. As it happened, the other driver, seeing the Italian sports car hurtling towards him, pulled over as far as he could towards the edge of the road while at the same time sharply applying his brakes. Disaster was averted for him, at least, if not for the sports car that slid off the road as if it had suddenly become covered in ice. Then, turning over completely, it landed back on its wheels and shot off to the side, ploughing through a fence and into a deep ditch, a donga, that cut through a neighbouring patch of scrub bush.

In the silence that follows the crumpling of machinery – that deep, shocked silence in which only the faint ticking of cooling metal might be heard, Mr J. L. B. Matekoni listened only for breathing – for his, and for Mr Malala's. Satisfied that both of them were still alive, he looked at the figure beside him, the diminished figure now forced back in his seat, smiling in a completely unexpected way. How could anybody smile after a brush with death? Well, perhaps to smile was an entirely natural reaction when you realised that you had cheated fate. Or was it more of a sheepish smile – the expression of one who had ignored advice and was now confronted with the consequences?

It now occurred to Mr J. L. B. Matekoni to say something. He might have said, 'I told you so,' which would be what most of us would like to say in such circumstances, but he did not, saying, instead, 'Are you all right, Rra?'

And Mr Malala, seemingly unashamed, replied, 'I am quite all right, Rra, thank you. That other driver was a very dangerous man. Did you see what he did?'

Mr J. L. B. Matekoni was too astonished to answer; and besides, Mr Malala, having started to unbuckle his seat belt, was attempting to open the door on his side of the car. After a brief struggle, he managed to manoeuvre himself out of the wreck. Mr J. L. B. Matekoni followed him, and was soon standing beside the car, looking balefully at what he imagined was a complete mechanical write-off. He took a deep breath; he was relieved to be alive – the destruction of the Italian sports car was regrettable, but it was, after all, only a car, and cars were replaceable in ways that human life was not. The thought cheered him up, and now, as he turned to address Mr Malala, he managed a smile. 'I am very pleased you are not injured, Rra,' he said. 'And it does not matter about the car. There are many cars; there are not many of us.'

Mr Malala considered this. 'That is true, Rra, but . . . ' An anguished look came over him. 'But what am I to tell my wife?'

Mr J. L. B. Matekoni frowned. 'I thought that your wife was unaware of this car, Rra. Or did you tell her after all?'

Mr Malala's misery seemed to grow by the moment. 'I did not tell her, Rra. What I am worried about is this.' And with that he turned his face sideways to reveal a large gash on his right cheek. In the excitement of their escape, he had not noticed the injury. He fingered at it now, wiping the blood away from the laceration.

Mr J. L. B. Matekoni gasped. Perhaps it had been too much to expect that one might walk away unscathed from such an accident. Instinctively his hand went up to his own cheek to check himself for a similar injury. He was unharmed. 'Oh, Rra,' he said. 'You are hurt.'

'It is nothing,' said Mr Malala. 'It is just a small cut. You do not die from a small cut.'

'It is not all that small,' said Mr J. L. B. Matekoni. 'You may need to get it stitched.'

Mr Malala groaned. 'She will notice it. How can she not see it, Rra? And then she will say, "Where did you get hurt like that, Malala?" I know her, Rra – she will say that. And I cannot say to her, "I crashed my new sports car." So, what will I say, Rra? You tell me.'

Mr J. L. B. Matekoni stared at him. This is what happened if you started to deceive your wife – deceptions grew like weeds until they covered the entire ground. The only answer was to tell the truth, and now he suggested that to Mr Malala, as gently as he could, bearing in mind that the poor man had just lost a cherished, if only briefly enjoyed, vehicle.

'I think you should tell her exactly what happened,' he said. 'It is always better to tell the truth, Rra – always.'

Mr Malala shook his head. 'I cannot, Rra. I cannot tell her. If you knew my wife, you would know why.'

'I cannot tell you what to do, Rra,' said Mr J. L. B. Matekoni. 'But I think that you should have that cut dressed.'

Mr Malala fingered his wound again. 'I do not want to go to the hospital,' he said. 'People will talk.'

Mr J. L. B. Matekoni thought this very foolish. 'It could get infected, Rra. Then you will be in worse trouble.' He paused. Mma Ramotswe always kept a bottle of strong antiseptic in the bathroom cabinet, along with sticking plasters. Puso was always scraping a knee and getting patched up in this way; she could do the same for Mr Malala, even if his injury was rather more serious. 'Perhaps you will let Mma Ramotswe put something on it,' he said. 'She is good at these things.'

Mr Malala thought this worth pursuing. 'Then I shall tell her that I fell,' he said. 'I shall tell my wife that I fell on some concrete steps and landed badly.'

Mr J. L. B. Matekoni said nothing. Mr Malala seemed to him to have very little difficulty lying. If it were him, Mr J. L. B. Matekoni, in this position, the telling of these casual untruths would cause him acute discomfort. Mr Malala, by contrast, seemed untroubled.

'I shall ask somebody to take us back into town,' said Mr J.

L. B. Matekoni. 'Some car will stop. We shall go to the house at Zebra Drive and see Mma Ramotswe. She will deal with your injury.'

Mr Malala nodded his assent. 'You are very kind, Rra.' He cast a mournful eye over the ruined car. 'And I am very sorry about your car.'

Mr J. L. B. Matekoni corrected him. '*Your* car,' he said. And he thought that he should have said 'your *late* car', but felt, on balance, that it would be a bit tactless to use such an expression so soon after the traumatic events of the last few minutes.

Mma Ramotswe was sitting in the shade of the veranda of her house on Zebra Drive when the car drew up at the front gate. This car was driven by a kind stranger – it was a Samaritan car, as Mr J. L. B. Matekoni put it subsequently – and it stopped to disgorge the sorry party of Mr J. L. B. Matekoni and a chastened and slightly bloodied Mr Malala. Mma Ramotswe could see at once that something was wrong, and she strode out to open the gate for them.

'Oh, Rra,' she exclaimed when she saw Mr Malala's face. 'You have been hurt.'

Mr Malala fixed his gaze on the ground. 'It is nothing, Mma,' he muttered. 'It is just a scratch. It is nothing more than that.'

'It is not a scratch,' said Mma Ramotswe firmly. 'It is a cut, Rra – and you should see somebody about it.'

'I thought you might look at it, Mma,' said Mr J. L. B. Matekoni. 'I thought that some disinfectant . . . '

Mma Ramotswe tut-tutted her disapproval. 'Disinfectant is not much use against tetanus, Mr J. L. B. Matekoni,' she said. 'But at least I can clean it. Then you can go and see somebody about it.'

She spoke in a tone that discouraged disagreement, and neither

Mr Malala nor Mr J. L. B. Matekoni were in a mood to argue. As they made their way back towards the house, she enquired how the injury had been sustained.

'I fell over,' said Mr Malala. 'It was a fall.'

Mr J. L. B. Matekoni caught his breath. He made his decision. He was not going to put up with this.

'Actually, Mma Ramotswe, what Mr Malala meant to say is that it was an accident. His car . . . '

He was unable to finish. 'My car went off the road,' Mr Malala blurted out.

Mma Ramotswe stared at him. 'Went off the road?'

'Turned right over,' said Mr Malala. 'But God was watching, and he turned us the right way up again.'

Mma Ramotswe glanced at Mr J. L. B. Matekoni. He had had enough.

'Mr Malala was driving a bit fast,' he said. 'Far too fast, in fact.'

'It was a very powerful car,' muttered Mr Malala. 'You put your foot down a little and then, ow, the car is going too fast. It is easily done.'

Mma Ramotswe pursed her lips. 'I am very sorry about this, Rra. I will wash that cut and put on some disinfectant. Then I shall phone your wife and ask her to come and fetch you. She can take you to a clinic.'

Mr Malala stopped in his tracks. 'Oh, please, Mma. Do not trouble my wife with this. It is such a small thing, and she has so much to do. She is a very busy lady.'

Mr J. L. B. Matekoni shook his head. 'There is no more time for all this nonsense,' he said. 'If you are too frightened to tell your wife what happened, then I think that Mma Ramotswe can do it for you.'

Mr Malala let out a small, simpering cry. 'I am such a foolish man,' he wailed. 'My wife will smack me very hard.'

Mr J. L. B. Matekoni stared at him in disbelief. 'I do not think that will happen, Rra. I think you are exaggerating.'

'No,' Mr Malala went on, 'She is a very strong woman, and I am just an average man. You don't know what it's like.'

Mr J. L. B. Matekoni was unprepared for what happened next. Mma Ramotswe had been ahead of Mr Malala on the path back to the house. Now she turned round and opened her arms to fold them about him. The small figure almost disappeared in her embrace.

'Oh, Rra,' she said, 'I can tell that you are frightened. You must not be. I shall speak to your wife. I shall make sure that everything will be all right.'

Mr J. L. B. Matekoni felt that he had to say something. 'It is best to let the ladies sort these things out, Rra,' he said. 'And I am sure that your wife will forgive you.'

Mr Malala was released from Mma Ramotswe's embrace. He had left a small bloodstain on her blouse. He dabbed at it ineffectively with the cuff of his shirt. 'You are very kind, Mma,' he said.

'It is best to tell the truth,' Mma Ramotswe said. 'If you tell the truth, then you will always be strong. That is well known.'

Mr Malala nodded. 'I know it now,' he said, adding, 'I think.'

He did not look strong, thought Mr J. L. B. Matekoni, but then sometimes those who looked strong were weak on the inside, and vice versa. And those who had been weak could become strong, which was also something that happened from time to time, and might just have happened here.

'Let us go inside,' said Mma Ramotswe. 'It is too hot to be standing out in the sun.'

They went into the house. In the bathroom, as she retrieved the bottle of disinfectant from the cupboard, Mr Malala suddenly said, 'I like the smell of disinfectant, you know. It takes me back to when I was a boy. My mother used to put Dettol on my knees if I fell over and grazed them. It reminds me of my mother.'

'I think of my mother when I smell freshly baked bread,' said Mr J. L. B. Matekoni, who was standing by, watching. 'She would make bread every week. She let me take it out of the oven for her, and I have never forgotten that smell. Never.'

Mma Ramotswe said nothing. She did not remember her mother, for she had been too young when she had died; her memories were of her father, that good man, Obed Ramotswe, whose kindness and love came back to her whenever she saw the sun turn the tops of the trees golden with its light and its warmth. That was how she remembered him.

Chapter Eleven

We Are Here for You at All Times

Mma Makutsi had taken to making flow charts – elaborate, pencil-drawn diagrams in which the steps of a proposed investigation were linked with each other in smooth progression. Suppositions were listed in boxes, along with the names of individual people, and these boxes were joined to others with arrows, culminating in a large box labelled *outcome*. Here and there on the margins a small question mark indicated doubt, while an exclamation mark recorded surprise at the vagaries of human nature. *Be surprised by nothing*, Clovis Andersen wrote in *The Principles of Private Detection*, but both Mma Makutsi and Mma Ramotswe had to admit that there were occasions when they encountered instances of human behaviour for which experience had not prepared them. People were infinitely resourceful, and also incorrigibly devious, and one should never assume, as Mma Ramotswe observed, that others would behave as expected.

When she went into the office on the morning after Mr Malala's unfortunate accident, Mma Makutsi decided to sit at Mma Ramotswe's desk. She felt entitled to do this because she was, for the time being, the acting managing director of the agency, and it was entirely appropriate that she should occupy that more commodious chair. On the desk in front of her she had a large sheet of paper on which she had carefully drawn a flow chart featuring the following pieces of information:

The Great Hippopotamus Hotel

Nature of business: hotel

That was in the first of the boxes, and it was linked by a neatly drawn arrow to a box in which was written:

Formerly owned by Mr Goodman Tsholofelo

Widely liked; no children, and for this reason the business has been passed on to . . .

Another arrow then took one to the next box:

Two nephews and a niece, now owners:

The nephews . . .

Two separate arrows led to a box with the words:

Nephews (brothers): Pardon Morapedi

And Mr H. J. Morapedi

Another box contained the name:

Diphimotswe (niece)

Both ownership boxes were then connected to a box labelled *Manager*. This contained a single name: *Quick Babusi (known as Babusi)*. This box was itself joined by a dotted line to another box in which was written *His opinions*, followed by a question mark. There were several other boxes dotted around the edge of the diagram. One said: *Waitress called Dolly, former employee*, while another said, *Persons currently unknown* and *Persons working in kitchen or with access to kitchen*. Finally, there was a large rectangular box edged in red ink, containing the name *Violet Sephotho*. Beside that was the name of Mr H. J. Morapedi. And directly underneath Violet's name she had written, *Suspect No. 1: almost definitely*.

She gazed at her diagram. She was pleased with her handiwork, although she recognised that the information it contained was spotty. It clarified, though, where various people stood in relation to the Great Hippopotamus Hotel; now all that she had to do was speak to these people and find out as much as she could about them. In particular, she would try to discover whether Violet Sephotho had any connection with the hotel – it was just too much of a coincidence that Violet should be linked with one of the owners.

Of course, she would still have to find a motive to explain why Violet should be organising these acts of deliberate sabotage. Could it be spite? It was possible, she thought, that Violet might resent the fact that her friend Mr H. J. Morapedi had only a one-third share of the hotel. If there was indeed a relationship between the two of them, then her proven greed might prompt her to try to get rid of Pardon and Diphimotswe, and in order to do that . . . She took her eyes off her chart and looked up at the ceiling. Of course! It was obvious, now that she came to think of it: if Violet made the ownership of the hotel stressful enough, then Pardon and Diphimotswe might become keen to get rid of their share. If they were to feel that way, then Mr H. J. Morapedi would be able to buy them out at an advantageous price. People who really wanted to get out of a business were often prepared to sell their share for less than it was worth. If that happened here, Mr H. J. Morapedi might pick up the shares cheaply and in this way take full control of the company. Naturally, if that were to happen, the run of bad luck experienced by the hotel would promptly come to an end and its reputation would be repaired.

The thought came to her so quickly and in such an unexpected way that for a short while she wondered whether it was one of those fleeting ideas that, on further examination, would appear ridiculous. She occasionally had such brainwaves just before she dropped off to sleep, and when she revisited them the following morning there was always a feeling of disappointment. Was this like that? She waited for the objections to emerge, but after a few minutes she decided that the situation she had envisaged was entirely credible. If her initial supposition was correct, and Mr H. J. Morapedi had ambitions to own all the shares in the Great Hippopotamus Hotel, then achieving that goal by getting his brother and cousin to sell their shares to him was a good way to go about it.

It was a moment of insight, and she rose to her feet in sheer delight at having so quickly discovered the solution to a complex problem. Her first instinct was to tell Mma Ramotswe about it; she wanted to share her discovery, and, if Mma Ramotswe saw its merits, to hear her say, 'Well, Mma Makutsi, that's a very fine good piece of reason – and you are absolutely right.' That would have been a boost. And for a moment she even imagined herself writing to the great Clovis Andersen, over in that place where he lived in America – Muncie, Indiana, they called it – to tell him about it; and getting a letter in reply, perhaps, in which he might say, 'This only goes to show, Mma, the benefits of thinking laterally, as I recommend in *The Principles of Private Detection*.' She had never quite worked out what lateral thinking was, but she knew that it was recommended by Clovis Andersen and she felt that whatever it was, she had probably been doing it for some time without realising it. Of course, some people would never be able to think laterally – Charlie was in that category, she thought: he was always getting things wrong because he thought back from the solution that he wanted to find, and then made the facts fit his desired conclusion. That was a very strange way of going about things, Mma Makutsi thought, and it came about because Charlie had never had any real education beyond his school-leaving certificate. That was enough to give one a basic grasp of subjects like mathematics and the physical geography of Botswana, but it did little to develop reasoning powers. That required tertiary education of some sort – such as that provided by the Botswana Secretarial College, or similar institutions. Poor Charlie – it was not his fault that he was who he was – and she had to remind herself, as she now did, that not everybody had the chance to better themselves.

She toyed with the idea of telephoning Mma Ramotswe, but decided against it. Mr J. L. B. Matekoni had made it quite clear that the doctor wanted Mma Ramotswe to have a complete rest, and that meant, surely, that the concerns of the office should not intrude in any way. So even if it would be helpful to have Mma Ramotswe's view on her theory, she would have to forgo that and trust to her own judgement. And that judgement, she thought, was obviously correct.

She sat down and picked up the pencil she had used to draw her diagram. At the bottom of the page, she now made a short list of the steps she would take. At the head of this would be a visit to Diphimotswe. There was a reason why she should be seen first. Women *noticed* things, thought Mma Makutsi. It was not that men went round with their eyes closed – men could be observant when they set their minds to it, but for much of the time men were just not very interested in what was going on around them.

And even when they were looking, men often missed what was going on below the surface – in the realm of feeling. Women, by contrast, were very interested in how people were feeling, and how these feelings affected what they did. As a result of this, Mma Makutsi had observed, men often thought that everything was going well when in fact it was not. So, if there were any undercurrents in the relationships among those who associated with the Great Hippopotamus Hotel, then these would be far more likely to have been spotted by a woman than by a man.

Not that I am being old-fashioned, Mma Makutsi said to herself: I am simply being realistic. There's no point in pretending that men and women were the same, she thought, when it was so patently obvious that they were not. To admit that, she felt, was not to run men down in any way: men did their best, and many of them were every bit as good as women at doing at least some of the things that had to be done (at others, she felt, they were not quite so good), but that did not mean that the sexes were the same. And that suited her: she did not want to be the same as men – she wanted to be what she was – a woman. But that did not mean that she accepted any male claims of privilege: men and women should have exactly the same chances, Mma Makutsi felt; they should have the same rights, the same opportunities. There was still some way to go to achieve that, she realised, but matters were heading in the right direction.

One of these days there would be a female president of Botswana, she told herself, and if she were ever to be asked . . . well, she would not actively seek that out, but she would rise to the challenge – for the sake of the country. An even better choice, though, she decided, would be Mma Ramotswe. She would make a wonderful, wise president, and would run the country carefully and humanely. She would be a credit not only to Botswana, but to

Africa as a whole. *President Ramotswe, a wise president* – she could see that headline in the *Botswana Daily News.* It would be a great day, that, for women throughout the country – a day of rejoicing and thanksgiving. She turned the idea over in her mind, revelling in its possibilities, but then an uncomfortable thought elbowed its way to mind: what if an entirely different sort of woman were to be elected? What if Violet Sephotho were to be attracted by the prospect of power? Mma Makutsi gave a shudder. That was the trouble with democracy: sometimes the wrong person won.

Or Mma Potokwani . . . What if Mma Potokwani were to take it upon herself to run for president? People would vote for her, Mma Makutsi thought, because she would remind them of their mother, and *everyone* would vote for their mother, if given the chance. Mma Potokwani would not be a bad president, and she would soon sort out any episodes of selfish behaviour. We would all have to tidy our rooms. The nation would be told to go to bed early, to eat plenty of green vegetables, and to remember to brush its teeth after every meal. There would be no harm in such policies, of course, but people might begin to resent them after a while. We need matron, Mma Makutsi admitted, because there is a small child within all of us, and matron understands that, but we also were uncomfortable about being told what to do all the time. There would be rebellion under a Potokwani presidency – sooner or later people would begin to behave like naughty children again. Mma Makutsi smiled.

Babusi had told her that Diphimotswe owned a dress shop, and now Mma Makutsi found herself pulling into a parking place directly outside Select Fashions. Switching off the car engine, she sat for a moment and took in the façade and window display before her. Painted along the face of the building, immediately above the display windows, was the wording: *Select Fashions: formal and informal outfits for all occasions.* The display windows reflected this philosophy, with some of the shop-models dressed in jeans and skimpy tops, while others demonstrated expensive-looking dresses. There were shoes too, which interested Mma Makutsi, although on first impression they struck her as being not the sort of shoes she would care to wear. But there was definitely something for all tastes, she thought, and the windows seemed to be attracting attention from passers-by.

Diphimotswe received her in her office at the back of the showroom. She was a tall, rather willowy woman, dressed in a loose-fitting blue dress of the sort that Mma Makutsi knew that Mma Ramotswe would approve of: she did not like clothes that clung too tightly. A colourful necklace and several gold bangles completed the impression of a woman who paid attention to what she was wearing, but who was not overdoing it.

Diphimotswe examined the card that Mma Makutsi had given her on being shown into the office. This card was an innovation: Mma Ramotswe had never bothered to have a card printed – 'I can just tell people who I am, Mma,' she had said – but Mma Makutsi had ordered one for herself, and was inordinately proud of it. She had shown it to Charlie, who had wrinkled his nose as he read it and then said, unhelpfully: 'So this thing says who you are, Mma. You can carry it around with you so that people will know who you are if you get lost. They can then send you back safely. Very useful, Mma.'

She had shaken her finger at him. 'That is not the point of these things, Charlie. You do not understand. A card is very important in business. People file it away and then when they need somebody to provide those services, they remember the card and call you. That is how it works.'

Charlie scrutinised the card. '*Grace Makutsi*,' he read. '*Dip. Sec. (97%, Bots. Sec. Coll.) Associate CEO, the No. 1 Ladies' Detective Agency*.' He paused, and looked at Mma Makutsi as if recognising her for the first time. 'Is that you, Mma? Are you this lady? And what is an Associate CEO? That sounds very important. Central Electricity Organisation?'

She snatched the card back from him. 'You are very ignorant, Charlie,' she said. 'It is very sad to meet somebody quite as ignorant as you.'

'Hah!' was all Charlie could say, although a few seconds later he managed another 'Hah!'

Now Diphimotswe was examining the card, and was duly impressed. 'I have heard of you people,' she said, as she put the card down on her desk. 'Please sit down, Mma.'

The young sales assistant who had shown Mma Makutsi into the room was sent off to make tea.

'These hot afternoons are very difficult without tea,' said Diphimotswe. 'I get up each day and think: surely the rains will be here soon. But they take their time, don't they?'

'As long as they come eventually,' said Mma Makutsi.

'They will,' said Diphimotswe.

She was looking at Mma Makutsi, who for a few moments felt that her clothes were being assessed. They were.

'I like your top,' said Diphimotswe. 'Those colours suit you, Mma. It is well chosen.'

'You are very kind, Mma. I have had this top for some time. I have always liked it.'

'Many people wear the wrong thing,' Diphimotswe continued. 'But you try to tell them that, Mma, and they don't like it at all. You cannot criticise somebody's clothes without causing big trouble.'

'No. I can imagine that, Mma.'

There was a brief silence. Then Diphimotswe said, 'I heard that you people were down at the Great Hippopotamus Hotel the other day.'

This was made as a simple observation, almost as an aside, but it took Mma Makutsi by surprise. 'Yes, Mma, we were there,' she began. 'But how did you . . . '

Diphimotswe smiled benignly. 'You know how this country is, Mma. You do anything – anywhere – and straight away, everybody knows about it. This person tells that person, and then that person tells this other person, and soon everybody knows. You may as well announce everything on the Radio Botswana national news.'

Mma Makutsi smiled. She was warming quickly to Diphimotswe, who had an appealing, friendly manner. 'We were asked to go down there because of some problems the manager had been having.'

Diphimotswe sighed. 'Poor Babusi. I think he is very worried.'

Mma Makutsi asked her if the manager had told her what had happened. He had, it seemed, and she listed the events that Mma Makutsi had heard about on her visit to the hotel, including the scorpion incident. 'How do scorpions get into bedrooms, Mma?' Diphimotswe asked. 'Sometimes they wander in, but I think that sometimes they are put there – that's what I think.'

Mma Makutsi agreed. It was always possible that things that bit or stung could make their way uninvited into a bedroom – she had herself found a cobra under her bed on one occasion – but when this happened alongside a whole chapter of unpleasant events, it began to look suspicious. Now she remembered the advice Mma Ramotswe had given her right at the beginning of her career, when she had said, 'If you want to know the answer to a question, just ask it: you'll be surprised at how many times that works.'

So now she said to Diphimotswe, 'Who do you think is doing these things, Mma?'

The other woman stared at her. Then she stood up and crossed the room to close the door.

'You have to be careful what you say,' she said as she returned to her desk. 'There are always ears listening, Mma. You should never forget that.'

Mma Makutsi felt a surge of satisfaction that her question should have prompted what promised to be a revealing response. Mma Ramotswe's advice – once again – was proving to be invaluable. Following the brief silence that followed, she said to Diphimotswe, 'You are right to be careful, Mma. When you are about to say something sensitive, always check to see who is listening.'

'That is true, Mma.'

'So?' prompted Mma Makutsi. 'Who do you think is responsible for all this?'

Mma Makutsi leaned forward. This was the moment of revelation, and for a moment she felt a pang of regret that Mma Ramotswe could not be there to witness the moment when her question elicited this crucial response.

Diphimotswe's voice remained low. 'I have no idea, Mma. None at all.'

For a moment Mma Makutsi thought she had misheard the response. 'Well, Mma,' she encouraged. 'Who do you think it is?'

Diphimotswe repeated herself. 'I said, I have no idea at all, Mma.'

'No idea?'

'No. None at all. I can't see why anybody would want to harm the good name of the Great Hippopotamus Hotel . . . other than . . .'

Again, Mma Makutsi leaned forward. 'Yes, Mma?'

'Other than some person with a grudge,' Diphimotswe said, with a shrug. 'Not that I can see who that might be.'

They looked at one another, both of them uncertain as to where the conversation might go. Mma Makutsi sighed: there had been no revelation, but she did not want to end this meeting without finding out something about Diphimotswe and what she felt about her cousins. 'Would you mind telling me a bit about yourself, Mma?' she asked.

Diphimotswe hesitated. 'Why do you want to know that, Mma? What has it got to do with what is happening at the hotel?'

Mma Makutsi explained that Diphimotswe was potentially one of the victims in this investigation. 'If the hotel is harmed,' she said, 'then the owners of the hotel are harmed too. You are one of the owners – therefore I need to know whether there is anybody who might want to harm you. That information could be useful.'

Diphimotswe looked surprised. 'But why would anybody want to harm me, Mma? What have I done?'

'There is always somebody who might take exception to any of us,' said Mma Makutsi. 'You never know what enemies you have until they strike.'

'But I have no enemies,' protested Diphimotswe. 'I am just an ordinary lady. I am not a politician or anybody like that. Why would I have enemies?'

'Everybody has an enemy somewhere,' said Mma Makutsi. As she said this, she realised that it might be true for most people, but not necessarily for everybody. Mr J. L. B. Matekoni, for instance, had no enemies – and she could not imagine anybody taking against him for any reason whatsoever. But Phuti had enemies – one or two business rivals and a couple of employees whom he had dismissed for dishonesty, and his enemies would presumably feel hostile to her, on the grounds that she was married to him. Such people would be inherited enemies – enemies you had to do nothing in order to acquire.

Mma Makutsi looked at Diphimotswe, who seemed genuinely perplexed that Mma Makutsi should be insisting that somewhere in the shadows there lurked an enemy who wished her ill. A different tactic, she decided, might be needed here.

'Just tell me about yourself, Mma,' Mma Makutsi began. 'Don't worry about people who may or may not be enemies. Forget all that. Just tell me about yourself and about how you became involved in the Great Hippopotamus Hotel.'

Diphimotswe seemed relieved not to have to think about enemies. 'From the beginning, Mma?'

'That is always a good place to start,' said Mma Makutsi, with a smile. 'Not that everybody starts there. Some people begin a story halfway through, and then go back to the beginning later on. Some people start at the end.'

Diphimotswe returned the smile. 'People are very strange, aren't they, Mma?'

Mma Makutsi agreed. 'Never underestimate how strange they are,' she said. 'People are very peculiar, and sometimes you think that *everybody* is peculiar – except yourself, of course.'

It was a joke, and, after a brief pause for that to be established, they both laughed. Mma Makutsi and Diphimotswe were getting on very well together. This is the beginning of a friendship, Mma Makutsi allowed herself to think. But then she reminded herself of her professional duty. Mma Ramotswe had often warned her to be careful not to allow her judgement to be clouded by feelings of warmth towards people she encountered in the course of her investigations. You may find yourself liking somebody, but remember that you may barely know them, and they may be wanting you to like them because they have something to hide. 'Do not be too mistrustful,' said Mma Ramotswe, 'but always be a *bit* careful. That is all. Be a *bit* careful – that's all.'

'My mother,' said Diphimotswe, 'was a very intelligent woman. But like many women in those days, she was not encouraged to make much of her abilities. It's sad, isn't it, Mma Makutsi, how they persuaded girls back in those days that they should concentrate on finding a husband and having children, rather than concentrating on their education. It was such a waste.'

'There were many wasted lives,' said Mma Makutsi. 'All those girls who could have gone on to do important things in the world ending up stirring the cooking pot.'

'And tilling the fields,' said Diphimotswe. 'And bringing in the crops. And feeding the children. And walking miles to get water in the days when there were no pumps and no taps. All of that, Mma.'

'Your mother's life was like that?'

Diphimotswe shook her head. 'It would have been, but she made up for the education that she never got. She worked very hard. She did not have much time to enjoy herself.'

Mma Makutsi sighed. 'I am sorry, Mma. That is very sad when that happens.'

Diphimotswe was silent for a moment. 'I do not think too much about it, Mma. There are many sad things in this life. It is best not to think about them too much or you will just spend your time with your head bowed down. You will not see some of the good things that are happening if you are looking down instead of up.'

That was true, thought Mma Makutsi.

'She married when she was very young,' Diphimotswe

continued. 'These days women marry much later. They allow themselves time to do things before they get married. They have a career. The things that men used to keep to themselves. It is all different now.'

Her father, she told Mma Makutsi, was a prospector. 'He did not have many paper qualifications – he had some sort of certificate in geology – but he had an amazing talent, Mma, for working out what was underneath the ground. You and I look at the ground and see just some earth – my father imagined the rocks underneath – deep underneath – and he was often right. He was a water diviner too. Have you seen those people working, Mma? Have you seen them?'

Mma Makutsi had seen a diviner looking for water up at Bobonong. He had been a wizened old man from over the border, from Bulawayo, and he had been brought down to Bobonong by a farmer who had despaired of finding a new borehole. They had watched him as he walked backwards and forwards across the fields with a twist of copper wire in his hand until the wire had suddenly dipped down, as if pulled by an insistent and powerful hand. Some people had been disbelieving – they were to be chastened when a drilling rig arrived and found water barely thirty feet below the surface.

She mentioned that incident. 'Yes,' said Diphimotswe. 'They are very good at finding water – if there is water to be found. Sometimes there is none, of course. They cannot help then, although my father would try and try before he gave up. He did not like to tell people that there was no water on their land.'

'That was not his real job, of course. The work that paid the bills was helping with prospecting teams that went out looking for gold. He spent a lot of time in Angola, because they were always hoping to find more gold there. He said that there was plenty of everything in Angola, but it was difficult to find it because it was a dangerous country and there were always people who would steal anything that you found. But the mining people over there liked him, because of his ability to tell them what lay underneath the surface.

'He died when he fell into an old mine shaft. They had many of these out in the bush. People dug them and then, when they didn't find gold, or when the gold ran out, they would just leave them. They were meant to block off the entrance, but nobody ever did that, which meant that people were always falling into them.'

Mma Makutsi gasped. 'Oh, Mma, that is a terrible way to go.'

She realised, almost immediately, that this was not the most tactful response, and so she quickly added, 'Although I am sure that he would have known nothing about it.'

Diphimotswe turned away at the painful memory. 'We came back to Botswana,' she continued. 'My late father had built up some savings. These were not enough to start a business, but my mother's brother, my uncle, Goodman Tsholofelo – you may have heard of him, Mma – helped her to buy this store. In those days it sold all sorts of clothing, including work clothes for men – you know, khaki shirts and so on – but she began to specialise in women's fashions, which were more profitable. My mother worked and worked . . . ' She paused and looked hard at Mma Makutsi. 'You know how women work in this country, Mma. You know how much there is for them to do.'

Mma Makutsi did know. 'It has always been like that, Mma.'

'She would be here,' Diphimotswe went on, 'first thing in the morning, when everybody was still in bed. She would be here getting ready to open the store. And she was always the last to leave in the evening. People think shops close at five. They may shut the front door, but there is still plenty of work to do – adding up the receipts, tidying the displays because customers are always moving things. You lay things out neatly on tables and they come and unfold them and move them round.'

Mma Makutsi assured her that she knew all about that. 'My husband has a furniture store,' she began.

'The Double Comfort Store? That big one with the red sign that lights up at night?'

'That is the one,' said Mma Makutsi. 'And he has a lot of trouble with people who come in and let their children swing on the doors of cupboards and sit on chairs and so on. And when it comes to beds in the bed department – oh, Mma, you wouldn't believe what goes on there.' She paused, as if unsure whether to continue.

Diphimotswe smiled. 'You can tell me, Mma. I am a married lady.'

'Well,' said Mma Makutsi, 'there are couples coming in because they are going to get married and some generous uncle or aunt is going to buy them a bed for their new home. They both get onto the bed and bounce around. They say they are testing the bed. It is very embarrassing for other customers, Mma – and it is not good for the bedsprings.'

Diphimotswe laughed. 'People are very odd, Mma. You know I had a lady come in one day and said that she was going to be married soon and she wanted to try on some pregnancy dresses. She was not yet pregnant, Mma – she was very thin, but she said that she was intending to get pregnant once she was married and she thought that she would get a pregnancy dress beforehand.'

'Oh,' said Mma Makutsi. 'You should not do that. What if you don't become pregnant?'

'Exactly. That's what I said to her, but she wouldn't listen to me.'

There was a brief silence before Diphimotswe continued her story. Through the office window, Mma Makutsi saw a Cape dove land on a small branch of an acacia tree directly outside. The branch bent under the weight of the bird, and the dove had to struggle to keep its grip. Once it had stabilised, it looked directly through the window, at Mma Makutsi. It did not flinch, and quickly became indifferent to what might be going on inside. Mma Makutsi thought of how her brother had aimed his catapult at those doves when he was a young boy, and she had remonstrated with him, pointing out that doves harmed nobody. And he had laughed and continued regardless, and now he was no more and she would never have the opportunity to forgive him for that, or for other acts of thoughtlessness to which boys seemed to be given. If only we could go back and cancel the misunderstandings and acts of selfishness that are like milestones in our lives, but we cannot, and so perhaps it is best for us to forget those things we cannot change.

She became aware that Diphimotswe was speaking again, and that she had missed part of the story. '... my mother, you see. Uncle told her that she could retire to her village and that she need not worry about me, because he would see to it that she had enough money to live on without taking it out of the business, out of the shop. He was so kind. I have heard of other kind uncles, but he is the kindest of them all. Do you believe in heaven, Mma Makutsi?'

Mma Makutsi sometimes did, and sometimes did not. It was safer, she thought, to believe in it, just in case, and so she answered, 'I think that we do not entirely disappear. Well, I mean we do disappear, the body we live in, but there is our soul, you see, Mma, and I think that might continue. Who knows? There might be a place up there where for all we know ...'

She had not thought much about that, although she had occasionally had a conversation with Phuti that became vaguely theological. Phuti said that there was more or less definitely a place where bad debtors and car thieves and the like went after they had finished causing inconvenience and trouble on this earth. 'Then there is a place for respectable people like us, Mma, and that will be a very good place to be, I think.' They had not discussed it much further; it did not do, Phuti thought, to take too close an interest in such questions, in case one's interest brought about a premature call from the next world. And Mma Makutsi agreed, although she would have liked to give further thought to what happened to the undeserving. She felt it was important for those who did their best to be good to at least know what advantage they were building up by keeping to the straight and narrow. It was a question of incentivisation, she thought. She had recently read about incentivisation and took the view that there was a great deal to be said for it.

'So, my mother packed up and went to her village,' Diphimotswe went on. 'She left me in charge of the shop, and I'm happy to say that business was good. I married the bookkeeper, Mma. He is a very fine man, and now we have two children who are five and three. I might have more, but I am not sure. We shall see.

'Uncle Goodman says that it is a good thing to have a lot of children, provided one can put enough food on the table to feed them. He says that if you do not have enough food, you should not have more than two children, as there is a risk they will go hungry if you do. He says that I can have as many children as I want because I have the shop and now I have part of the hotel. He loves that hotel, by the way. I never believed that anybody could love a business so much, but he does. I think that at night he dreams of the Great Hippopotamus Hotel. He would like to be buried there, he says, near an old mango tree at the back. He says that that is where he would like to go when his time comes. I do not like to think of it, but I'm sure we shall honour that wish.'

Mma Makutsi was pleased that they were getting back to the subject of the hotel. She pressed Diphimotswe on her cousins. 'Did you know Pardon and Mr H. J. Morapedi when you were younger?' she asked. 'Were you close?'

'Yes, I spent a lot of time with my cousins when we were children,' Diphimotswe said. 'We went out to the lands together with our grandmother. But then we drifted apart later on. We went to different schools, and that always makes a difference when you are young. By the time we were eighteen, I saw them very little. We were always together at family weddings and so on – but otherwise we led separate lives.'

'You got on well?' asked Mma Makutsi.

Diphimotswe hesitated. 'Most of the time,' she said. 'I got on a bit better with Pardon than with H. J. I don't like to compare them, and I don't want to say anything against H. J., but Pardon is gentler, I think. He is one of those people who asks you how you are feeling – H. J. never does that. I think he is far more – how shall I put it? – a bit more self-centred than his brother. I suppose you might say that Pardon is *nicer* than H. J.'

Mma Makutsi waited. This was exactly the sort of thing that she was hoping she would hear. It was a small step from saying that somebody was not so nice to identifying him or her as a malefactor. Was that the point they had reached?

Diphimotswe frowned as she went on. 'I wasn't surprised, you know, when H. J. took up with that woman – what is her name, Mma?'

'Violet Sephotho.'

'Yes, Violet Sephotho. That's the one. Do you know her, by any chance?'

Mma Makutsi drew in her breath. She knew that when you were questioning somebody you should not give vent to too many of your own opinions, but there were occasions when you simply could not avoid doing exactly that. 'Do I know her, Mma? Oh, Mma, I could tell you so much about Violet Sephotho, starting way back when she and I were students together.'

Diphimotswe looked interested. 'At the university? You were students together at the University of Botswana?'

Mma Makutsi waved a hand. 'It was at a different . . . ' She almost said *university*, but stopped herself. There was nothing to be ashamed of in being a graduate of the Botswana Secretarial College. 'I was at the Botswana Secretarial College. You may know the place, Mma – it is one of the main centres for secretarial studies in all of southern Africa.'

'Oh, I know the place,' said Diphimotswe. 'It is a very fine college, Mma. I have heard many good things about it. You were very fortunate to go there.'

Mma Makutsi felt a rush of affection for this woman, with her impeccable judgement. 'Thank you, Mma,' she said. 'I do believe I was very fortunate. And I hope that my results showed my appreciation.'

'You did well, Mma?'

Mma Makutsi hesitated. 'Actually, Mma, I did – now that you ask. Ninety-seven per cent in the final examinations. I do not speak about that too much, but you raised the issue.'

'That is remarkable, Mma,' said Diphimotswe. 'I would never get ninety-seven per cent – for anything.'

Mma Makutsi assured her that she might surprise herself. 'Always set your sights high, Mma – then you will very likely do very well. Even if you did not get ninety-seven per cent, you might still get a mark somewhere in the high eighties. You never know, Mma.'

Diphimotswe laughed. 'I would be lucky to get that,' she said. She paused, and then, 'You did not form a very high opinion of this Sephotho lady?'

'I did not,' said Mma Makutsi. 'And since then, I have come across her in many different contexts – all of them extremely negative, I must say. If trouble brews up, I say that there is at least a fifty-fifty chance that Violet Sephotho is behind it. Somewhere in the background, you will see her hand. I have found that time and time again.'

Diphimotswe looked thoughtful. 'Then you think it is Violet who is causing these things to go wrong at the hotel?'

Mma Makutsi decided to nail her colours to the mast. There was a time for hypothesis to become a working explanation. That time, she decided, was now.

'I am sure of it, Mma,' she said. 'Violet wants to wreck the hotel so that you and Pardon will sell your shares to Mr H. J. Morapedi at a knock-down price. A failing business, with all the guests scared away, will not be valued at much. You and Pardon might be pleased to get rid of the shares – at any price. That is more or less certainly her plan.'

Diphimotswe stared at her, her expression a mixture of astonishment and disgust. 'She would do that, do you think, Mma? She would stoop so low?'

'There is no need for her to stoop, Mma,' said Mma Makutsi. 'She is already very low. If you are very low, you do not need to stoop. You are already down there.'

Diphimotswe shook her head. 'And H. J. knows all about this?'

Mma Makutsi hesitated. She had not thought of the possibility that Mr H. J. Morapedi was innocent, and that Violet might be acting of her own accord. But why would she do that? A possible answer occurred immediately: Violet might be acting without his knowledge. For his part, Mr H. J. Morapedi might have no intention of acquiring the shares of the other two owners, but would nonetheless be encouraged by Violet to do so. If she intended to get him to leave his wife for her, then it would be in her interests for him to be as wealthy as possible. Once he had bought out his brother and his cousin and the hotel was his alone, Violet would turn the business round and reap the rewards. That would be the plan I would make if I were Violet Sephotho, thought Mma Makutsi.

Diphimotswe looked thoughtful. 'Will you tell Pardon about this plan that Violet has?'

Mma Makutsi shook her head. 'I do not think I should tell him just yet,' she said. 'At the moment, it should be kept just between you and me.'

'Very wise,' said Diphimotswe. 'He might say something to his brother, and then it would get to Violet.'

'Precisely. But I should go and have a word with those two – with Pardon and H. J. – just to build up a picture. I also need to talk to the staff. Violet will not be acting alone. She will have her accomplices in there somewhere.'

Diphimotswe gave an involuntary shudder. 'Oh, Mma, it is very worrying to think that there is a snake in the house – not a real one, of course, but a human one. It is not a nice thought.'

'It is not,' agreed Mma Makutsi. 'But that is what we are here for, Mma. The No. 1 Ladies' Detective Agency is here to protect good people from the doings of people who are not so good. That is our mission statement, so to speak. *We are here for you at all times.*' That was made up on the spur of the moment, but it was rather a good mission statement, thought Mma Makutsi – better than the one that Mma Ramotswe had come up with at the very beginning: *For the problems of ladies and of others.* That was true enough, in its way, but was not as reassuring as the one that Mma Makutsi had just coined. *We are here for you at all times* sounded very good, although, in order to avoid misunderstanding, one might need to add *except for Saturday afternoons, Sundays and public holidays.* Mission statements tended to sound enthusiastic, and that was usually acceptable, but they should not mislead, especially with regard to opening hours.

Chapter Twelve

Kindness, Forgiveness, Errant Husbands

The house occupied by Mr Mo Mo Malala and his wife, Sheila Malala, a former beauty queen, stood well back from the road in an expensive part of town. Mr Malala was a man of some means, and took the view that those who were able to build on a substantial scale should do just that. If they were unwilling to spend at an appropriate level on the house itself, then they should, at the very least, make sure that they had expensive gates: a mediocre house, he felt, could be enhanced by elaborate gates that showed to any passer-by that the person within had achieved something in life.

More than mere ostentation lay behind this view. Not only did a large house remind anybody who needed reminding of the depth of the pockets that commissioned it, it also provided a substantial amount of work for tradesmen. The Malala house satisfied these requirements, as well as being a comfortable family home for Mr Malala and his wife, along with her aged parents, who were accommodated in a suite of rooms attached to the kitchen. Behind the house a grove of paw-paw trees ensured a regular supply of fruit for the Malala breakfasts, as did a beneficent avocado tree. At the front of the house was a wide veranda under the shade of which Sheila Malala grew herbs for kitchen use. A patch of kikuyu grass at the front of the house was the legacy of an attempt at a lawn, the boundaries of which were marked by white-washed stones of the sort that used to be popular outside every government building in Protectorate days.

Sheila Malala had been Miss Mahalapye decades earlier, but had allowed child-bearing and prosperity, and possibly also gravity, to bring about a fundamental change in her figure. She was now what Mma Ramotswe would describe as an *extremely* traditionally built woman, considerably taller and wider than her husband. When photographed together on family occasions, it was common practice for Mr Malala to stand on an orange box, or on a convenient step, to avoid being dwarfed by his wife. But even with that assistance, he was markedly smaller than she was, and in his demeanour and expression clearly the junior member of the partnership.

'I can see your wife sitting on the veranda,' said Mma Ramotswe, as she turned the tiny white van into the drive that led up to the house.

Sat beside her, Mr Malala made a sound that could have been the beginnings of a sentence, or, more likely, of a whimper.

'You must not worry,' said Mma Ramotswe. 'I will speak on your behalf, Rra.'

This did not reassure Mr Malala, who let out a low groan. 'This is very bad, Mma. I am in big trouble now.'

Mma Ramotswe had taken him to a clinic, where the cut on his cheek had been expertly sewn up. A tetanus injection and a small dressing had completed the treatment.

'You are going to be fine, Rra,' Mma Ramotswe said as she parked the van at the head of the drive. They were being watched now from the veranda, and this had the effect of increasing Mr Malala's nervousness.

As they emerged from the van, Sheila spotted her husband and gave a cheerful wave. Then she rose from her chair and went to stand at the top of the steps leading up the veranda. It was there that she noticed the dressing on her husband's face.

'What have you done to your face, Mo Mo?' she asked.

There was concern, rather than reproach, in her voice, but that did not seem to lessen Malala's anxiety. 'It is nothing,' he stuttered. 'Just a cut.'

Sheila looked at Mma Ramotswe. There was unspoken accusation in her expression. 'You are Mma Ramotswe, aren't you?' she said. 'You are the garage man's wife?'

'I am,' said Mma Ramotswe. 'And I am bringing your husband home, Mma, on behalf of Tlokweng Road Speedy Motors.'

Sheila frowned. 'On behalf of the garage, Mma? What is this nonsense?'

They had reached the top of the steps and Sheila was peering suspiciously at her husband's dressing. She turned again to Mma Ramotswe. 'I do not understand, Mma.'

'There has been an accident,' Mma Ramotswe said. 'Your husband had taken delivery of a new car, and unfortunately there was an accident. That is why I am bringing him home.'

Sheila looked puzzled. 'But we did not order a new car, Mma.

We have a perfectly good car behind the house. Your husband ordered it for us two years ago. It is still in very good condition.'

'Ah yes,' said Mma Ramotswe. 'Well, sometimes people decide that they need two cars . . . '

'We do not,' said Sheila firmly. 'Why would we need two cars? I don't go out much and my brother lives two doors down the road. He can drive me if I need to get anywhere while Mo Mo is using our car.'

'What if he is busy?' asked Mma Ramotswe. 'What then?'

'He is never busy,' snapped Sheila. 'My brother is a very lazy man. He never does anything.' She paused before continuing, 'You should not have bought a car without discussing it with me, Mo Mo. I shouldn't have to tell you that. You must ask Mr J. L. B. Matekoni to take it back.' Her voice was heavy with reproach.

This brought silence. Mr Malala glanced at Mma Ramotswe, and then lowered his gaze. Mma Ramotswe watched him: rarely had she seen a husband so openly and completely in thrall to his wife. It was sad, she thought – sad and undignified. It was not just because he was a man – one did not expect men to be so submissive – what made the situation particularly uncomfortable was his lack of courage. Mma Ramotswe thought that there was a minimal amount of courage that we all should have, whatever our circumstances – and Mr Malala came nowhere near that threshold. He was weak.

But she looked at him, and saw, with fresh eyes, his diminutive stature. What was it like to be small, to always have to look up at people? Was that harder for a man than for a woman, she wondered? Women did not bother about such things, she thought, but it was not like that in the world of men, where size and strength had traditionally been admired. Boys had always been encouraged to grow up strong, and although there had been changes in attitude towards so many things, those views were still widely held. She sighed. Women had been doing their best to stop, or at least take the edge off, certain male attitudes, but there was still a lot of work to be done. There were still men who wanted to dominate their wives, to bully them – for that was what it was – simple bullying. And there were still many women who lived in fear of the violence that some of these men were capable of using. She herself had suffered in that way at the hands of Note Mokoti, during her first, short-lived marriage. She had escaped from that, but many women could not, and remained trapped.

She had occasionally wondered whether there were many cases in which those unhappy roles were reversed, and men found themselves mistreated in this way by their wives. She imagined that there might be such cases, but they were probably kept concealed by male shame at being seen to be weak. Or through fear, for fear was the ally of so many bullies. Now it occurred to her that Mr Malala might be just such a case – that this large former beauty queen, with her brisk and rather pushy manner, might be a bully, and this small man, with his rather nervous manner, might be her victim. She glanced at him now, and noticed for the first time the small beads of sweat that had appeared on his brow. She saw too the clenching and unclenching of his right fist, and that, more perhaps than the sweat, confirmed that Mr Malala was frightened of his wife.

This, she realised, explained so much. When she had first been told by Mr J. L. B. Matekoni of the fast and expensive sports car, she had put that down to the desperation that middle-aged men felt when they realised, usually rather late, that youth was well behind them. Now, it seemed that this might be something different. The secret purchase of the car was a break for freedom from a controlling spouse – it was Mr Malala's assertion of his independence.

And Mma Ramotswe found that she could not be entirely disapproving of that. She had often said to Mma Makutsi, 'Put yourself in the shoes of other people, Mma,' and now, putting herself in the shoes of poor Mr Malala – and what small feet he had, now that she looked at them – she felt that she understood what made him behave as he did.

Yet understanding things was not the same thing as excusing them. It was as wrong for Mr Malala to deceive his wife as it was for her to browbeat or intimidate him.

She took a deep breath. 'It will not be possible for Tlokweng Road Speedy Motors to take that car back,' she told Sheila Malala. 'That car is no more, Mma.'

Sheila Malala fixed her with an intense glare. 'I do not understand what you are saying, Mma. Are you telling me it has been sold?'

'It has been destroyed, Mma,' replied Mma Ramotswe. 'My husband tells me that it is beyond repair.'

Sheila Malala transferred her glare from Mma Ramotswe to her cowering husband. 'Is that true, Mo Mo?'

Mr Malala opened his mouth to reply, but no sound emerged.

Mma Ramotswe answered for him. 'It is true. Yes, it is true.'

Sheila Malala swung round. 'He has a tongue, Mma. He can speak for himself.'

Something within Mma Ramotswe snapped. She was not sure what it was, but it made the same sound that an elastic band makes when it is stretched to breaking point. Perhaps, she thought, we have invisible elastic bands within us, and these are the things that control our temper. Perhaps this is the sound they make when we are goaded beyond endurance and they snap. Of course not, she thought, but that was how it sometimes seemed.

She looked Sheila Malala in the eye. 'I know he has a tongue,

Mma,' she said. 'But sometimes people cannot use their tongue because they are frightened. Sometimes they cannot speak because there is somebody who is listening who will shout them down, whatever they say.'

The other woman froze. Nobody moved or said anything until Mma Ramotswe broke the silence. 'I would like to speak to you alone, Mma,' she said.

Sheila Malala bristled. 'What do you have to say to me that cannot be heard by my own husband?' she retorted.

Mma Ramotswe delivered her answer quietly. 'Rather a lot, Mma.'

Again, there was an awkward silence, ended this time by Mr Malala, who sidled away, muttering an indistinct apology.

Sheila Malala turned to Mma Ramotswe. 'Well, Mma,' she said. 'Now it is just the two of us. Now it is just two ladies – as you wanted it to be.'

Mma Ramotswe never sought confrontation. She preferred the negotiated solution, the compromise that enabled people to avoid the humiliation that resulted when one side bettered another. She had often said that one did not change people by shouting at them, and she still believed that. At the same time, though, Mma Ramotswe was confident not to be intimated by somebody like this former beauty queen. If Mr Malala could not stand up for himself, then she would have to do it for him – not to provoke a show-down but at least to attempt to get this headstrong woman to think again.

'Your husband,' she began, 'is a good man. He is not like many men you meet who go off drinking or chasing after women. He does none of these things, Mma.'

Sheila Malala looked at her with disdain. 'Do you think I don't know that, Mma Ramotswe?' she snapped.

'You may know it, Mma,' said Mma Ramotswe, 'but I think you do not behave as if you know it.'

This brought a narrowing of Sheila Malala's eyes: if war had not yet been declared, it could not be far away. Now Mma Ramotswe had no alternative but to persist. 'Yes, Mma,' she went on. 'He is a good man, I think, but I think I am right in saying that you make all the decisions. I also think I am right in thinking that you do not tell him that you are proud of him, or that you think he is a handsome man, even if a bit small. You do not say things like that, Mma; you do not say anything nice to your husband. You have forgotten how to do that, perhaps. Maybe you should now remember because if you do not, Mma, I can tell you one thing that is definite: you will lose this man. Yes, Mma, you will lose him.'

As she came to the end of this admonition – or denunciation, for that is what it sounded like – it occurred to her that Sheila Malala might simply show her the door, as was her right. But something very different happened: the former Miss Mahalapye seemed to deflate before Mma Ramotswe's eyes. It was as if somebody had taken a pin to an inflated rubber bladder, letting it fold in on itself. Had there been the hissing sound of escaping air, Mma Ramotswe would not have been surprised.

'Oh,' said Sheila Malala, and then, 'Oh' again.

'You see,' Mma Ramotswe continued, pressing her advantage, 'it is very easy to forget how other people feel. Perhaps you did not know that your husband wanted you to look up to him – even just a little bit. Perhaps you did not know how he felt about being a smaller man surrounded by bigger men. Perhaps you thought that didn't matter – but it does, Mma, it does. Sometimes people like that feel that there is a knife inside them, cutting, cutting. Perhaps you did not realise that you made things more difficult for him.'

Sheila Malala looked away. 'I have never wanted to hurt my husband,' she said.

Mma Ramotswe waited until the other woman looked back at her before she responded. 'We never want these things,' she said quietly. 'We never want to make other people feel bad, but we do it all the same. We do it because we do not think, Mma Malala.'

Silence ensued. Then Sheila Malala asked, 'How do you know these things, Mma?'

Mma Ramotswe shrugged. She was unsure how to answer the question. Did she know these things because she had read Clovis Andersen's great work, which was full of practical wisdom from cover to cover? Did she know them because she was the daughter of a wise man, the late Obed Ramotswe, and had acquired from him, from all the talks they had had together, a feeling for the way the world worked? Or did such understanding as she had come from the experience of human nature she had acquired through running the No. 1 Ladies' Detective Agency? That brought her into contact with all sorts of people, and these people often opened up to her about their inmost thoughts. You learned about life that way – you could hardly avoid doing so.

She tried to answer Sheila Malala's question, but she felt she did not do it very well. After a few references to how it was generally best to trust one's feelings about people, and about how such feelings often proved to be correct, she sighed and remarked that there were occasions when one might know something without realising how one came to know it. Rather to her surprise, this might have been enough for Sheila, who nodded and said, 'That is true, Mma.'

They looked at one another, each expecting the other to say something more. Eventually Mma Ramotswe broke the silence. 'You do know that your husband loves you, Mma? You know that, don't you?'

Sheila remained silent.

'And he is proud of you?'

The silence persisted, but now Mma Ramotswe noticed a quivering of Sheila's lips. She assumed that she was right about Mr Malala loving his wife, and she thought there was at least a chance that he was proud of her. But there were times when it was right to embroider or take a chance with the truth when good might result. This, she thought, was such a time.

She had one more conversation to add. 'Men can do foolish things at times, Mma – they can be very foolish.'

A flicker of a smile came to Sheila's face. 'Oh, they can. But . . . '

'But what, Mma?'

'I think we must forgive them.'

It was what Mma Ramotswe wanted to hear. She could hardly believe it, but sometimes people responded to having very simple things pointed out to them. It sometimes happened.

Sheila, though, had a proviso to add. 'Within limits,' she said.

Mma Ramotswe smiled. 'But of course, Mma. We must do everything within limits.'

She thought of some of the limits that bounded our lives. There were many of them. She thought of Mma Potokwani's fruit cake – to be enjoyed within limits. She thought of the pleasure that came from treating oneself to some longed-for item – also one to be parcelled out carefully. Then she thought of love, for which there probably should be no limits. You could allow yourself to love with all your heart because that was always the right thing to do, in whatever circumstances. There were people who warned that you had to protect yourself from the hurt that might come from loving too readily, but Mma Ramotswe did not think they were right. You loved those with whom you shared the world, those whom you encountered on your way through life – you loved them with all your heart, freely and generously, and you should not worry about holding back, because the time we have is not a lengthy one, and is over before we know it.

Mma Ramotswe drove home, deep in thought. She was not sure how she felt about the events of the morning. She had done what she had promised Mr Malala she would do: she had spoken on his behalf, and had stood between him and an immediate reckoning with his formidable wife, but she was uncertain whether she had protected him from Sheila's ire. Certainly, Sheila's demeanour had changed, and she had become less forbidding, but would the attitudes of a lifetime change that quickly? Mma Ramotswe thought it unlikely.

By the time she reached the gate on Zebra Drive, she had decided that all she had done was put off for Mr Malala the uncomfortable moment when he would be obliged to explain to his wife what he was doing buying an expensive sports car in the first place and how he was going to get his money back. To these questions, Mma Ramotswe had no solution. The inescapable truth of the matter was that Mr Malala had no escape and would probably have to bear whatever punishment was being prepared for him. That was unfortunate, and she wished she could have helped him, but there was only so much that any woman could be expected to do.

Chapter Thirteen

May the Light Shine Upon You

'Pardon is the one who can tell you about what's going on,' said Diphimotswe to Mma Makutsi. 'Of the three of us, he has always been most interested in the hotel. He will know what's what.'

Mma Makutsi replied without really thinking about what she was saying. 'That will be useful,' she said. 'If you know what's what . . . ' She paused, uncertain as to how to complete her observation. Eventually she finished, 'If you know what's what, then you will miss nothing.'

Even as she said this, she doubted that it was true. It was too easy not only to miss minor details, but also to pass over the glaringly obvious. And it was true that even the best informed of people could come to entirely the wrong conclusion in circumstances in which a badly informed person might get things right.

Even Charlie, whom Mma Makutsi considered to have the wrong idea about most things, was occasionally proved to be right about something or other – a fact that Mma Makutsi admitted, even if somewhat reluctantly.

Mma Makutsi had been interested to hear that Pardon was the cousin who took the closest interest in the Great Hippopotamus Hotel. She did not know very much about him, but had managed to garner a few background details that suggested he was just the sort of person to take a sober view of a family business. If you inherited a family business, you implicitly took on responsibility for employees whose livelihood depended on that business. Building up a business was a matter of hard work, often over many years, but it was only too easy for somebody who did not care, or who was simply not interested, to undo everything that had been achieved – sometimes within days of taking over. Phuti had told her of one such case in the furniture business, when the son of a chair manufacturer in Gaborone, on assuming control of the business, had let slip at a business conference that he found his family firm's chairs gave him backache after he had sat in them for more than half an hour. 'Don't buy our chairs if you have a bad back,' he had jokingly observed – within the hearing of a passing journalist. The remark had not been intended to be taken seriously, but it had appeared in the journalist's weekly column and had been widely circulated. The resultant drop in the company's turnover – twenty-seven per cent – had taken two years to repair, and led to the loss of four jobs.

Diphimotswe had further praise for Pardon. 'Pardon is Uncle Goodman's favourite,' she said. 'Now, I know that an uncle should not favour one child over another, but uncles are human, after all, and sometimes you can tell which one they like the most. In this case, it's Pardon – although Uncle has always been very good to me.'

Mma Makutsi sensed that the fact that H. J. had not been mentioned was significant.

'And H. J.?' she asked. 'What about him?'

Diphimotswe's reply was hesitant. 'Uncle is a good judge of character. Uncle can tell.'

'Tell what, Mma?'

Diphimotswe's voice rose. 'He seemed to be doubtful about H. J. I'm not saying that is what I thought, Mma – all I'm saying is what I think Uncle felt. I'm not sure that he liked him as much as he liked Pardon.'

Mma Makutsi absorbed this information. Of course, it was hardly in H. J.'s favour that he was involved with Violet Sephotho – that told one something about him. But even as she thought this, she realised women like Violet were quite capable of turning the heads of good men, and for this reason she should be careful not to make the sort of assumption that Clovis Andersen warned against in *The Principles of Private Detection*. Had he not written, *The obvious conclusion about somebody is often the wrong one*? And then, at another point, if her memory served her correctly, he had warned, *Do not accept without question an assessment of character made by another person. What if that person is wrong? What if that person has a reason to mislead you as to the character of a third party?*

She remembered the precise words that Mr Andersen used, including the term *a third party*. She had liked those words, and repeated them now to herself. *A third party* . . . H. J. was a third party, and one over whom there seemed to hang a bit of a question mark. But what if Diphimotswe disliked him for reasons of her own? The rivalries and dislikes of childhood can survive into adult life – everyone knew that – and that might be what was happening here. *I know so many cases where cousins have bad relations with one another because of the past.* That was what she told herself now, but then she stopped, realising that she did not really know of any such cases, or at least could not think of them now, not by name. That was the problem, she thought: we think that we know things that, on closer examination, we do not really know. Mma Ramotswe, of course, solved that problem by simply saying, *That is well known*. There was something to be said for such an approach, even if at times Mma Makutsi felt like challenging her to explain *how* it was well known.

Now she asked Diphimotswe a simple question. 'Are you sure how your uncle felt about H. J., Mma?'

Diphimotswe's expression changed. 'I am not sure, Mma. And I may be wrong about him. H. J. may not be perfect, but we can't all be Nelson Mandela. And everybody has at least some good points.'

Mma Makutsi considered this. 'Good points?' she enquired. 'Such as, Mma?'

Diphimotswe frowned. 'I am not sure, Mma. But the fact that I cannot name any of H. J.'s good points does not mean that he has none. I would not say that.' She paused. 'Perhaps you could ask Pardon, Mma. He might be able to tell you of good things that his brother has done. Perhaps.' She frowned again, and then concluded, 'You never know.'

It was, thought Mma Makutsi, a good way of ending any discussion. *You never know*. On one thing, at the end of the day, we might all agree: that you never knew.

Pardon Morapedi lived in a house near Kgale Hill. It was a house of a type that Mma Makutsi would describe as *middle-income* – not too ostentatious or expensive, but several rungs above the economical two-bedroom places in which somebody like a middle-ranking government servant – say, a tax inspector or a head of a section in the Department of Water Affairs – might live. In her reports she usually wrote something about the setting in which she interviewed somebody, as this gave context to the encounter, which could be useful in drawing a conclusion. And there were times, too, when the setting was in itself a piece of evidence, as when, in any case involving dishonesty or corruption, one might see somebody enjoying a standard of living well above that which their station in life might warrant.

An example of that had been when she and Mma Ramotswe had been asked by the trustees of a church to investigate an inexplicable shortfall in diocesan funds. The two of them had gone to visit the church treasurer in his house on the Molepolole Road, and had been invited to have a cup of tea with him in his sitting room. Being married to Phuti Radiphuti, Mma Makutsi knew all about furniture and what one would pay for a five-seater sofa in dyed blue leather. She had a good idea, too, of what one would pay for a fitted carpet of the quality of the one on which the sofa stood, or for a surround-sound stereo system of the type that was prominently displayed under the velvet picture of a lion that occupied most of the wall above the composite-stone fireplace.

The treasurer had left them sitting in the living room while he went off to order tea from the kitchen maid.

'Twenty-five thousand pula,' Mma Makutsi had whispered to Mma Ramotswe, pointing an accusing finger at the luxurious sofa.

And then, as Mma Ramotswe cast her eye over the shameless piece of furniture, Mma Makutsi gave an informal valuation of the surround-sound stereo system that she said could not have been purchased for anything under thirty thousand pula, given the size of the speakers and the brand name emblazoned on the turntable. 'These things are not cheap,' she had said to Mma Ramotswe, her voice full of disapproval.

The conversation with the treasurer had touched on the losses in the church accounts, which the treasurer put down to the carelessness of the clergy.

'I never like to criticise men of God,' he said, as if in a confidential aside. 'But their minds are so often on higher things, *Bomma*. They are thinking of things like angels and so on and they forget to ask for receipts for any church expenditure. And then when I come along and try to make sense of the accounts, I cannot see where the money has gone. It is very irritating, I can tell you. I cannot make up figures out of thin air – no treasurer can do that.'

'Of course not,' said Mma Ramotswe. 'You are so right about that, Rra.'

If you want to get people to talk, wrote Clovis Andersen, *tell them that they are right. They love that, and will tell you more and more. You can never nod your head too much!*

'It is kind of you to say that, Mma,' said the treasurer.

'This is a very comfortable room, Rra,' commented Mma Makutsi. 'I like leather sofas. They are easy to clean. Fabric covers – oh, my goodness – especially if you have children. I always say: do not buy a fabric-covered sofa until your children are at least sixteen. That is the advice I give, Rra.'

'This time it is you who is right,' said the treasurer, with a grin.

'And I always say this, Rra,' Mma Makutsi continued. 'It doesn't matter that they are so expensive. Buying an expensive sofa is a good investment – even if you have to borrow the money to do so.' She paused. 'Not that I think you had to do that, Rra. Even if you are only a bookkeeper at the hospital – and not even the head bookkeeper. Even if you are only that, it is worth getting hold of the money to buy good, well-made things for your house rather than cheap items that will not last long.'

Mma Ramotswe felt that this remark was rather heavy-handed,

and tried to catch Mma Makutsi's eye. She did not succeed, but Mma Makutsi's direct approach was to be vindicated, as the treasurer, made nervous by these allusions, soon made contradictory and incriminating comments that led to his dismissal. The church did not press for prosecution, as it was keen to avoid scandal, but the treasurer was obliged to sell his ill-gotten goods and make reparation for his misdeeds.

Now, as she walked up the short path to the front door of Pardon Morapedi's *middle-income* house, she looked about her for anything that might indicate inappropriate wealth. But then she stopped herself: this was not about that; Pardon was not suspected of anything – at least by her. She was hoping to get information from him about his brother, H. J., whose guilt was what she was expecting to establish.

Pardon had agreed to meet Mma Makutsi that same afternoon, after her visit to Diphimotswe, who had telephoned to make the appointment. 'My door is always open,' he said. 'It is never shut – except at night-time, of course.'

'That is what he is like,' said Diphimotswe when she reported this conversation to Mma Makutsi. 'He is a man who observes the traditional courtesies – unlike many people these days.'

'That is good,' said Mma Makutsi. 'There are too many people who have no time for anything these days.'

And when Pardon greeted her at the door, he followed the prescribed form, enquiring after Mma Makutsi's health and general welfare, and listening to her reply appreciatively, as if being vouchsafed information of some significance.

The formalities over, Mma Makutsi was admitted to a comfortably furnished living room where she was invited to sit down. A tea tray had been placed on a table in the centre of the room, and on this there was a plate of fat cakes, an array of sandwiches and some sliced beef. Pardon poured the tea and passed her the plate of small fat cakes. She selected one of these and put it on the edge of her saucer.

'I cannot resist fat cakes,' said Pardon, as he helped himself. 'These are made by the lady who works in our kitchen. She would win prizes if there were any prizes for fat cakes. She would win every time.'

Mma Makutsi took a bite of her fat cake, and readily agreed with her host. 'Just right,' she said. She looked about her. There was nothing exceptional about the furnishings in the room, and it was to the pictures on the wall that her eye drifted. These seemed for the most part to be of religious gatherings, and Pardon featured prominently in all of them.

'I see that you are looking at our pictures, Mma.'

Mma Makutsi looked away guiltily. 'I'm sorry, Rra. You must think I am very nosy.'

Pardon smiled. 'But you must be nosy, Mma. That is your job, is it not? Shouldn't anybody who comes from the No. 1 Ladies Detective Agency be nosy?'

'I suppose that is right, Rra,' said Mma Makutsi. 'But we should also be discreet.'

Pardon pointed at one of the larger pictures – a framed photograph of himself standing beside a river. A number of people, mostly dressed in white, were beside him, while a pastor, arms held out in blessing, stood slightly apart.

'That was taken last year,' Pardon announced. 'I went up to Maun for a ceremony. We took sinners up from Gaborone, to join sinners up there in the Delta. There was a big baptism ceremony conducted by a visiting reverend from Ghanzi. It was a ceremony for the whole country – paid for by me.' He paused, looking at her as if he was keen to establish that she had heard what he said.

'I paid for everything, Mma. Buses for the sinners – meals while they were there – everything, Mma.' He allowed himself a small smile. 'Sinners can have good appetites, Mma.'

Mma Makutsi was fulsome in her praise. 'That was a very good thing to do, Rra.'

He accepted this as his due. 'Thank you, Mma. I am always looking for good things to do.'

She gave him an appraising glance. She did not particularly like people who wore their good deeds on their sleeves, and he was clearly one of those.

'I hope that you find them, Rra,' she muttered.

He seemed pleased. 'Oh, I find them all right, Mma. I find good things to do every day, or almost every day.'

She decided to change the subject. Pardon, she suspected, would be prepared to talk about himself at some length, and there was not much that she needed to know about him. She wanted to discover his views on H. J.

'Your younger brother,' she began, 'is he always engaged in good works – as you are?'

Pardon hesitated.

'You can speak to me in confidence,' Mma Makutsi assured him. 'I am interested only in protecting the hotel – and I believe that that is what you want too.'

He responded quickly, and with enthusiasm. 'Oh, I am always thinking of the hotel, Mma Makutsi. I think of it every day. And all I want is for it to be an even bigger success than it has been when it was run by my dear Uncle Goodman Tsholofelo.'

'I am sure that he knows that,' said Mma Makutsi.

'He does. I have always been the one he has talked to about the hotel. He has always known that I will be a big defender of his beloved hotel. He has known that all along, Mma.'

Mma Makutsi absorbed this. Then she said, 'A defender against what, Rra?'

For a brief moment Pardon looked uncomfortable. 'Against bad decisions, Mma – against the bad decisions of my brother.' He paused. 'Look, he cannot help being a sinner. I have offered him many opportunities to walk in the ways of righteousness, and he has always turned his face away from me. He does not want to be a good man, Mma. He does not want to secure his business-class ticket to heaven. Oh, now he wants to go dancing with those women he meets in bars – in bars, Mma. Those places are full to the ceiling with sinners. The sinners go there to drink and then dance – and do sinful things after they have finished dancing. I have seen it, Mma. I have seen it with my own eyes.'

Mma Makutsi made a disapproving sound.

'Yet he is my brother,' Pardon went on. 'You cannot say of your own brother: *I will have nothing to do with this man because he is sinful.* You cannot do that. You must carry on saying, *This man is my brother in spite of all his failings.* Your brother is your brother from the day he is born until the day he becomes late and goes to heaven – or in this case, I am sorry to say, Mma, to the other place.'

Mma Makutsi inclined her head in sympathy. It must not be easy imagining that your own flesh and blood was heading for eternal damnation – a stiff fine, perhaps, or two weeks in prison, but not eternal damnation . . .

Pardon sighed – a loud, somewhat deliberate sigh, but Mma Makutsi felt that he had good reason to express his frustration. She had once tried, without success, to get a delinquent cousin up in Bobonong to change his ways, and she remembered giving vent to just such a sigh.

'And now,' Pardon went on, 'now he is carrying on with that

Sephotho woman.' He shuddered. 'Violet Sephotho – perhaps you know her?'

Mma Makutsi did not reply immediately. She wanted him to anticipate her response, so that when she made it, he would understand just how profound and well-grounded was her antipathy towards Violet.

'Do I know her, Rra?' she said at last. 'Do I know Violet Sephotho? Oh, Rra, I have known that woman ever since I came to Gaborone – ever since that first day at the Botswana Secretarial College. I saw her then, and I knew straight away what sort of person she was. Remember, Rra, that I had come down from Bobonong and I hadn't seen many people like Violet before—'

Pardon interrupted her. 'Oh, I can imagine that, Mma. I can imagine that you were hard-working and polite, because that is what Bobonong people are like, in my experience. And you came here to this city and you saw all these people who were the opposite of what you were – people like Violet Sephotho.'

The complimentary reference to the good qualities of Bobonong people was just the sort of thing that Mma Makutsi liked to hear, and she nodded her head in agreement and gratitude.

'I found it hard to believe that anybody could sit there and paint her nails while the principal was talking,' Mma Makutsi said. 'The principal himself! Can you believe it, Rra?'

'Oh, I can believe anything when it comes to sinners,' said Pardon. 'Sinners are always painting their nails.'

Mma Makutsi decided to press Pardon for his explanation of what was going on. 'Do you think that Violet Sephotho is playing a role in what is happening at the Great Hippopotamus Hotel?' she asked.

Pardon leaned forward in his chair. He glanced over his shoulder, as if to confirm that nobody could hear them, although they were clearly alone in the room.

'Do I have a theory? Is that what you are asking me, Mma Makutsi?'

'In a word, yes, Rra. Can you think of what Violet might be doing?'

Pardon lowered his voice, so that Mma Makutsi had to struggle to hear it.

'I do not think we can be overheard,' she said.

He looked over his shoulder. 'You can never be too careful, Mma.'

'Well?' she encouraged.

The theory was quickly and crisply set out. 'All right,' said Pardon. 'So, there are three of us who own the hotel now – fifty-fifty.'

Mma Makutsi held up a hand. 'Excuse me, Rra, don't you mean in three shares? It would be fifty-fifty if there were only two equal owners.'

Pardon made a *silly me* gesture. 'You are right, Mma. I was not thinking. So there are three owners who are equal – one third of the shares each. That is what Uncle Goodman Tsholofelo wanted because he has always been very fair. I know that he would like to have given me the controlling share, but he did not. One day he said to me, 'Pardon, you are the best of the bunch, but I must be fair to the weaker brethren, so to speak.' By that, he meant not only H. J. but also Diphimotswe. She is a good woman, but not very bright, I'm afraid. She can sell ladies' clothes, of course, but she could never do anything more than that. She could never be a teacher or a chemist or anything. Ladies' dresses are just right for her, I think.'

Mma Makutsi felt a strong urge to voice an objection to this astonishing level of condescension, yet she said nothing. She could say something to Pardon about his out-of-date attitudes later on, but for the moment she wanted to encourage him to share with her his theory.

Pardon cleared his throat. 'You know what I think, Mma?' he began. 'I shall tell you. The person behind all these problems is Violet Sephotho. H. J. is one of the lost sheep, but she is the one who has put him up to all this. She wants him to get full control of the hotel. She wants to get us out – that is, Diphimotswe and me. She thinks she can do this by wrecking it.'

Mma Makutsi was quite still. She hardly dared believe it, but Pardon was coming up with exactly the same explanation that she herself had worked out. It was uncanny.

Pardon noticed the effect that his theory was having on Mma Makutsi. 'Are you all right, Mma?' he asked. 'You look surprised.'

'I am,' said Mma Makutsi. 'I am surprised because you seem to have exactly the same idea as I have.'

Pardon took this in his stride. 'That is probably because we both know Violet. We understand the way she thinks.' He shook his head, as if in disbelief. 'Her plan is that we both will be prepared to take a very low price just to get rid of the shares. If the hotel is not worth much, then he gets it without having to pay very much. Then it is all his.'

Mma Makutsi thought about this. She was pleased that Pardon seemed to endorse her own theory – having reached his conclusion independently – but now it occurred to her that there was an obvious flaw to this shared theory. Pardon and Diphimotswe might simply decline to sell – and would be particularly likely to do this if they realised what H. J. and Violet were up to. She raised this with Pardon, who nodded as she spoke. He had anticipated this objection, but had a way round it.

'He can force a sale,' he said. 'There is a provision in the company's articles of association that if any of the owners offers a sum that is twice the value of the shares at the time of such an offer, then the owner must sell. That was Uncle Goodman Tsholofelo's idea. I suppose he wanted to make it possible for one of us who is very keen on the hotel to get the chance to run it without the others – something like that.'

Mma Makutsi thought about this. Perhaps Goodman Tsholofelo was not as even-handed as he appeared to be; perhaps he really did have a favourite – probably Pardon – and was paving the way for him to get sole control. He might not have realised, though, that the right he had created might be used by H. J. – and in an underhand way.

'It is a very strange provision,' Pardon continued, 'but it is there. And, of course, if the value of the shares is very low – because the hotel has lost its clientele – then twice very little is still very little.'

'He is being very cunning,' said Mma Makutsi.

'He is like that,' agreed Pardon. 'Cunning – and bad. Or rather *she* is being cunning. I have never doubted that she is the one behind this, Mma – that woman Violet Sephotho. There are her fingerprints all over this, Mma – all over it.'

Mma Makutsi imagined Violet with her long, painted nails leaving her fingerprints on all that she touched. She shuddered. Merely thinking about Violet made the back of her neck feel warm, which annoyed her, as Violet's ability to interfere in this way with her body temperature represented a victory of a sort for the other woman, and that was a matter of great regret. But life could be like that, she told herself: it was often the case that the worst people came out on top. That happened time and time again – so frequently, in fact, that one might wonder if there was much point in trying to battle against such outcomes. That doubt had to be dispelled, and Mma Makutsi now made a mental resolution to that effect. She would foil Violet in her diabolical schemes; she would defeat her in her machinations and send her packing. She would do that and tie this matter up neatly before Mma Ramotswe came back to work. Then she would be able to say, 'That Great Hippopotamus Hotel business, Mma Ramotswe – all sorted out now.' And Mma Ramotswe would look at her with admiration and say, 'I don't know where we would be without you, Grace Makutsi' – or words to that effect: it does not matter too much how praise is expressed, as long as it is unambiguous. That, as Mma Ramotswe would have no hesitation in saying, is well known.

Pardon asked her what she proposed to do about H. J. and Violet Sephotho. 'It is very important to stop all these incidents at the hotel,' he said. 'But you will have to find out how they are doing it, I imagine. Then you can swoop.'

Mma Makutsi pictured herself poised and ready to swoop. She liked the idea of *swooping*. She would be wearing a cape of some sort and she would descend in just the manner in which a hawk falls upon its prey. Yes, she would swoop, but not just yet. If you were going to swoop, you had to have everything ready – and then you could act, firmly and decisively, unmasking wrongdoers and dealing with them as easily as one brushed aside a fly that had been pestering you for too long.

Mma Makutsi exchanged a few final observations with Pardon, and then said that she had to go.

'God bless you,' said Pardon as he showed her to the door. 'May the Light illuminate your enquiries.'

Mma Makutsi thanked him. 'And may the Light shine upon you too,' she said, not quite sure whether it was the right thing to say. It sounded polite anyway, and that was the important thing.

'Oh, it already does,' said Pardon.

Chapter Fourteen

Never Declare Victory Prematurely

Mma Ramotswe announced the next day that she would be returning to the office shortly.

'I shall be coming back the day after tomorrow,' she said to Mma Makutsi. 'I am feeling much better now.'

Mma Makutsi expressed pleasure at the news that she was feeling better, but urged her not to return to work too quickly. 'That is what high-achieving people like you do, Mma – you never take enough time off when you are ill. It is always work, work, work.'

Mma Ramotswe laughed down the line. 'High-achieving people, Mma? That is very kind of you, but I am not such a person. I am an ordinary lady – that is what I am.'

Mma Makutsi did not want to argue. She thought that both of them – Mma Ramotswe and she herself – were high achievers: together they had created a successful – well, slightly successful – business, and over the years they had both helped numerous people with the problems in their lives. In her view, that was enough of an achievement to merit such a description. The problem with Mma Ramotswe, she thought, was that she was too modest. Modesty was a good quality, but you could be too modest, and that was as bad, in its way, as being too boastful. A person who was too modest was a bit like a mouse, and nobody paid much attention to mice. If you did well in this life – so well as to get, for purposes of argument, ninety-seven per cent in your final examinations – it was wrong not to mention the fact. Mentioning it helped other people – it gave them a goal to which they might aspire. That was why she was ready to mention her own ninety-seven per cent from time to time: it motivated people, it urged them on to achieve their personal goals. Poor Mma Ramotswe, she said to herself; she had left school early, without her Cambridge certificate; she never had the chance to get ninety-seven per cent in anything. What a pity that was. But would she have got such a mark if she had had that chance? Mma Makutsi felt herself inclined to say no, but then she realised that she was being too grudging. Mma Ramotswe was undoubtedly intelligent, and she had good judgement too. She could easily have got something like ninety-six per cent had she been given the chance. Yes, ninety-six per cent would have been about right.

After she had finished their telephone conversation, Mma Makutsi sat and thought. She did her best thinking when seated, and now, sitting at the table in her kitchen, she considered the next step in her investigation into the happenings at the Great Hippopotamus Hotel. It was one thing to know who was behind the occurrences – Violet Sephotho, beyond a shadow of a doubt – but it was quite another to know what to do about it. It was tantalising to think that she had worked out exactly what

Violet's plans were and yet to realise that so far she had nothing but surmise to support her conclusion. She needed evidence, hard evidence, and there was nothing of that sort that she would be able to put before Mma Ramotswe once she returned to the office. She could just imagine what Mma Ramotswe would say: 'Yes, Mma Makutsi, that is very interesting, but we need hard facts to go on, and at the moment . . . Well, I am very sorry to say, I do not see any hard facts here.' And in saying that, in dowsing her colleague's theory in cold water, Mma Ramotswe would be doing exactly the right thing, as even Mma Makutsi would have to admit.

Thinking through the issue, Mma Makutsi hoped that a solution would come to her in the same way as it had done when she had first developed her theory. She closed her eyes, hoping that this might help, but it did not: all she could think about, it seemed, was what she would be cooking for dinner that night. And when, with an effort of will, she put that out of her mind, the thought that replaced it was of the need to buy Phuti a new toothbrush, as he had complained that morning that his existing one was now showing its age.

And it was at this point that the telephone rang, which, in the circumstances, was something of a relief. It was Mma Potokwani, who asked Mma Makutsi if she could possibly come to the Orphan Farm to hear something that she thought she should hear in person.

'It is something that is hard to talk about on the phone,' she said. 'It would be better, Mma, if you could come.'

Mma Makutsi required no persuasion. She would be there, she said, in half an hour, possibly less. Mma Potokwani was pleased, and hoped that it would not be an inconvenience. 'The diary can be cleared,' said Mma Makutsi, picturing what she knew was an entirely empty page. It was an expression that she liked using from time to time: *the diary can be cleared* made people feel that their concerns counted for something, and to give that impression was a matter of courtesy rather than mendacity.

'It's one of the housemothers,' said Mma Potokwani.

Sitting in the matron's office, a cup of tea and a generous slice of fruit cake on the table beside her, Mma Makutsi waited for Mma Potokwani to reveal more.

'Mma Oteng,' continued Mma Potokwani. 'She is a very good housemother – one of our best – although she has not been here all that long.'

Mma Makutsi had heard of her from Mma Ramotswe, when she had told her of her last trip to the Orphan Farm. 'I have heard the name of this lady,' she said. 'Mma Ramotswe has met her, I believe.'

'Yes,' said Mma Potokwani. 'And that is why I called Mma Ramotswe earlier on and spoke to her. She said that she is not back at work yet because of her stomach. She said you were dealing with that hotel carry-on.'

'I am in charge of the enquiry,' Mma Makutsi said. 'I shall be very interested to hear any information anybody might have.'

Mma Potokwani nodded. 'Well, our Mma Oteng has some important information for you, Mma. I have asked her to come over here and speak to you. She will be here shortly, I think.'

Mma Makutsi took a sip of her tea. This was very promising, and timely, too, in view of the imminent return of Mma Ramotswe. She had a report to write and at present she had little more than the few scraps of information she had received from Diphimotswe and Pardon. That could be contained in a paragraph or two, which would make for a rather light report. Now here was the prospect of something meatier, and she felt relieved. She sensed now the prospect of resolving this rather unusual case, although she knew it was important that she should not become complacent. There were many obvious and important pieces of information that were missed where investigators thought they had solved a case when they had not, in fact, done so. *Never declare victory prematurely*, Clovis Andersen counselled – advice that, as was always the case with the great man from Muncie, Indiana, was both pertinent and wise.

Mma Oteng arrived a few minutes later, just as Mma Makutsi finished the final crumbs of her fruit cake. Mma Potokwani invited her in and introduced her to their visitor.

'This is Mma Ramotswe's assistant,' she said.

It was not intended, but the misdescription made Mma Makutsi act as if she had been touched with an electric prong. 'Colleague,' she hissed.

Mma Potokwani looked puzzled. 'That is what I said, Mma.'

'No, you did not,' said Mma Makutsi. 'You said *assistant*, Mma Potokwani, and I am not Mma Ramotswe's assistant. I am joint managing director. *Joint*.'

Mma Potokwani did her best to placate her. 'I am very sorry, Mma. I did not mean to demote you. I should have said that you worked for her. I should not have said that you were a junior member of staff.'

This required correction, if not retraction. 'But I do not work *for* her,' Mma Makutsi insisted. 'I work *with* her. There is a big difference.'

'Of course, of course,' Mma Potokwani said quickly. 'I am always getting these things wrong. I will try harder in the future. It is a small thing, though.'

That was a mistake. 'It is not a small thing,' protested Mma

Makutsi. 'Something that looks like a small thing can be a big thing, you know. And then, before you know where you are, there is a major problem.'

Once again, Mma Potokwani sought to placate her. 'The important thing is that you are here, Mma, and you are prepared to listen to what Mma Oteng has to say.'

She turned to Mma Oteng and invited her to tell Mma Makutsi her story. The housemother hesitated, her natural reticence temporarily getting the better of her desire to share what she had recently learned.

'Mma Makutsi is very keen to hear about this,' Mma Potokwani urged.

Mma Oteng took a deep breath. 'I look after a young boy,' she began. 'He is a good boy, although he has trouble with one leg and is very shy about speaking. He will speak to me, though.'

'He is happy here,' said Mma Potokwani. 'One day he will speak. I have seen that happen before.'

Mma Oteng continued with her tale. 'He is always looking at what is happening about him. People think that he does not know anything, but he does. He knows all about birds and the small creatures that you see scurrying around under the bushes. There are always things down there, Mma Makutsi – if you look for them. He knows how to find them.

'Now this boy, whose name is Khumo . . . '

'I have met him,' said Mma Makutsi.

'Well, Khumo goes at weekends to my sister, who works at a hotel that way, Mma.' She pointed in the direction of Lobatse, although Mma Makutsi knew, even before she did so, that this would be the Great Hippopotamus Hotel. 'He goes down there sometimes on Friday. I put him on a minibus that goes that way and the driver drops him off. He walks to the hotel, where my sister gives him a meal. He is starting to talk to her now – a few words, and maybe he will say more in the future.'

'He will definitely do that,' said Mma Potokwani.

Mma Oteng nodded. 'Last night Khumo suddenly told me something that made me worried. He said very little to begin with, but I had to prise it out of him, and slowly I learned more. He said that he had been asked to find a snake for somebody at the hotel. He also said that he had found them two large scorpions before. He gave them to them in a box, and he said they were very pleased. Now they want a snake – a small puff adder. They know that he can find these snakes and can also put them in a box for them.'

Mma Makutsi and Mma Potokwani exchanged glances. The matron held up a hand. 'When Mma Oteng told me about this, Mma Makutsi,' she said, 'I remembered what we heard when we went down to the hotel – you, me and Mma Ramotswe. I remembered how the manager down there – Babusi – told us about scorpion problems. Do you remember that?'

Mma Makutsi inclined her head gravely. 'I remember that well, Mma Potokwani.' Now she turned to Mma Oteng. This was her chance to discover who, within the hotel, was acting on behalf of Violet Sephotho. 'Who was this person who got the scorpions from Khumo?' she asked.

Both Mma Potokwani and Mma Makutsi waited, both trying not to push Mma Oteng too obviously. They were both prepared for a disappointing answer. But the answer they received was as clear as they could possibly have wanted.

'The manager,' she said. 'They call him Babusi. It was that man.'

Mma Makutsi gasped. 'But he is the one who asked Mma Ramotswe to look into this. Khumo must have confused him with someone else. It must have been H. J. Morapedi.'

'He said that it was a man who wore glasses with clear frames,' said Mma Oteng. 'You know the sort. I asked my sister who wears glasses down there, and she said that the manager is the only one.'

Mma Makutsi struggled to make sense of what she had heard. 'Did he say anything else?' she asked.

Mma Oteng nodded. 'He said that it was the same man who has asked him for a snake. But this time, Khumo said, there was another man with him. It was the brother who is one of the owners.'

Mma Makutsi felt that she had to interrupt. 'Mr H. J. Morapedi.'

'Yes,' said Mma Oteng. 'When I asked my sister about it, she said that that man is called Morapedi.'

It was now clear to Mma Makutsi what had happened. It was surprising, but it was blindingly clear. Mr H. J. Morapedi, urged on, she believed by Violet Sephotho, was acting together with Babusi, who would, presumably, be rewarded by a promotion or pay-off once H. J. was in charge of the enterprise. That was straightforward enough. But now came the twist that made the plot so brilliant. In order to cover his tracks, one of the main conspirators had been detailed to invite external investigation. That was where Mma Ramotswe came in. The fact that she had been asked to investigate by Babusi himself would mean that nobody would suspect him. It had all been thought out very carefully.

Mma Makutsi brought the meeting to an end. She thanked Mma Potokwani and Mma Oteng, and asked them to say nothing about this to anybody else. Mma Oteng then asked whether Khumo should go to her sister at the hotel, as planned. His next visit was to be the following day – that Friday.

'He should go,' said Mma Makutsi. 'But he should not try to find a snake for them. He should show them in some way – he can use signs, I assume – that although he found a puff adder, it had escaped. Could he do that?'

He could, said Mma Oteng. He was an intelligent boy, she explained, as would become apparent to more people once he became more confident about speaking. 'He will have a lot to say then,' she said, a note of pride creeping into her voice. 'We shall all see that.'

They talked for a short time longer, but Mma Makutsi had difficulty in concentrating on what was said and she soon brought the meeting to an end. She was struggling to find a solution to this case. She believed that she had found out what was going on, but the decision as to what to do was far from simple. The crux of the matter was that the client – Babusi – was also, it seemed, the perpetrator. That was a highly unusual situation, and one that she had never thought she would encounter. In normal circumstances, when you uncovered the wrongdoer, you went to the client so that he or she could take appropriate action. But how could she go to Babusi and announce to him that the person he was looking for was, in fact, himself? This was a real conundrum – one which even Clovis Andersen would be hard put to resolve. For a moment she entertained the possibility of contacting the great authority himself and asking him what he would do, but she would never be able to do so in time to get an answer before Mma Ramotswe returned to work.

As she drove back into town, it occurred to her that one way of dealing with this situation was to go to H. J. Morapedi and tell him that his plot had been discovered. He would realise the futility of trying to proceed with it when the potential victims, his brother and cousin, were aware of what he was up to. She would then go on to confront Violet Sephotho and warn her that it would be futile for her to make any further attempts to secure control of the hotel, as not only would she and Mma Ramotswe have informed the other owners, but they would also have gone to tell Mr Goodman Tsholofelo about what had happened. He would put his weight behind Pardon and Diphimotswe, which would leave H. J. Morapedi isolated. It was probably also the case that H. J. would be loath for his uncle to hear of his treachery, as he presumably still admired him as head of the family. If H. J. thought that Violet had been responsible for Uncle Goodman's turning against him, then that would not help their relationship.

She made up her mind as she reached the turn-off to the old Gaborone Club. She would confront Mr H. J. Morapedi the following morning and ... She stopped herself as she realised that tomorrow morning was Friday and that young Khumo would be visiting his aunt – staying with her in the staff quarters behind the Great Hippopotamus Hotel. Babusi and H. J. would be expecting something from him – a snake, no less, to create a further shocking incident. How could they? How could they put guests at risk by introducing a creature like that into one of the hotel rooms, presumably to be discovered with great fanfare and fuss, and reported in guests' reviews. Word got round quickly when bad things happened in hotels – reputations were rapidly lost.

She seethed in her outrage. Violet had behaved reprehensibly in the past, but this was sheer wickedness – there was no other word for it. She would confront both conspirators there, catching them virtually red-handed. That would be a particular pleasure, she thought, as it was always good to witness the look of surprise, and often regret, that came upon a wrongdoer unmasked and made to face justice. The only pity was that Violet Sephotho would not be there, and that her downfall would have to wait a while. But it would come – oh yes, it would come, thought Mma Makutsi, and great would be the weeping and gnashing of teeth on Violet's part as her perfidy was laid bare. And none too soon: it was some years since Violet had first burst onto the scene with her ploys and poses – in a better-ordered world she would have been dealt with more swiftly, but better late than never, thought Mma Makutsi. Her thwarting now would be for all those occasions on which she had got away with it; this would be the payback for all those times she had mocked Mma Makutsi for being diligent in an assignment at the Botswana Secretarial College; this would be revenge for all those women whose husbands Violet had flirted with and tried to lure away; this would be what comes to you when you were so shameless in all your doings. This would be a repayment for years of selfishness, ostentation and sheer obnoxiousness. This would show, to anyone who cared to notice, what happens when you behave like Violet Sephotho.

Chapter Fifteen

She Saw Botswana

That Saturday, Mma Makutsi said goodbye to Phuti, kissed her son, Itumelang, and set off through the morning traffic for the Lobatse Road and the Great Hippopotamus Hotel. She drove slowly, not just out of caution, but because she could not help but feel some trepidation when she thought about what lay ahead of her. Mma Makutsi was no coward, afraid of speaking her mind to power; nor was she slow to stand up for what was right. But even with this resolution, she feared that the script for her confrontation with Mr H. J. Morapedi was a thin and shaky one. He was a man with a position in life – he was no tongue-tied minor figure, ready to wilt when faced with an unexpected broadside. What if he simply chose to refute her accusation, or even simply laughed at her? She had satisfied herself of the strength of her case, but it was not much more than an assumption, backed up by the second-hand testimony of a young boy. Faced with a challenge from Mr H. J. Morapedi, a boy like that could hardly be expected to do anything but cower in fright.

Yet she had to do it. Not only was it her duty to her client, she told herself, and that meant ... She stopped, reminding herself that she had no client now. What had started as a commissioned investigation was now one of those *pro bono* affairs of the sort undertaken by Mma Ramotswe that she herself sometimes criticised on the grounds that they did nothing to bolster the finances of the agency. Yet, if she had been unsympathetic to such cases in the past, she now harboured no reservations about the importance of seeing this through. This was for every victim of Violet Sephotho's sharp tongue and devious ways; more than that, this was for Botswana.

Renewed resolve made her pick up speed, with the result that by the time she reached the turn-off to the Great Hippopotamus Hotel she almost shot past it. She slowed down just in time, though, and was soon driving gingerly over the unpaved track that led to the hotel and its oasis of trees. She noticed that there were several cars in the parking area, one of which, she assumed, would belong to Mr H. J. Morapedi. She cast her eye over them, trying to work out which looked as if it might be driven by a prominent businessman and joint owner of a boutique hotel. She failed. That was something that Mr J. L. B. Matekoni could do instinctively; he often spoke of the almost inevitable match between driver and make of car, but she was at a loss as to how he did it. A purple car nudged under the shade of a handy thorn tree, though, stood out for its suspiciousness. That was just the sort of car that would appeal to Violet Sephotho ... She smiled. It was a ridiculous thought – car profiling was a dubious science, as well as being a distraction. Violet was not here, and there were plenty of people who might drive such a car in spotless innocence.

She sat down at one of the tables on the veranda. Only two of the tables were occupied, and those already there had been served with tea or long, icy drinks in tall glasses. When a waitress appeared, Mma Makutsi ordered a pot of tea.

She addressed the waitress before she went off to fetch her order. 'I hope you are well, Mma,' she said.

The waitress answered the enquiry with a warm smile. 'I am very well, Mma. And I hope you are well too.'

Such exchanges could go on for some time, and could encompass enquiries as to the health of parents and dependents. So Mma Makutsi cut it short with a direct question. 'Is Mr Morapedi here, Mma?'

The waitress nodded. 'He is here, Mma. He was in the kitchen. They are putting in a new fire-alarm system. Now I think he is somewhere outside. He is always moving around – this place, that place. You know what some men are like.'

Mma Makutsi pretended indifference. 'Do you know him well, Mma? If you have worked for him for some time, then you must know what he is like.'

The waitress hesitated. 'I have been here for only three months. I have not seen much of him. There are three owners, you see.'

'I know that,' said Mma Makutsi.

'There is him, and then there is his brother. And there is a lady, too, who is a cousin.'

'Diphimotswe,' said Mma Makutsi, hoping to assure this waitress by her knowledge that she was an insider with whom opinions might safely be shared.

'Yes, that is the lady,' said the waitress. 'The owners are here from time to time, but not all that much. The day-to-day management is done for them by a manager.' She paused. 'He is friendly with Mr Morapedi.'

Of course he is, thought Mma Makutsi. They were not only friends, they were partners in crime, and partners in crime were often very close to one another.

'And is there a lady on the staff here,' Mma Makutsi asked, 'who sometimes looks after a boy for her sister – a very quiet boy?'

The waitress thought for a moment. Then she said, 'Yes, there is such a lady, Mma. The boy has a limp and is very quiet. I have never heard him talk.'

'Is she here now?' asked Mma Makutsi.

The waitress nodded. 'It is her day off. She will be sitting with that boy round in the quarters. She tells him stories and she is teaching him how to weave a basket. Boys do not normally learn that, but times are changing, Mma. All over the world, I think, boys are learning to do useful things again.'

'That is a very good thing,' said Mma Makutsi. 'Our sisters are learning to fly planes now. Air Botswana is training them. It is very good progress.'

She stopped. The waitress was looking over the lawn towards the tennis court. She could see two men walking around the periphery of the court, deep in conversation. She turned to Mma Makutsi. 'You see those two over there?' she began. 'That is the manager, and the man with him is Mr Morapedi.'

Mma Makutsi strained her eyes, and when it became clear to her that they were not deceiving her, she whispered to the waitress, 'That is a different Morapedi. That is his brother.'

The waitress frowned. 'No, that is the one, he is the one who comes here quite often. He is a big friend of Babusi. There is another one who hardly ever turns up. He is called Mr H. J. Morapedi.' She paused. 'That one – H. J. Morapedi, they call him – is very kind to us when he comes round here. He is a gentleman, you see. And he has a very nice friend. She has been good to us, here. She made them give us a bonus – that was her doing.'

Mma Makutsi struggled to get the words out. She almost failed, so great was the choking reflex. But eventually she managed. 'And this lady is called Violet, Mma?'

The waitress shook her head. 'No, she is called Miriam. She is from a village up in the north – near Francistown.'

'So where is Violet?' asked Mma Makutsi, addressing the question, it seemed, to herself.

'I do not know this Violet,' said the waitress. 'There is no Violet.'

Mma Makutsi caught her breath. It was still possible that there was an innocent explanation here: Babusi, as manager, obviously had to speak to all three owners about the affairs of the hotel. Perhaps that was all that was happening.

And then it occurred to her. What if Mr H. J. Morapedi was deceiving Violet Sephotho, and seeing this Miriam while he was still conducting his affair with her – that is, with Violet? Oh, that would teach her! Jezebel cheated on. Oh, what justice!

Mma Makutsi's head was reeling. How could she have been so wrong?

She asked the waitress a final question: 'Where are the staff quarters, Mma?'

'At the back,' said the waitress. 'That is where they always put us, Mma. At the back, where nobody can see us. That is where you go if you are ordinary people these days, Mma. At the back.'

'Do not give up, my sister,' said Mma Makutsi. 'Your life may get better.' She paused. 'I hope it does.' And then she said, 'I must cancel my order for tea, Mma. I have to go and speak to that lady with the boy who does not speak very much.'

The waitress smiled. 'I am glad to have talked to you, Mma. Thank you. People sometimes don't talk to us because they think we are nothing people – just waiting staff, there to help them all the time. *Do this, do that.* You know how it is, Mma. But we are not.'

'No,' said Mma Makutsi. 'You are not, Mma. Definitely not.'

She made her way round to the back of the Great Hippopotamus Hotel. There, as the waitress had told her, several simple buildings housed the hotel staff. In front of one of these, a large umbrella, pensioned off from swimming-pool usage, and fraying at the edges, had been erected to shelter several rickety chairs. On one of these chairs, Mma Makutsi saw a middle-aged woman, dressed in a blue dress, with, at her feet, the figure of a young boy. Another of the chairs was occupied by a woman in a chambermaid's unform, appearing, at that distance, to be either asleep or close to it.

She approached the woman sitting with the boy. She greeted her formally before continuing, 'You are Mma Oteng's sister, Mma?'

The woman shaded her face with a raised hand. 'I am that woman, Mma. I am also called Oteng. I have no husband.' She sighed, and made a gesture of helplessness. Mma Makutsi wanted to say something to her, to tell her that it was not her fault, but she did not. Instead, she asked, 'Did she tell you about . . . '

Mma Oteng interrupted her. 'I think I know who you are, Mma. She told me.'

'And she told you about what we think is happening here?'

Mma Oteng shook her head with disgust. 'It is very bad, Mma. And they tried to use this poor boy.'

'There is no excuse for that, Mma,' said Mma Makutsi. 'But tell me one thing, Mma: does the boy remember who asked him to get them the snake?'

Mma Oteng was sure that he did. 'He is a very intelligent young boy,' she said.

'Could he point them out?' asked Mma Makutsi.

For a moment Mma Oteng looked doubtful. Then she said, 'I don't see why not.'

They stood by the side of the hotel, shaded by the leafy branches of an exuberant creeper that clung to the wall. There was a good view of the tennis court, where the two men she had seen a few moments ago were still engaged in conversation.

Mma Oteng pointed towards the court. 'Khumo, are those the two men?' she asked. 'Are those uncles the ones who asked you to find them a scorpion?'

The boy stared. Mma Makutsi found herself looking at his legs. There was no doubt: he was wearing shorts and the twisted shape of his left leg was painfully obvious. Now he made a noise – something between a sigh and a word, thought Mma Makutsi. She turned to Mma Oteng.

'What was that, Mma?' she asked.

Mma Oteng bent down to repeat the question. Now she added, 'You can show us by nodding, Khumo. If it is those men, you can do that.'

The boy hesitated. He was staring at Mma Makutsi – and suddenly he smiled at her. He found his tongue. 'You are that nice lady,' he said.

Mma Makutsi returned the compliment. 'And you are the nice boy I met at Mma Potokwani's place. I remember you.'

'You had shoes that talked.'

Mma Makutsi made a gesture to silence him. 'No, Khumo, I don't think so.'

Mma Oteng looked surprised. 'Who has shoes that talk?'

'This lady,' said Khumo.

Mma Makutsi laughed. 'The things that children say, Mma.'

Khumo gave her a reproachful look, and she relented. 'Well, maybe it sounds as if they're talking, but they aren't really. Sometimes we get mixed up about where sounds are coming from. That happens, you see.'

'Very odd,' said Mma Oteng.

'Yes,' said Mma Makutsi, and then quickly continued, 'Are you sure that is the other man with Babusi, Khumo?'

The boy nodded. 'His name is Pardon,' he said. 'I have heard them calling him that.'

Turning to Mma Oteng, Mma Makutsi said, 'That is the same man, isn't it? Pardon Morapedi?'

'Of course, it is,' answered Mma Oteng. 'He is a very big church man.'

Mma Makutsi struggled. What was the term: *hypocrisy*? And did this mean that Violet Sephotho had nothing to do with what had been happening at the Great Hippopotamus Hotel?

She heard a small voice – and it came from down at ground level. *Violet had nothing to with any of this, Boss. You are looking at the two men who did, Mma. They are the ones, Mma. Those two.*

'How do you know?' Mma Makutsi muttered.

Khumo watched. He said nothing, but his eyes were firmly fixed on Mma Makutsi's feet.

But there was no answer from the shoes. And, from Mma Oteng, there came only, 'How do I know what, Mma?'

'Nothing,' said Mma Makutsi. 'I was just thinking.'

The shoes had a further observation to make. *You see, Boss. Don't jump to conclusions. Just don't.*

'Did you hear something?' Mma Makutsi asked Mma Oteng.

'Nothing,' she replied. 'But then I'm rather deaf these days.'

Mma Makutsi looked down at her feet. It was all in the mind. That was the only thing to conclude. Shoes did not talk, but sometimes we talked to ourselves, and we were not above putting our own words into our shoes' mouths.

But none of this mattered. What counted was that she now had a result, even if it was not the precise one that she had anticipated.

Those two are rotten, said a small voice from down below. *We can tell these things, Boss. We see things from the ground up. We could have told you.*

'Well, you didn't,' muttered Mma Makutsi, adding 'And you just remember who's boss.'

It was a timely admonishment, and silence resulted.

She left shortly after that, resisting the temptation to sit on the veranda of the Great Hippopotamus Hotel with a pot of tea. There was not much more she could do there, she decided; what she needed to do was to present the case to Mma Ramotswe, which she could now do with confidence. She was relieved, not only at bringing the enquiry to a conclusion, but also being able to pass on to Mma Ramotswe the decision as to what to do with the information she had uncovered. She thought that the best approach might be to go to Mr Goodman Tsholofelo and lay the facts at his feet. It was a member of his family, after all, who had caused all this trouble, and if there was anybody who had the authority to put a stop to Pardon's nefarious plans, then surely it must be the senior uncle. But Mma Ramotswe might have different ideas, and she was quite happy to wait and see what she proposed.

She reached the edge of town and made the turn that would lead her off in the direction of Zebra Drive. As she approached Mma Ramotswe's house, she was pleased to see that both the tiny white van and Mr J. L. B. Matekoni's truck were parked in their usual places, which meant that both were at home. Now, stopping to open the gate so that she could drive into the yard, she saw that Mma Ramotswe had been sitting on the veranda and had risen to her feet to wave to her.

'You are my first visitor,' Mma Ramotswe exclaimed as she welcomed Mma Makutsi on the front steps. 'I have been sitting here for a few days now, Mma, hoping that I would have some company, but all my friends have been told that I must have complete rest. They have been good, and have stayed away. And Puso and Motholeli have been off at a school camp up in the Delta. So my only friends have been the birds – they have been singing to me from the trees.'

'Are you better, now, Mma?' asked Mma Makutsi.

Mma Ramotswe assured her that she had completely recovered, and that in her view it had all been a storm in a teacup. 'You know what doctors are like, Mma,' she said. 'They shake their heads and tell you to stop doing anything. Except when they tell you to take more exercise – then they want you to go everywhere at the double.'

Mma Makutsi laughed. 'And there is that marathon now,' she said. 'All those people running and running, trying to go faster than other people. What's the point of that, I ask myself. I do not have an answer.' She shook her head. 'You will not find me running in a marathon, Mma.'

'Nor will you find me doing that,' said Mma Ramotswe. 'Although I think you would be faster than I would be, Mma. I think you might come in . . . ' She almost said *ninety-seventh*, but stopped herself in time. There were some things you did not joke about.

'Come in what?' asked Mma Makutsi.

'Come in near the top,' said Mma Ramotswe quickly.

Mma Makutsi smiled modestly. 'Oh, I do not think so,' she said. 'But maybe halfway. Perhaps I would come in around the middle somewhere.' She paused and gave Mma Ramotswe a discreet glance. 'You are looking well, though, Mma.'

They talked for a few minutes about matters of no real importance, and then Mma Makutsi said, 'I have dealt with that unfortunate business down at the Great Hippopotamus Hotel. I think I have found out what is going on.'

Mma Ramotswe listened intently as Mma Makutsi gave her an account of her investigation. She left out no details, with the exception of any reference to the role played by her shoes: nothing was said of their ill-mannered – in Mma Makutsi's opinion – intervention. Not that she believed they talked, anyway; it was all in the mind, she told herself, and, when she found herself inadequately convinced of that, she repeated it. *All in the mind* ...

That's where you're wrong – again, Boss, said a small voice, almost a whisper. It had not been heard by Mma Ramotswe, although Mma Makutsi noticed a slight flicker of an eyelid on Mma Ramotswe's part as the unsolicited comment was ventured.

At the end of Mma Makutsi's account, she spread her hands in a gesture of completion. 'So there we are, Mma Ramotswe,' she said. 'I freely admit that I was wrong about Pardon Morapedi. He is a big hypocrite – possibly the biggest hypocrite in Botswana. He has been plotting with Babusi to ruin the business so that he can acquire it cheaply. He was prepared to do down his brother – his own brother, Mma – and his cousin, Diphimotswe.'

Mma Ramotswe looked thoughtful. 'Very possibly,' she said.

'Very possibly? No, Mma – very definitely.'

Mma Ramotswe smiled. 'Perhaps I should say – it is most likely. In fact, I think we can act on the assumption that you have got to the heart of the matter, Mma, and that we can report to . . . ' She stopped.

'To Goodman Tsholofelo?'

Mma Ramotswe considered this. 'He is an old man, now,' she said. 'Would it be kind to burden him with all this bad behaviour on the part of one of his nephews?' She answered her own question: 'I don't think that would be helpful, Mma.'

Mma Makutsi waited for her to expand on this.

'You see,' Mma Ramotswe continued, 'sometimes it is best to let people believe what they want to believe about members of their family. They may be quite wrong about them, but they may be more comfortable thinking about them positively. We do not always want to know the truth about our family.' She paused, and then added, 'Or ourselves.' That was true, she thought, much as we might wish that things were otherwise.

'So, what do we do?' asked Mma Makutsi.

Mma Ramotswe was silent while she considered her response. Then she said. 'We go to see Mr H. J. Morapedi, and we tell him what we have found out.' She paused to correct herself. 'What *you* have found out, Mma – through a fine piece of work, Mma. It is your good work that has led to this. It is your ability to consider possibilities and then look at them closely that has produced this result.'

Mma Makutsi lowered her eyes. She loved praise, and to be praised by somebody like Mma Ramotswe, who was one of the most insightful and intuitive women in all Botswana, was high praise indeed. Now she said, 'You are very kind, Mma – too kind, in fact.'

Mma Ramotswe shook her head. 'I am only giving praise where it is due, Mma. That is all. And I should ask you if I can come with you to see this Mr H. J. Morapedi. I would be interested to do that, but this is your enquiry and you may want to complete it yourself.'

Mma Makutsi thought for a moment, but she did not really need to think very much: she had made up her mind. 'Of course you can come, Mma. Of course you can.'

Mma Ramotswe made them a cup of tea each – redbush for herself, and plain tea for Mma Makutsi, who liked Five Roses English Breakfast Tea, although she always felt slightly guilty drinking it on occasions other than at breakfast. She knew she did not need to feel bad about that, but it had always struck her as being a breach of the rules, an ignoring of the instructions, so to speak, to drink breakfast tea in the late morning or afternoon.

After their tea, they went out to get into Mma Makutsi's car to make the journey to Mr H. J. Morapedi's house, Mma Ramotswe having obtained the address from his listing in the telephone directory. As they walked towards the car, Mr J. L. B. Matekoni appeared from behind the house, where he had a small workshop in which he did woodwork and carried out the occasional household repair.

'Don't tell me I'm not well enough to go out,' said Mma Ramotswe. 'I am fully recovered now.'

Mr J. L. B. Matekoni laughed. 'I can see that, Mma – I do not think the doctor would want to keep you in.'

'Good,' said Mma Ramotswe. 'Because Mma Makutsi and I are going off on a bit of business.'

He nodded, and then smiled.

'What's so funny, Mr J. L. B. Matekoni?' asked Mma Makutsi.

'I have had a call,' he said. 'I have been called out.'

'To deal with a breakdown?' asked Mma Ramotswe.

'No. It is to find a car.'

They looked at him in puzzlement. 'Somebody has lost their car?' asked Mma Makutsi.

'No. It is to look at a car for a client.'

Mma Makutsi frowned. 'Which client?' she asked.

'A certain Mr Mo Mo Malala,' answered Mr J. L. B. Matekoni.

This brought a shriek from Mma Ramotswe. 'Not another sports car, Rra? Not another Italian car that goes one hundred and twenty miles an hour, maybe more?'

Mr J. L. B. Matekoni assured them that it would be an entirely different sort of car. 'It will be a very sedate car,' he said. 'It will be a very slow one.'

They waited.

'I am going to look at a car with Malala and his wife.'

There was a sharp intake of breath. Then Mma Ramotswe turned to Mma Makutsi. 'His wife is coming too, Mma.'

'Quite right,' snapped Mma Makutsi.

'Are they reconciled after that business with the red sports car?' asked Mma Ramotswe.

'Completely,' said Mr J. L. B. Matekoni. 'I am going to show them an old Mercedes Benz. It has white tyres, but it will not go very fast.'

'So, Malala has had his mid-life crisis and come out on the other side,' said Mma Makutsi.

'That seems to be the case,' said Mr J. L. B. Matekoni.

'Hah!' said Mma Ramotswe. 'He will be happier now, I think.'

'And so will she,' Mma Makutsi observed.

Mr H. J. Morapedi received them in his sitting room. He was sitting in a large armchair, his right foot propped up on a stool. They were shown into the room by a housemaid, a woman from Bobonong whom Mma Makutsi vaguely recognised. The two of them exchanged a few snippets of Bobonong news before they were led down the corridor to the living room.

'His wife is not here,' said the housemaid. 'She has gone to stay with a friend out at Mokolodi. Her friend has built a new house and she is helping them settle in.'

'It is a good friend who does that,' said Mma Ramotswe.

They entered the living room, where they saw Mr H. J. Morapedi sitting in a large easy chair, his stockinged right foot up on a stool.

'I have had an attack of gout,' he said, after he had greeted them. 'It started three days ago. That's why I have to sit like this. Gout is very painful.'

'I have heard that,' said Mma Ramotswe. 'Would you like us to come back some other time?'

Mr H. J. Morapedi shook his head. 'No, I have taken painkillers and something they gave me to reduce the swelling. It is getting much better – as long as you don't expect me to dance.'

'We have not come here to dance,' said Mma Makutsi.

Mma Ramotswe glanced at her. Mma Makutsi had many talents, but an understanding of irony was not one of them.

'We have a very complicated story to tell you, Rra,' Mma Ramotswe began. 'It is about your hotel.'

'The Great Hippopotamus Hotel? I would like to hear your story, Mma. Not everything has been going well at the hotel, I believe.'

Mma Ramotswe indicated to Mma Makutsi that she should tell the story, which she did there and then. She laid out her theory of how Pardon and Babusi had conspired to destroy the hotel's reputation and drive down its value. He listened carefully to that, initially with disbelief, but then with a growing realisation that it all made sense.

His dismay was evident. 'My own brother!' he exclaimed. 'He

has been a big one for telling other people how to behave and all the time he has been doing this. Oh, it is very sad, Mma Makutsi. It is very, very sad.'

When she came to telling him of her suspicions as to Violet's involvement, she decided she would not say anything. But Mma Ramotswe did. 'There is an aspect that almost led us to the wrong conclusion, Rra,' she said. 'We had reason to believe that you were involved with a certain woman . . . '

'My wife,' said Mr H. J. Morapedi quickly.

'No,' said Mme Makutsi. 'One Violet Sephotho. I take it that you know her. We believed she was involved in this plot to damage the hotel.'

Mr H. J. Morapedi stared at her, and Mma Makutsi wondered whether she had crossed some unwritten boundary. After a few moments, though, he simply let out a sigh and began an explanation that took them completely by surprise. 'Violet and I were friends,' he said. 'We were close friends.'

Mma Makutsi said nothing, Mma Ramotswe watched Mma Makutsi – it was important everybody was careful here.

'I said *were*,' he continued. 'Then, not long ago, I realised that she was meeting somebody else. I told her that she must stop, because that was not right.'

Mma Makutsi was staring at him wide-eyed. She could hardly believe what she had just heard. 'You told her to stop because it was wrong to see two people at the same time?'

Mr H. J. Morapedi was oblivious to her scorn and incredulity. 'That's correct, Mma. It's not right. One woman, one man. That's what I say.'

Mma Makutsi drew in her breath. 'But you, Rra – what about you? You are married, I believe, and yet you were seeing Violet at the same time.'

'That is different,' said Mr H. J. Morapedi. 'It is different for men.'

Mma Makutsi was visibly riled. 'Why is it different for men?' she challenged.

Mr H. J. Morapedi shrugged. 'It just is.'

Mma Ramotswe sought to dampen the rapidly encroaching disagreement. 'I don't agree with you, Rra, but that is another matter.' She gave him a piercing look. 'So, Violet has gone?'

He drew in his breath. The look on his face, thought Mma Ramotswe, was one of self-disgust. 'I have been very foolish, Mma,' he said. 'I thought . . . '

Mma Makutsi interrupted him. There was triumph in her voice. 'Oh yes, Rra,' she crowed. 'You have been very foolish. Big-time. If they had Olympic Games for foolishness or stupidity, you would be leading the parade of the Botswana team.' She put on a different accent. '*And here they come, ladies and gentlemen, representing Botswana, and led by Mr H. J. Morapedi, the well-known fool . . .*'

Both Mma Ramotswe and Mr H. J. Morapedi looked at her in astonishment. If he was expecting an apology, though, he would have to wait.

'You see,' said Mma Makutsi unapologetically. 'That's what happens when you get involved with Violet Sephotho.'

Mr H. J. Morapedi was staring down at the floor. Suddenly, with no warning, he began to cry.

'I am a very foolish man,' he said. 'You are right, Mma; you are very right. I have a good wife, who is very strong, and who has given me three fine children. I have gone off with another woman because of her painted fingernails and her short skirts and . . . '

'And all that rubbish,' interjected Mma Makutsi, adding, 'that makes men behave like little boys.'

This only increased his sobbing. 'So stupid,' he stuttered, between wracking sobs. 'So stupid.'

Mma Ramotswe now did something that took both Mr H. J. Morapedi and Mma Makutsi by surprise. She stood up, went to crouch beside his chair, and put her arms around him. 'Oh, Rra,' she said. 'Do not cry. Do not. We all do foolish things – all of us. The important thing is that you have realised that you were wrong and know that you can do something to make up for it. You can say sorry to your wife.'

'I have done that,' he said, wiping away his tears. 'I have done that. And she has forgiven me – which makes me feel even worse, Mma. Women do so much forgiving, Mma – far more than their fair share, I think.'

Mma Ramotswe renewed her embrace. 'You have done the right thing, Rra. Now you must let time do the rest.'

He looked at her. 'You are very kind, Mma Ramotswe.'

She patted his shoulder. 'We are just doing the job that has been given to us in this life. That is all.'

'But you are still very kind.' His sobbing subsided. 'I deserve to have gout,' he said. 'I deserve for my toe to swell up to the size of a tennis ball. That is my punishment.'

'Carry on taking the pills,' said Mma Ramotswe.

'But what about my brother?' asked Mr H. J. Morapedi. 'What can I do about him? I don't know if I can face him now.'

Mma Ramotswe looked thoughtful. 'It is a very bad situation,' she said. 'You cannot let him get away with it.'

'Definitely not,' said Mma Makutsi.

Mr H. J. Morapedi sighed. 'But he is my brother. I cannot change that fact.'

'No,' said Mma Ramotswe. 'It is true – he is your brother. And when brothers or sisters do something wrong, it is best to speak to them. It may be hard, but I think it is the only way, Rra.' She gave him a sympathetic look. 'We can't divorce our brothers and sisters, you see. They are with us for life, I'm afraid.'

Mr H. J. Morapedi stared at the floor, misery written across his face. 'I don't know what to say to him, Mma. I don't know how to speak about something this serious.'

For a few moments Mma Ramotswe was silent. Then she said, 'Would it help if we went with you, Rra?' She nodded towards Mma Makutsi. 'Mma Makutsi and I could go with you to speak to him. He is at the hotel, Mma Makutsi says.'

'Right now?' asked Mr H. J. Morapedi.

Mma Ramotswe nodded. 'It is always best to do unpleasant things the moment you think of them. If you put them off, then you will never do them. It's rather like going to the dentist.'

Mr H. J. Morapedi instinctively touched his jaw. 'I have not been to the dentist for a long time,' he said.

'You should go tomorrow,' Mma Makutsi admonished him.

Mma Ramotswe did not like to add to Mr H. J. Morapedi's suffering. 'There will be time for dentists later on,' she said quickly. 'We should concentrate today on what has been going on at the hotel.'

'Yes,' said Mma Makutsi firmly. 'We must sort that out right now.'

Mr H. J. Morapedi was largely silent as the three of them made their way down the Lobatse Road to the Great Hippopotamus Hotel. Mma Ramotswe glanced at him from time to time, and saw that he looked anxious, as if he were a man on his way to an appointment with an uncomfortable destiny – which he was, she thought. It was difficult to predict what might happen in the encounter with Pardon. It was likely that he would deny everything, and she could envisage that leading to a shouting match with Mma Makutsi. And she was unsure, too, as to how Mr H. J. Morapedi would respond to an outright denial by his brother. She rather suspected that he might cave in, rather than face a confrontation, and that would mean the whole situation would remain unresolved. They would then have to see whether Diphimotswe was prepared to tackle her errant cousin. She might be, but once again, it was impossible to be sure. Family disputes often played out according to rules of their own, as the old business of childhood, ancient jealousies and insecurities came to the fore. There was just no telling what would happen.

Pardon had seen them coming, and waved to them from the veranda as they emerged from Mma Makutsi's car.

'Oh, there is my brother,' said Mr H. J. Morapedi, with a groan. 'I'm not sure, Mma Ramotswe . . . '

Mma Makutsi was not one for backsliding. 'That is good, Rra,' she said. 'We can speak to him directly.'

'But . . . '

Mma Makutsi took his arm, and began to walk towards the steps that led to the veranda. Mma Ramotswe followed close behind – there were times when she admired Mma Makutsi's brisk determination, and this was one of them.

'Well, well,' said Pardon as they joined him on the veranda. 'This is very nice. Here we all are together.'

'Not so nice, Rra,' snapped Mma Makutsi. 'Not so nice at all.'

Pardon looked surprised. 'Is there something wrong, Mma?' he asked.

'Everything is wrong,' replied Mma Makutsi. 'Everything is one hundred per cent wrong.'

Pardon glanced at Mma Ramotswe and then at his brother. 'H. J., is everything all right?'

'Well . . . ' began Mr H. J. Morapedi.

'Everything is not all right,' snapped Mma Makutsi. 'You and that manager of yours . . . '

'Babusi?'

'Yes, that is his name,' said Mma Makutsi. 'You and Babusi are the ones who have caused all the trouble round here.'

Pardon froze. Then, his voice small and broken, he said, 'What are you talking about, Mma? What is all this nonsense?'

Before Mma Makutsi could reply, a door at the back of the veranda opened and Babusi emerged, holding a teapot. He stopped, surprised to see the group before him. After a moment or two, he regained his composure. 'I was bringing tea. I can get some more cups . . . '

Mma Makutsi gave the manager a withering look. 'You have arrived just at the right time, Rra,' she said. 'We are talking to Pardon here about what has been going on. He has told us all about your plan to destroy this hotel's reputation.'

Mma Ramotswe recognised immediately what Mma Makutsi was doing. This was straight out of *The Principles of Private Detection*, from the section where Clovis Andersen reveals how to trap a collaborator into an admission by telling him that his friend has confessed to everything. *It almost always works*, the great authority had written. *They think that the beans have been spilled and they proceed to provide confirmation.*

And that is what happened. Babusi spun round to face Pardon. 'You told them, did you?' he snarled. 'Well, now they're going to find out about you. Oh yes, they're going to hear about every last pula you took to make those bets of yours. Every last pula. I warned you.'

Mma Ramotswe raised a hand. 'Hold on, Rra.' And to Pardon she said, 'Am I right in thinking that this man has been threatening you, Rra?'

Pardon looked up at the ceiling. Mma Ramotswe noticed that his lower lip was quivering. 'I'm right, am I not, Rra? You have been gambling, and then . . . '

'He took money from the business,' Babusi blurted out. 'And then he made me do these things to wreck the hotel.'

Pardon gasped. 'I did not make you do anything, Babusi. *You* were the one. It was your idea.'

'Nonsense,' said Babusi. 'I did not. It was you.'

Mma Ramotswe looked at Babusi, and then at Pardon. There were times when, faced with two incompatible stories, one just had to decide between their authors. She knew whom to believe. Pardon's reaction had been genuine – he had been shocked by Babusi's lie.

She leaned forward to place a hand on Pardon's arm. 'Could you come with me, Rra? Come with us and your brother. I would like to walk round the garden.'

Pardon looked undecided. 'But . . . '

'Just come,' Mma Ramotswe urged. 'It will not take long. Just a short walk.'

'And me?' asked Babusi.

'I think you should go back to your office,' said Mma Ramotswe. 'Presumably you have work to do, Rra.'

They made their way towards the tennis court. By a bed of drought-resistant plants – waxy green cactuses and small grey shrubs, they paused while Mma Ramotswe asked her questions.

'Why did you do it, Rra?' Mma Ramotswe asked.

Pardon remained tight-lipped.

'I am your brother, Pardon,' said Mr H. J. Morapedi. 'What have I ever done to you?'

Pardon shook his head. 'You have done nothing. You have always been a good brother to me.'

'Then why?' asked Mr H. J. Morapedi.

Pardon looked away. It was difficult for him, but it seemed that he had decided to speak. 'I have a bad habit,' he said at last. 'I am a gambler. I am a very big gambler. I could not stop.'

Mma Ramotswe shook her head. 'It is a very powerful thing, that,' she said. 'It is like a snake that winds itself around you.'

Pardon liked the metaphor. 'Yes, it is just like that, Mma. A python. And once it gets you . . . ' He shrugged. 'You'll do anything to get money to place the next bet. And you think that the next bet will enable you to pay it all back, but it never works that way.'

'How much?' asked Mr H. J. Morapedi.

'Lots,' said Pardon. 'But I shall try to pay it back, H. J. I feel very bad about what I have done.'

'So you should,' said Mma Makutsi.

Mma Ramotswe asked how Babusi had discovered what was happening.

'He saw me,' answered Pardon. 'He saw me taking money from the safe. He said that he had an idea that would work very well for both of us. He said that if we got the hotel on very favourable terms, he would buy me out. I would be able to pay off the people I had borrowed money from – the betting people. Then the hotel would be his.'

'And you gave in?' asked Mr H. J. Morapedi.

Pardon nodded. 'I did not want anybody to find out – especially my brother.' He paused. 'Or the neighbours. They all think I am a good person. They would be very shocked.' He paused again. 'I only meant to borrow the money. I would never steal anything.'

'So you started to sabotage the hotel?' pressed Mma Makutsi. 'You decided to do those dangerous things?'

Pardon shifted his feet uneasily. 'I did not do it myself,' he said. 'It was Babusi. He said . . . ' He faltered.

'He said what?' asked Mma Makutsi.

'He said I was a coward. And I think he's right. He did all those things – put the scorpion in the room, washed the salad in dirty water and so on. He was the one.'

Mr H. J. Morapedi shook his head. 'You are not a coward, my brother. You were frightened – and we are all frightened of something.'

Pardon looked at him with gratitude. 'I am very sorry for what I have done,' he said. 'But there is this thing inside me, you see – this gambling thing.'

'There are people who can help you with that,' said Mma Ramotswe. 'Gambling is like a big snake – you said so yourself. But snakes can be dealt with if you know what to do.'

For a few moments nobody spoke. Then Mma Ramotswe said, 'I think that we can go back now.'

'And Babusi?' asked Pardon.

'He is out of here,' said Mr H. J. Morapedi. 'His job is over with immediate effect.'

'I think we should get him to pay our fee,' said Mma Makutsi. 'He agreed to do that right at the beginning when he brought us in on the case. Now we have done a lot of work on this case. He can pay out of his own pocket.'

Mma Ramotswe laughed. 'That's a good idea,' she said. 'And half of it, I think, can go to Mma Potokwani's orphan fund, because it was that little boy who set you on the right trail, Mma Makutsi.'

'Yes, he did,' agreed Mma Makutsi. She would have liked to take all the credit, but she realised that Mma Ramotswe was right. At least ten per cent of the credit belonged to young Khumo – maybe slightly more. Twelve per cent, perhaps.

*

It was a week later that Mma Ramotswe, Mma Potokwani and Mma Makutsi drove down together – with Mma Makutsi at the wheel – to have lunch, on the invitation of Diphimotswe, at the Great Hippopotamus Hotel. It was, Diphimotswe told them, to be a thank-you for all they had done.

'We love this hotel,' said Diphimotswe. 'And the people who come to stay in it love it too. Now everything is back to normal, and we have already interviewed a new manager. All is well now.'

'And your cousin's gout?' asked Mma Ramotswe.

'He is walking comfortably again. He is much happier. He and Pardon have spoken to one another a lot.' She paused. 'They have fought a bit in the past, but now they have started to talk.'

'And?' asked Mma Ramotswe.

'And they are discovering that it is easier to talk than to fight – much easier.'

'So much can go wrong in families,' said Mma Ramotswe. 'But then so much can be sorted out by talking about what has gone wrong, too. That is well known, I think.'

'You are right,' said Diphimotswe. 'And you are also very kind, Mma Ramotswe. That is well known too.'

And she had more to tell Mma Ramotswe. She had taken Pardon to see a friend of hers in one of the local clinics. This friend knew all about addictions, and was already treating several people for gambling problems. Pardon had joined a group, and was making good progress. 'There is every chance that he will become better. It will be a long haul, but they are hopeful.' There is always something you can do, Diphimotswe said. It may only be a small thing, but each small thing counted.

'And Babusi? What about him?' asked Mma Ramotswe.

Diphimotswe was cautious. 'We shall see, Mma. We discussed handing him over to the police, but H. J. was in favour of giving him a chance. He has a wife and two children, and he did not want them to suffer. H. J. found him a job with a construction firm. He mixes concrete now. It is very tough, physical work, but we think that he knows he is lucky to have it. I think he may have learned his lesson.'

Mma Ramotswe approved of that. 'It is always possible that people will change,' she said. 'But you have to give them a chance to do so. You can't change if you don't get a chance. That is well known, I think.'

'Yes,' agreed Diphimotswe. 'That is certainly well known.'

After their lunch, they went for a walk in the gardens of the Great Hippopotamus Hotel. Mma Ramotswe wandered off briefly while the others inspected a new planting of vegetables for the hotel kitchens. She made her way to a section of the garden planted with succulents – dry-land plants that could withstand a poor rainy season. She stared at the plants in their delicate beauty, and their persistence. Then she looked up at the sky – the sky that was also a part of Botswana, she believed, although it floated so high overhead, stretching out towards places far to the south, to the lonely shores of Namibia and the distant Cape, the very tip of Africa. She saw blue. She looked out towards the hills in the distance. She saw green, and more blue. She saw Botswana, the country she loved with all her heart, with all her heart.

Alexander McCall Smith is the author of over one hundred books on a wide array of subjects, including the award-winning The No.1 Ladies' Detective Agency series. He is also the author of the Isabel Dalhousie novels and the world's longest-running serial novel, *44 Scotland Street.* His books have been translated into forty-six languages. Alexander McCall Smith is Professor Emeritus of Medical Law at the University of Edinburgh and holds honorary doctorates from thirteen universities. He was knighted by the King in 2024.

Help us make the next generation of readers

We – both author and publisher – hope you enjoyed this book. We believe that you can become a reader at any time in your life, but we'd love your help to give the next generation a head start.

Did you know that 9% of children don't have a book of their own in their home, rising to 12% in disadvantaged families*? We'd like to try to change that by asking you to consider the role you could play in helping to build readers of the future.

We'd love you to think of sharing, borrowing, reading, buying or talking about a book with a child in your life and spreading the love of reading. We want to make sure the next generation continue to have access to books, wherever they come from.

And if you would like to consider donating to charities that help fund literacy projects, find out more at www.literacytrust.org.uk and www.booktrust.org.uk.

Thank you.

hachette CHILDREN'S GROUP

little, brown BOOK GROUP

*As reported by the National Literacy Trust